A HUNDRED SWEET PROMISES

SEPEHR HADDAD

APPLEYARD & SONS PUBLISHING

Disclaimer

This novel was inspired by a story my grandmother told me on the eve of the 1979 Islamic Revolution in Iran. Even though I recreated events and conversations from what she shared with me over forty years ago, in certain situations, I have added fictional conversations inspired by historical figures.

These conversations and interactions are a product of the author's imagination, and any resemblance to actual conversations or events is purely coincidental. In some instances, I have changed the names of individuals and locations and other identifying details, such as physical properties, occupations, and places of residence.

Book Cover Design by ebooklaunch.com

Cover photographs: Sepehr Haddad

APPLEYARD & SONS PUBLISHING
5557 Baltimore Ave., Suite 500-1108
Hyattsville, Maryland 20781
AppleyardandSonsPublishing.com

ISBN 978-1-7325943-0-2

Dedication

For my two sons, Kian and Riyan,
hoping that they always remember their Persian roots.

ACKNOWLEDGMENTS

I thank my late grandmother, Mami, for telling me this story, and thank Moana, who encouraged me to write this book and assisted in editing it. I am also grateful for Gertrude Lowthian Bell's timeless translation of Hafez's poetry over a century ago, which I have used herein.

TABLE OF CONTENTS

"For One Moment Our Lives Met, Our Souls Touched"—

Oscar Wilde

CHAPTER 1

A FRIDAY TURNS BLACK

Tehran, Iran, 1978

"Move away now! I repeat, move away at once!" the soldier yelled in Persian through the bullhorn. I peered curiously through the window of my grandmother's bedroom onto Shah Reza Avenue in downtown Tehran to see what the commotion was all about.

It was Friday, September 8th, 1978, the first full day after martial law had been declared in Tehran and other cities in Iran. No one could have imagined that just several months later, the Islamic Revolution would ultimately overthrow the shah's government. My family was visiting my grandmother Mami for lunch, as many of our extended family often did on Fridays. (Fridays were the traditional day of rest.)

On this day, it was only my immediate family who showed up. We assumed others stayed away due to the uncertainty of the situation under martial law.

From my view through the window, I noticed there was a lot of unusual activity. There were armored vehicles and tanks stationed at each corner of the square. Soldiers were enforcing the new rules that forbade gatherings, and they broke up any group of more than two people walking together or just hanging around. Gun-toting soldiers were backing up the regular traffic cops. I felt nervous and excited to see the troops out and about, having never witnessed anything like it except in the movies.

This day, the one thing the soldiers, police, and civilians all had in common was a sense of uneasiness, and it seemed everyone was on edge. Demonstrations cropped up all over the city while the shah's military tried to stop them before they got out of hand. I watched from the window as soldiers went from group to group, attempting to break up any perceived collaboration. This action seemed hopeless since just as one group dispersed, another quickly formed.

I strained to see whom the soldier was yelling at, not able to see all directions from the window. As I leaned in closer with my nose pressing against the glass, I suddenly realized the soldier with the bullhorn was addressing me, and this time he angrily ordered, "*Baraye akharin bar az panjereh boro kenar!*" ("This is the final warning, move away from the window!")

Standing beside him was another soldier with a G3 automatic rifle pointed directly at me. My brother, Kaveh, who had heard the commotion outside, rushed into the bedroom and forcefully pulled me from the window. Being singled out by the soldier was so shocking that I had frozen and could not move out of fear. If not for my brother's quick thinking to drag me away and assuming the soldier's threat was valid, the day could have ended very differently.

Up to this point, the developing political crisis had not directly affected me. However, suddenly it had, and I anxiously wondered if the soldiers would enter the apartment building and try to find me.

Kaveh and I looked at each other, and I sensed that he was worried too, so we rushed to the front of the apartment, cupping our ears behind the door, trying to detect the soldiers' footsteps in the stairwell. We could only hear muffled yelling in the distance to others on the street below and realized the coast was clear. We took a few moments to collect ourselves and went into the living room, where Mami was sitting. She had the television on, listening to the news while knitting in her typical rhythmic motion, oblivious to what had just happened outside her bedroom window. My parents had stepped out to go to the apartment next door, where my cousin lived, so it was only the three of us in her living room at the time.

Mami slowly raised her head, looking at us from above her eyeglasses, which had slid almost to the tip of her nose, and asked, "Are you boys hungry?"

Feeling as though I had dodged a bullet, I had no appetite, and we excitedly told her what had just happened. She probably thought we were exaggerating since she did not take the matter as seriously as I had expected. Sitting down next to her, I was grateful to watch events on television away from what was happening just outside. As time went on and my anxiety subsided, I began to pay more attention to the constant news updates being broadcast.

Every few minutes, the announcer would repeat all the guidelines the public had to follow not to be in breach of martial law, reminding the viewers that the military government expected strict adherence to these new rules.

As the reporter read the latest news, I kept hearing him mention "Khomeini," a name I had never heard before. He said that Khomeini's anti-shah sermons were reproduced on cassette tapes and distributed to mosques to influence people as they came to the houses of worship for prayers. These inflammatory sermons against the monarchy ran the gamut from accusing the government of not respecting Islam, to pronouncements against foreign influences on the country, particularly by the United States.

Since I had never heard of him, I asked my grandmother, "Mami, who is this Khomeini?"

She replied, "He is a cleric who gave fiery sermons against the shah in the holy city of Qom about twenty years ago. One thing led to another, and he was eventually exiled to Iraq."

3

At hearing this, I assumed the shah had thought, *Out of sight, out of mind,* hoping that Khomeini could no longer spread his message in exile. The shah's government could control messages through the airwaves and newspapers, but not through the system of mosques where clerics gave their sermons every Friday and on religious holidays.

I wondered why I had never heard of Khomeini since I had attended the International School in Tehran. Unlike in typical Iranian high schools and even the University of Tehran, we had access to controversial reading material. These publications even included what was banned on the street, but somehow, I never read anything about Khomeini.

When Mami told me of Khomeini's past, I was surprised to hear that someone had dared to overtly disagree with the shah, because growing up in Iran, we saw the shah as all-powerful. He was portrayed as such in the media, and it was unheard of for anyone to quarrel with him so publicly. Statues of the shah and his father, Reza Shah, were strategically placed in public squares in the capital and other cities. The shah's portrait was everywhere. It was on all paper money and coins, in every schoolbook, all public buildings, and every movie theater near the projection screen. This portrayal of the shah gave us a larger-than-life impression of him.

I told my grandmother, "I am amazed. I cannot believe that there was no mention of Khomeini in our history class or on radio, television, or even in casual discussion. How could it be that we did not know about him?"

She replied, "No, Sepehr, it is not that amazing, since there are many things you do not know. Things as close as your own family!"

I paused in thought, wondering what she was referring to. Was there something everyone else knew but me, and I was the last to find out? Or was this a family secret that she had felt hesitant to reveal to anyone up until now? Her comment seemed strange, so I asked, "Mami, what do you mean?"

"Your grandfather, for instance. He fell in love with a Russian princess many years ago. I am sure you did not know that!"

When Mami mentioned this, my eyes locked with hers with sincere and profound curiosity, signaling my eagerness to hear more.

One would think she would have displayed envy or perhaps embarrassment in this confession, but I did not detect even a hint of it. Instead, without any awkward silence, she seemed to want to carry on, as if telling me a story about someone else's husband, not her own, and his love for another woman.

However, we were suddenly interrupted by a special news bulletin announcing clashes between government forces and demonstrators near Jaleh Square, which was just a few miles away. My parents returned from my cousin's apartment, having also heard the news, and they said we had to go, not wanting us to be caught up in the melee. We rushed off, and Mami's story about my grandfather had to wait for another day.

The car ride home was exciting, at least for the first few blocks, as we drove amongst army personnel carriers and tanks. The force of soldiers and police with guns at the ready was a sight to behold, especially considering my very recent encounter with a soldier.

But the farther we got from downtown, the fewer soldiers were present. After a while, it was like nothing was going on, and everything appeared as usual. Tehran is unique in that way; there is a clear north-south divide. The southern section of town is congested, hot, and polluted, and the people who lived there were more traditional and religiously observant. This part of the city was where most of the clashes were taking place.

In contrast, the northern portion of the city, where the more affluent and less traditional Tehranis lived, was closer to the Alborz mountain range and therefore had a colder climate. Even in the old days, my mother would tell me how the whole family would pack up their belongings and move to the northern part of the city to pass the hot summer months. This part of town was also home to a significant international presence. Here one could see women wearing the latest fashions from Paris and Rome, including miniskirts, while in the southern parts of the city, women mostly wore the traditional head-to-toe covering, the *chador.* On this day, the quiet north of town displayed no outward indication that martial law had even been declared.

As we got closer to home and things quieted down, I thought of what Mami had said before our sudden departure, and I asked my mother, "Did you ever hear Mami tell a story about your father falling in love with a Russian princess?"

She turned around and faced me in the backseat, caught off guard by my question. "A Russian princess?" She paused for a moment and then added, "I know my father studied music at the conservatory in Saint Petersburg, but about a Russian princess, no, Mami never mentioned it."

Then she curiously asked me, "Well, what did Mami say about him?"

I told her I had not found out since we had to leave so quickly. It made me wonder even more what Mami was going to say to me.

When we got home, we were fixated by the television news and heard the calamitous result of the day's events. The army, which comprised untrained recruits, had opened fire on the demonstrators at Jaleh Square, and hundreds of people had been shot to death. This bloody scene was a tragic turning point in the unfolding political turmoil. The massacre was dubbed Black Friday, and it made any future compromise between the shah's government and the demonstrators impossible.

CHAPTER 2

A LUNCH WITH MAMI

Ten days had passed since Black Friday, and a strange new normal descended upon Tehran. This included people sharing rumors, with a dose of their own opinions, as to what had transpired and what was to come, but most went back to business as usual. I had just a few days left before returning to California for college, and I wanted to visit my grandmother one last time before my departure.

I took a taxicab to Ferdowsi Square, in the southern part of the city where she lived. Sitting in a shared taxi in Tehran was like listening to a radio talk show where all kinds of news, opinions, and unsolicited advice were offered. On the way downtown, all the talk was about martial law, who was to blame for Black Friday, and views on the economy.

Today this frustrated driver complained that he had to wait in an awfully long line at the gas station due to the fuel supply shortage resulting from the workers' strike at the country's major refinery. He grumbled, "The minute it was my turn to pump gas after the long wait, the power went out, and the pumps couldn't operate, so I wasted half a day where I could have been driving my cab," as he lamented the lost income.

We all commiserated with him, agreeing that things seemed to be taking a turn for the worse. One of the younger passengers, sitting beside me in the cramped front seat, hopelessly exclaimed, "I wish I could move to Europe or America," anxious about his future. An elderly gentleman in the backseat offered some fatherly advice, with a kind smile and in a comforting tone: "Young man, don't worry so much. Things are going to get better; this is just a rough patch!"

It appeared that the driver was trying to make up for his downtime at the gas station by cramming in as many passengers as he could along the way. He drove recklessly fast to deliver each rider to his destination quickly, attempting to recoup the income he could have made earlier in the day.

Even though I was intrigued by the conversation, being packed in tightly with strangers in the stifling heat of the claustrophobic cab made me feel queasy. So I decided to get out and walk the rest of the way to get some fresh air. When I got to Mami's apartment, she had just finished setting the table for lunch.

Mami and I were remarkably close; I was the youngest of her twelve grandchildren and the son of her youngest daughter. She was a kind-hearted but strong lady. She lived a simple life but had not had a simple life. She was married at a young age to my grandfather Nasrollah Minbashian and had been widowed earlier than most, raising five children by herself. For many of the ensuing years, she lived with her mother, my maternal great-grandmother, Mrs. Davamolmolk Vaziritabar, known to the family endearingly as Khanoom Bozorg, literally meaning "Grand Lady."

Khanoom Bozorg had lived to the ripe old age of ninety-eight, having died just a few years earlier. While alive, she was the matriarch of the family and was quite strong-willed.

Khanoom Bozorg had been instrumental in Mami's arranged marriage to Nasrollah. In the many years that they were married, Nasrollah had brought Mami a sense of fun that filled her life, and she was always grateful to her mother for that.

Mami had managed to raise highly successful children, at least in terms of their careers. Of note were two of my uncles. The eldest had risen to the highest rank of the army as a four-star general and commander of the Iranian Armed Forces. The other was appointed the first-ever minister of culture and fine arts of Iran by the shah.

Mami loved her apartment, filled with sunlight and family mementos, even though it was a simple two-bedroom flat showing signs of age. Her apartment held many unforgettable memories for me as the Friday meeting place where we visited with relatives whom we would not regularly see. She had two helpers who could prepare food for thirty-plus people in no time, but today, it was only Mami and me.

As we sat at the lunch table, I had no idea that this would be the last time I would ever see her again. After a few minutes of small talk, I reminded Mami of the story she was going to tell me about my grandfather's love for a Russian princess.

She smiled and said, "Oh yes, you left in such a rush that day, I never got a chance to tell you about it. Your grandfather shared this story with me a short while after we married!"

I appreciated the excitement with which Mami began to tell me the story. As she recalled this tale, it seemed as if she had been at my grandfather's side every step of the way.

CHAPTER 3

THE RELUCTANT RETURN

St. Petersburg, Russia, 1905

"I did not come here of my own accord, and I can't leave that way.
Whoever brought me here will have to take me home"
— Rumi

Nasrollah rode in a private *droski*, a horse-drawn carriage, on his way to the train station. He was embarking on the first leg of his trip from St. Petersburg through Moscow to his final destination, Tehran.

Spring of 1905 in St. Petersburg had come so suddenly that only a few days earlier, the beautiful Neva River had been totally frozen. On this travel day, not an inch of ice remained as the city basked in the warm sunshine. The ducks had also returned on the Neva, and Nasrollah considered this an auspicious beginning to his long journey.

The most famous thoroughfare of Russia, the Nevsky Prospect, which ran through the heart of the city, was spectacular. The droski rolled leisurely along a single track on the side of the avenue where strips of smooth wood pavement were reserved for such carriages. Workers of all kinds carried bulky loads in the middle of the road on cobblestone since they were not allowed to walk on the sidewalks. Kiosks were abundant, selling everything from papers to tobacco on every busy corner. Street-cars, wagons, and carriages all shared the same busy Nevsky, albeit haphazardly.

Nasrollah knew how much he would miss this magnificent city where he had lived for the past seven years. Passing the Great Morskaya, another famous street of St. Petersburg, he encountered the usual battalion of Russian troops playing the martial music he enjoyed, which often echoed throughout the capital city many times a day.

Nasrollah had a fondness for military music, undoubtedly due to growing up in a military household with a father who composed such pieces.

In 1898, when Nasrollah was just thirteen, his father, Gholam-Reza Minbashian, known as Salar Moazaz, had brought him along to Russia to study music at the famed St. Petersburg Conservatory. (The honorary title of *Salar Moazaz* was given to Gholam-Reza Minbashian by royal decree for his contributions in the field of music.)

Salar Moazaz himself was a pupil of the Russian composer Nikolai Andreyevich Rimsky-Korsakov, having studied composition and orchestration under his tutelage.

Father and son were together for five years studying music in St. Petersburg until, in 1903, Salar Moazaz left Russia and traveled back to Persia. His return was to answer the king's call of creating the new music department at the Dar al-Funun (the Tehran Polytechnic), Persia's first modern school.

After his father's departure, Nasrollah had remained in St. Petersburg for an additional two years to finish his music studies. It was now his turn to return to Persia, although he was doing so reluctantly, having spent his formative teenage years in this beautiful city. Nasrollah was not yet ready to leave since he wanted to add the mastery of music theory and orchestration to his repertoire at the conservatory, under the guidance of Rimsky-Korsakov.

Despite his wishes, the revolutionary upheavals of 1905 in Russia had suddenly interrupted these plans. Rimsky-Korsakov, a lifelong political liberal, sided with the demonstrating conservatory students demanding the establishment of a constitutional monarchy. In March, he had been dismissed from his professorship, along with the expulsion of many of the student protestors.

This event somewhat lessened Nasrollah's unwillingness to return to Persia, now that the academic year had ended so abruptly. He decided to leave for home and planned to come back to St. Petersburg when the situation in Russia settled down.

The winter of 1905 had not been kind to St. Petersburg due to the riots and student demonstrations occurring throughout the city. These protests culminated with the painful Bloody Sunday on a fateful January afternoon, where upward of one thousand demonstrators were killed and many more were wounded.

Soldiers of the tsar's Imperial Guard fired upon unarmed protestors as they marched toward the Winter Palace to present a petition to the emperor. The public outrage and resulting strikes had not had a softening effect on the regime. Instead, these demonstrations had prompted the tsar's government to crack down even more violently on the protesters. There was a palpable feeling of unrest in the city.

Notwithstanding the current political turmoil, there were many things about St. Petersburg Nasrollah knew he would miss. Notably, the enchanting summers with extremely short nights due to the city's far-northern location. As the locals say, "In St. Petersburg, daylight lasts until daylight comes again!"

The long and cold winters were a different story, for Nasrollah did not enjoy the cold climate. Still, he would remember with fondness the essential ingredient of all winter celebrations— vodka. He would reminisce about the times he spent with other students at the café, heatedly discussing the "new music."

Living in the capital city had also afforded Nasrollah many unique opportunities. One such instance was being invited to the apartment of Rimsky-Korsakov with several other foreign students to discuss the composer's ideas about music. That one time, Rimsky-Korsakov had confessed, "I believe that to become a musician in the full sense of the word, it is not necessary to even be at the conservatory. I think that much of what they teach is nothing other than trivia that is only required by the school!"

The professor felt that he could impart so much more to the students through individual tutoring. This was the main reason why Nasrollah wanted to study privately with him. Nevertheless, unlike what the professor suggested, Nasrollah did appreciate being a student at the prestigious St. Petersburg Conservatory of Music. Here he studied amongst some of the best and brightest musical minds of Russia.

The conservatory also attracted aspiring talent from Europe and around the world who were drawn by the opportunity to learn from these masters. Nasrollah's association with this pride of Russia cast him amongst the artistic elites of the world, and he loathed to walk away from it all.

However, as all Persian sons of strong-willed fathers were taught, he had no choice but to comply with Salar Moazaz's request to return home. At his father's behest, Nasrollah would assist him in developing the country's music department at the Dar al-Funun.

It was a fourteen-hour overnight journey from St. Petersburg to Moscow on the fastest train in Russia, the courier train. This train traversed the four-hundred-mile distance at speeds double that of ordinary passenger trains, making stops along the way and consisting of only a few first-class carriages.

Nasrollah was fortunate to be sharing one of these carriages with another passenger, as the company and conversation made the trip less tiresome. The train followed a straight line through desert and marshes with not much to see.

Nasrollah introduced himself to his fellow passenger and asked, "Monsieur, may I ask if you know why the train line was constructed in such a linear manner?"

The man, who seemed eager for conversation, offered Nasrollah a firm handshake and introduced himself as Rustam Somkhishvili (the surname meaning "child of Somekhi" or "Armenian" in the Georgian tongue).

He responded, "Well, the rumor is that the tsar had willed it so by laying a ruler on a map and drawing a straight line from the new to the old capital city and demanding it be built in this fashion!"

Somkhishvili was an older, fashionably attired businessman with a well-cut and well-fitted coat, displaying his decidedly good taste. He was handsome with thick, bushy gray brows that shaded his deep-set blue eyes and a long gray mustache that completely covered his upper lip. He was heading to his hometown of Tbilisi, the capital of Georgia, after a brief stay in Moscow.

When Nasrollah asked him his profession, Somkhishvili took a long draw from his cigarette, and as a spiral of whitish-gray smoke curled above his head, replied, "I am an iron merchant and have been supplying materials for the ever-expanding Russian railway network; that is why I am familiar with the rumor of the tsar's desired railway route."

Somkhishvili added with a chuckle, "You know, several routes had been suggested by his ministers, but the tsar suspected ulterior motives on their part and therefore made the final decision the way he did, with a ruler!"

Nasrollah laughed and asked, "Are you by any chance of Persian descent?" recognizing Somkhishvili's Christian name, Rustam, as the hero of the Persian epic *Shahnameh*, or *Book of Kings*.

Somkhishvili replied, "No, I am not Persian. I am a Georgian, named after the famous bodyguard of Napoleon Bonaparte, Rustam Raza. He was also born in Tbilisi to Armenian parents, like me."

Nasrollah's companion was a gregarious man with a delightful and entertaining character and seemed to have a good sense of humor. Traveling in a private carriage had its benefits when it came to Somkhishvili expressing his true feelings far from curious ears. He mentioned that his father, being Armenian and living in Georgia, had disdain for Russia's domination and territorial desires. Even though both Armenia and Georgia were Christian countries, they never identified with Russia as a big brother.

Somkhishvili added, "My father, God rest his soul, believed that the enemy of your enemy is your friend, and therefore he admired Napoleon, naming me after the French emperor's Georgian-born Armenian bodyguard!"

Nasrollah's great-grandfather, the head of the Minbashian clan, was also born in Georgia, back when it was part of Persian territory and called Gorjestan in Persian. *Minbashian* means "one thousand heads" since Nasrollah's ancestor commanded one thousand men.

Nasrollah revealed, "Even though I also have a Georgian heritage, I have never visited, but I will be passing through Georgia on my way to Baku on the Caspian, as part of my next leg home."

Somkhishvili declared, "In this whole world, there is no country more beautiful than Georgia!"

As everyone speaks about their own homeland like this, Nasrollah had a feeling this was just typical bragging.

Sensing this, from the look on Nasrollah's face, Somkhishvili added, "You see, Monsieur, Georgians tell the story of how it was that they came to possess the most beautiful land in the world."

Smiling proudly, he continued, "When God was distributing land to all the different peoples of the world, the Georgians were having a party and had too much to drink, and hence arrived a bit late to where God was portioning out the land. When they mentioned they were late because they were drinking in praise of Him, God was pleased and gave the Georgians the part of the world that He had been reserving for Himself!"

Nasrollah laughed along with Somkhishvili when he finished telling him this tale. With a common heritage and many hours of laughter and conversation, the two men bonded, only sleeping for a few hours during the overnight train ride.

Once they arrived in Moscow, Somkhishvili convinced Nasrollah to stay at the Bolchaya Moskovskaya Gastinitsa. Nasrollah was to stop over for one week before continuing his trip to Persia, while Somkhishvili was planning to remain in the city of the Muscovites to attend several business meetings. Nasrollah agreed to join him at this attractive caravansary since he had not yet arranged a place to stay.

Luckily, the seven years Nasrollah had lived in St. Petersburg had offered him fluency in the Slavic tongue. He was often mistaken for a Russian, mainly because he spoke the language with no hint of a foreign accent. In the native Russian *Gastinitsa*, which in every way was thoroughly Russian, this ability was a necessity. This gave Nasrollah an advantage over other foreigners who were the target of unscrupulous locals, looking to take advantage of newcomers' ignorance of the language and local customs.

After settling in at their hotel, Nasrollah and Somkhishvili went for a short walk to stretch their legs after the long train ride. They bought some cigarettes at the tobacco kiosk nearby and returned to the hotel since they were still tired. They had a quiet dinner and began planning the next day's schedule.

Somkhishvili told Nasrollah, "Tomorrow morning, I have to attend to some business, but we should meet up at the Sandunovsky baths later to seek refreshment and rejuvenation, after a long day of meetings for me and sightseeing for you."

The Sandunovsky baths were considered some of the best in the world, and Nasrollah eagerly agreed to Rustam's offer since he wanted to experience the spa, drink, and socializing that the venue offered during this brief stopover in Moscow.

The next day after breakfast, each went his own way, with Nasrollah spending his time visiting the splendid monuments, museums, and churches of this grand city. However, his visit to one place left a deep impression on him: The Cathedral of Christ the Saviour. The Russians built the cathedral as a sign of their gratitude that Napoleon Bonaparte had retreated from Moscow during the 1812 Patriotic War.

This building held a particular interest for Nasrollah since it had been the scene for the world premiere of the famous 1812 Overture by Tchaikovsky. This was a source of pride for Nasrollah because Tchaikovsky, who was considered a Russian national treasure, had also graduated from the conservatory in St. Petersburg.

While exploring the incredible cathedral, a tour guide who mentioned he was from the town of Vilnius began explaining the history of the war to Nasrollah. The guide, who displayed an apparent dislike for Napoleon, said, "Near my town, there is a simple monument bearing two plaques. On one side, facing towards Russia, it is written, *Napoleon Bonaparte passed this way in 1812 with four hundred thousand men,* while on the other side, leaving Russia, are engraved the words *Napoleon Bonaparte passed this way in 1812 with nine thousand men!*"

He then added with a sense of pride, "It's a tragic depiction of how many men the French lost trying to defeat the Russians, don't you agree?"

Nasrollah agreed with a nod of his head, but at the same time thought, *Somkhishvili's father would not have liked to hear this story,* recalling what Rustam told him just yesterday about his father's love for the retreating emperor.

Later that day, as planned, Nasrollah and Somkhishvili met in front of the bathhouse, a stately structure that was three stories high and covered a whole city block. Nasrollah noticed that Somkhishvili seemed rather well-dressed for a simple visit to a spa. As Nasrollah had just come back from a day of sightseeing, he wondered if he should have upgraded his attire.

The Sandunovsky provided various kinds of baths, from the cheap scrubbing for ordinary customers to the luxurious private suites fitted with all sorts of devices for cleansing. These included dry heat, showers, and massages, a treatment costing many rubles but well worth it for pampering the well-to-do to rid the body from a full day of tiredness.

They waited at the counter to pay upfront for the services they desired and to be given numbers, based upon which they would be ushered into their private suites for bathing and massage. Even though they had arrived together, Somkhishvili was given a low number, while Nasrollah was given a much higher number, which meant a longer wait for him to get in. He attributed this to Somkhishvili being a return customer, an older gentleman, and perhaps because he was better dressed. Nasrollah guessed there had been an assumption on the part of the proprietor of Somkhishvili's higher station in life, which could lead to an ample gratuity for each service provided.

The establishment was busier than usual this evening. The short-handed staff seemed to be rushed and inattentive, so much so that Nasrollah had to wait half an hour after Somkhishvili had already gone in to be assisted. To add to his disappointment, the bath attendant and masseur were rough and seemed lacking in their service, performing their tasks in a perfunctory way. Nasrollah did not feel so much attended to, but more like a chore to be gotten over with quickly. He was surprised as to why the bathhouse had garnered such excellent accolades.

Once his bath was over, he met up with his friend, who was waiting in the cool-down room, sipping a freshly squeezed, chilled pomegranate juice. When Nasrollah ordered a similar drink, to his surprise, it was a warm and stale libation.

Somkhishvili, totally unaware of what his friend had just experienced, inquired, "Monsieur Minbashian, how did you enjoy the spa?"

Nasrollah replied, "Unfortunately, it did not meet my expectations!"

Somkhishvili, who was a regular customer at the bathhouse whenever he visited Moscow, had always enjoyed the best attention while there. That is why he was genuinely surprised to hear of the unprofessional and hurried service Nasrollah had received. He wondered if maybe Nasrollah was exaggerating the level of his discontent.

Sensing this, Nasrollah offered his drink to Somkhishvili, saying, "Take a sip of my drink to see what I mean."

After drinking some of Nasrollah's pomegranate juice, Somkhishvili's mouth flooded with the warm, sour taste, as he smacked his lips theatrically to show his displeasure with the flavor. He immediately got up from his seat with great purpose, and Nasrollah asked him, "Where are you going?"

Somkhishvili, who had suggested coming to this bathhouse, felt terrible and replied, "I'm going to complain to the proprietor for the disrespect they have shown towards you!"

Nasrollah was surprised to see how upset Somkhishvili was and calmly stated, "My friend, please do not bother yourself; there is no need to complain."

Nasrollah thought for a moment as his eyes began to glow with excitement, adding with a sly smile, "I have another idea. Let us have some fun with them instead."

Somkhishvili sat back down, curious to see what Nasrollah planned to do. When the time came for payment of the gratuity to each provider, Somkhishvili believed that Nasrollah, to show his displeasure, would either pay nothing and give them each a scolding or, at the absolute best, pay them each a kopek or two. To Somkhishvili's astonishment, Nasrollah gave each attendant a gratuity that was much more than they had expected, even if they had provided the best service.

The attendants began to apologize for their lackluster service, now realizing they had mistaken Nasrollah for someone of lower stature and thereby had paid him little attention in their rush.

When the attendants left, a confused Somkhishvili, mystified at Nasrollah's unexpected action, asked, "I thought you wanted to have some fun with them. What happened? Why did you pay them so much? They will only get more spoiled, being rewarded for a job not well done. But never mind; next time, we will go to another bathhouse that shows more respect!"

Nasrollah replied, "If you do not mind, I actually want to come back here again. I don't think they will make the same mistake a second time."

Several days later, on the eve before Nasrollah was to leave for Baku, he asked Somkhishvili to join him at the bathhouse once more. As they entered the establishment, the attendants recognized Nasrollah from his visit a few days before. He was promptly given immediate attention, and every step of the way, he was treated with the best care and utmost respect. Somkhishvili soon realized why Nasrollah had wanted to return to the same place, since now the attendants knew he was a man who would grease their palms, especially if they gave him excellent treatment.

When their bath was over and the time came for the attendants to receive their gratuities, they were surprised when Nasrollah gave them each a kopek, an insulting sum.

When the proprietor noticed this, he politely asked Nasrollah, "Monsieur, I beg your pardon, was there something lacking in the service, or were you not satisfied for some reason during your visit? I ask since I noticed each attendant was trying to offer their finest courtesy."

Nasrollah responded graciously, "On the contrary, Monsieur, I am delighted with the excellent service I have received this day, and I thank you and the attendants for a job well done."

The confused proprietor then further inquired, "So, may I ask why you offered such a disproportionate gratuity for their service today if you were satisfied?"

Nasrollah replied with a smile, "That is because today I am paying for last time's service, and the last time, I paid for today's service, and now all accounts are squared away!"

The disappointed proprietor bowed his head with a hand on his chest in a gesture of apology. He slowly walked back toward the curious attendants who were waiting nearby. Nasrollah and Somkhishvili were within earshot as he explained to the now sour-faced attendants the reason behind the lack of a gratuity.

Having witnessed this bold move by his friend, Somkhishvili could not contain his excitement, giving Nasrollah a congratulatory pat on the back and exclaiming, "Brilliant idea, Monsieur!"

Nasrollah chuckled. "Take a look at their faces; I think we have had enough fun with them. I feel bad for them, but they should have known that it's not the clothes that make the man."

So Nasrollah then called the proprietor back, at which point he handed him a generous tip to give to the anxious attendants. The man, now realizing Nasrollah had no ill intent, offered his full apologies, asserting that he would make sure the servers learned their lesson to not judge a patron by his appearance.

As they left the bathhouse, a bewildered Somkhishvili excitedly said, "That was an interesting way of getting even."

Nasrollah flashed a gratifying smile, enjoying the compliment, but admitted that he did not deserve credit for the idea. "To be honest, I just reenacted a story from a fable about a wise man, Mullah Nasrudin, the Persian version of Aesop. Mullah Nasrudin had also been treated poorly in a bathhouse and had done the same thing to settle accounts. The only difference is that unlike what I just did, Mullah Nasrudin did not pay a large gratuity the second time he visited."

Realizing that in his attempt to just make a point, he had, in fact, paid a hefty gratuity twice, Nasrollah laughed at himself, adding, "Although it seems in this case, the attendants got the better end of the deal. Nevertheless, we Persians learn much about life through such stories."

Since it was their last evening together in Moscow, they decided to go to dinner and settled on the exquisite restaurant at the aquarium. The restaurant was lighted like a cathedral, with beautiful stained glass, and had a stage where entertainment of all sorts was taking place. This included troupes of acrobats dancing and singing national ballads to opera singers performing their art. Many drinks were had to toast this newfound friendship, as they learned much about each other's lives and families. The two men began to share a closer bond than expected after being acquainted for only one week.

As the night wore on, Nasrollah confided to Somkhishvili with great frankness, "Honestly, I am not ready to go back to Persia, even though I do miss my mother, who I have not seen for the past seven years. You know, I came here at the age of thirteen with my father, but now I will be returning to my country as a man. I tell you, as God is my witness, the first chance I get, I will return to St. Petersburg. This is where I truly feel at home, especially since there is still much for me to achieve in my musical pursuits."

At this point, Somkhishvili, recognizing a special kinship with Nasrollah, insisted, "Please, my friend, with the next toast, use Rustam instead of my surname," for the formality that was typical in their initial introduction had by now fallen by the wayside.

Nasrollah complied with a toast to Rustam's health, vowing to return for another toast upon completing his short journey back to Persia.

Recognizing Nasrollah's double-mindedness, a struggle between what he wanted to do and what his duty to his father was, Rustam gave him this friendly advice, "From my own experience, sometimes in life, you have to play the cards you have been dealt, even if the hand seems unfavorable."

Nasrollah replied with the hubris of a younger man, "I do not want to only be a passive spectator in life, but rather an actor that makes his own destiny!"

Hearing this, Rustam began to tell Nasrollah the story of his namesake, Rustam Raza, the famous bodyguard of Napoleon.

He said, "At the age of thirteen, the same age that you came to Russia with your father, Rustam Raza had been kidnapped in Georgia and sold as a slave in Cairo. From that day on, he had vowed that he would escape and return to his family in Georgia. But the sheik of Cairo presented him to General Napoleon Bonaparte to serve as his bodyguard. Rustam Raza found great success as a bodyguard of the emperor, living the rest of his life in France, never having fulfilled his vow to return to Georgia."

Rustam added, "So you see, divine providence is under no obligation to be kind to us all. Destiny had a different plan for the slave-turned-bodyguard, even though he believed he would also make his own destiny."

Nasrollah replied, "But the difference between him and I, my friend, is that I am not a slave."

Rustam took a final sip of his vodka, knocking the bottom of his glass to the top of Nasrollah's drink, signaling it was time to leave, and added, "Everyone is a slave to something or other, but without a doubt, we are all slaves to the whims of fate!"

The next morning Rustam accompanied Nasrollah to Moscow's Kasansky railway station, from where he was to begin the second leg of his journey home through Baku. This would be the end of the line for travel by train, and from Baku, Nasrollah would have to catch a ferry to Bandar Anzali (Port of Anzali), on the Persian shore of the Caspian Sea.

After saying their goodbyes, as Nasrollah took his last step onto the train, he stopped and turned, facing Rustam. He chuckled as he told him, "My friend, I will for sure know when the train is passing through Georgia since it will probably be the most beautiful land I have ever seen," alluding to Rustam's earlier story about his homeland's unrivaled beauty.

CHAPTER 4

CROSSING THE CASPIAN

Baku, Russia, 1905

After two days on the train, Nasrollah finally arrived in Baku, a city that had changed hands between the Russians, Ottomans, and Persians several times. Baku was forever lost to the Russians after the end of the Russo-Persian wars in the early 1800s. In many ways, Baku reminded Nasrollah of Persia, a city where the Persian language and culture were still very much alive.

Baku was swarming with Persians, both resident and migratory, and they were seen everywhere as shopkeepers, mechanics, masons, carpenters, and businessmen. The name Baku itself was derived from the old Persian name of the city, Badkube, meaning "wind-pounded city," due to its renowned harsh winds. It was these same winds that made traveling by boat quite uncomfortable in rough weather on the Caspian Sea.

Nasrollah booked his passage on one of the Russian steamers that carried mail back and forth between the two countries, leaving that evening and scheduled to arrive in Bandar Anzali two days later.

The best of the Caspian mail-boats was most uncomfortable in rough weather. It was not uncommon during inclement weather for three or four attempts at leaving Baku for Bandar Anzali, only to return from less than a mile off the port, back to Baku. Nasrollah was not expecting a comfortable ride, especially after hearing the stories his fellow passengers shared. He became anxious when he heard that for some travelers, this was their second attempt, and even for a few others, their third try to get to Persia.

Fortunately for him, the journey was not a long one. The steamer was dirty, and the mosquitos sharing Nasrollah's sleeping cabin were plentiful and voracious, not to mention the bed bugs inhabiting his mattress that made sleeping difficult.

During the second night of the trip, before they were to arrive, the weather turned stormy. The water became exceedingly choppy, as the size of waves on the treacherous Caspian sometimes rivals the height of oceanic waves, reaching above twenty feet. The movement of the boat in a rolling sea was tremendously disturbing for Nasrollah.

Every moment it seemed as if the trembling ship was going to break up beneath the force of the waves. Nasrollah was terrified and nauseous by the motion of the vessel. Wondering if he would ever see his family again, he questioned whether an early grave was waiting for him at the bottom of the Caspian. The little time he did close his eyes and let his mind wander, he was disturbed by visions of being hurled into the deep, with seaweed wrapped around his face, sinking to rise no more.

Lucky for him and the rest of the passengers, his worst fears were not realized. In the morning after the rough night, the storm had abated, but his seasickness had not. He went outside to take some air. As he stood on the deck with the view of Persia now in sight, he hoped that on his return to Russia, he would not have to traverse the Caspian ever again. He vowed from then on to take trains for travel whenever possible. As he stood there, breathing in the fresh air, he began to feel better but could not wait to take leave of this ship and pursue his journey on land.

Standing close by was an officer, who, unlike most onboard, was not a Swede or a Finn but a Greek. He was waiting to see if the ship could steady itself enough in the winds the storm had left behind to allow the flatbed rowboats to approach for transferring the cargo and passengers to port. The two men acknowledged each other and began to talk about the last evening's storm. The Greek officer mentioned that having traveled this route so many times before, he was used to the Caspian's temper tantrums.

As they continued chatting, the officer said, "You know, whenever I cross the waters of the Caspian towards Persia, I always wonder how it would have been traveling with Alexander the Great, on his expedition to Persia two thousand years ago."

Nasrollah, still feeling queasy, responded with little patience, "My dear sir, to a Persian, there is nothing great about Alexander, the man who destroyed our ancestors' realm. We Persians refer to this man as Alexander of Macedonia, nothing more!"

The Greek officer, who was not expecting Nasrollah's defensive reaction, felt offended and countered boldly, "So, Monsieur, please tell me then, why is it that many Persians name their sons after conquerors who have destroyed their country?" He continued, "You have children named Iskandar, the Persianized form of the same Alexander you just belittled, or they name them Chengiz, I assume in honor of Genghis Khan of the Mongols. I have always wondered why? Was it not he who brutally slaughtered your ancestors?"

Nasrollah, impressed that the man knew so much about his country's history, realized he might have been somewhat unpleasant in his initial reply. So, he smiled and said, "This is the paradox of the Persian: on the one hand, he despises the conqueror for the destruction he causes, while at the same time, he admires him for his ability to conquer."

The Greek officer laughed and mentioned he had a relative living in Persia, right in Anzali. He said, "My cousin came to your country many years ago and has fallen in love with it the same way Alexander did, and like the Macedonian, he also decided to stay for a while. But instead of destroying anything, he built something in your land, a hotel. If you wish to get breakfast before continuing your journey, he does serve a tasty fresh salmon. It will be the best remedy to rid your body of seasickness."

Even though the winds were still strong enough to hinder the rowboat from attempting to reach them, a well-seasoned and enterprising navigator finally made his way to the steamer, and Nasrollah hired the boat on the spot. Once his cargo was loaded on the small vessel amidst the constant bumping into the ship, he got on and made his way to shore, riding on top of the breakers, getting soaked every time the rowboat's nose dipped into the waves.

After a harrowing thirty-minute turbulent boat ride, the expert rower finally got them to shore safely. Nasrollah, still feeling under the weather, took the Greek's advice and had breakfast at the officer's cousin's hotel. He then left for Tehran through Qazvin by carriage, traveling on the cart road that had just recently been constructed by the Russians. The building of this road, however, was not out of the kindness of the Russians' hearts but more as a system of quick communication between their Caspian base and the capital city, Tehran.

Two days later, and after a tiresome journey of two hundred miles, Nasrollah finally arrived in his hometown with an ever-increasing excitement that he had surprisingly lacked when departing St. Petersburg weeks earlier.

CHAPTER 5

THE HOMECOMING

Tehran, Persia, 1905

In 1865, Tehran was first connected by a telegraph line to Moscow and St. Petersburg through Tbilisi. While in Russia, Nasrollah had only communicated by letter with his family, and the first time he telegraphed a message was to acknowledge his father's request to return home. The second telegram he sent was from Baku, informing them of his impending arrival in Tehran before the week was out.

Nasser Al-Din Shah of the Qajar dynasty had instituted The Persian Telegraph Department, a symbol of technological innovation for the country. This department also functioned as a secret agency, which the king used to get reports from the far reaches of the land through the service of the telegraph master. In this way, the shah made his power and presence felt in the distant parts of his realm.

Another innovation of Nasser Al-Din Shah, a great patron of music, was the founding of the Cossack Brigade Military Band, several years before his assassination. This orchestra was conducted by Nasrollah's own father, Salar Moazaz.

Salar Moazaz was an extraordinarily talented and creative man. He played and taught the piano and various wind and brass instruments and was considered an expert at playing the Persian *tar.* In 1898, he had the foresight to leave Persia and take his young son to study music at one of the most prestigious schools in the world. This move was quite unique since Persian attitudes toward music were ambivalent, with many disapproving of music as a career choice. In Persia, music-making, including teaching, was mostly a private affair, with individual classes held at a master's house. Therefore, the concept of general music education was a totally foreign idea.

Salar Moazaz had studied at the St. Petersburg Conservatory, and he was eager to set up a similar system of music education in his own country. He was a pioneer who intended to transform the Persian music scene from traditional instruments and religious hymns to what he considered "new music." Salar Moazaz was also the first person to introduce the Western notation system to his country.

The new music Salar Moazaz envisioned would be based on Western-oriented symphonies and orchestras, with complementing instruments such as pianos, clarinets, violins, and woodwinds. In this quest, he needed the assistance of other classically trained musicians, of which there were only a few in Persia. As his own son was included in this select group, he was eager for Nasrollah's return.

Nasrollah arrived at his family home in Tehran before noon on Friday, the day of rest. As was customary, a lamb was sacrificed to give thanks for his safe return from the long journey, with the meat from the slaughter distributed to the poor as charity. This was one of the traditions Nasrollah had not missed while in St. Petersburg. Though he had no quarrel with the charity, he did not appreciate the street-side butchery of the animal and considered this act a superstitious ritual.

This would not be the last time Nasrollah would find himself rejecting what he considered backward traditions. This event somehow reflected his own transformation from the child who had left Persia to the European-influenced man who had now returned.

After greeting his mother, Khata Khanoom, his two sisters, and his youngest brother, Gholam-Hossein, who at a very young age was a musical prodigy himself, Nasrollah attempted to greet his father.

But instead of hugging his eldest son and welcoming him back home, Salar Moazaz gestured to Nasrollah to instead go and sit at the piano. In all of Persia, there were only a handful of people who had such an instrument, and this particular piano had become a symbol of pride in the Minbashian home, having been gifted by Nasser Al-Din Shah to Salar Moazaz. This was one of the four pianos the shah had purchased and brought back to Persia after visiting Europe.

Salar Moazaz said to his son, "Nasrollah Khan"—sir—"before any welcomes, I want to make sure the many years you spent in St. Petersburg have not gone to waste. I want you to perform the piece of music I have chosen and left for you on the piano!"

Nasrollah was surprised by his father's request, but at the same time, did not mind showing off his skills at the keyboard. He took a few moments to warm his fingers and take in the musical notes and then proceeded to play the piece. After he finished delivering an impassioned performance, tears of joy began to flow from the eyes of his proud—and now satisfied—father.

Once Nasrollah finished, Salar Moazaz hugged his son, kissed him on both cheeks, and said, "Congratulations, my son. Welcome home!"

Salar Moazaz had big plans for his son, as he and Nasrollah had grown quite close during their stay in Russia. Salar Moazaz hoped his son would follow in his footsteps, first as a military musician, and then as a professor at the Dar Al-Funun.

However, in the two years since Salar Moazaz left Russia and Nasrollah had lived alone in St. Petersburg, the son felt he had become his own man, and he had other ideas for his future. Nasrollah harbored the desire for a quick return to Russia to continue his studies at the conservatory with Professor Rimsky-

Korsakov. His domineering father would soon realize he was dealing with a different-minded son than the one he had left in Russia a few years back.

After a few weeks of settling in, Nasrollah became acutely aware that his father was irritated with him. Salar Moazaz was surprised that Nasrollah seemed to lack interest in teaching the new music. Every time Salar Moazaz had tried to discuss his son's future plans, Nasrollah was able to either change the subject or politely excuse himself when he felt the conversation was leading in that direction. But Nasrollah felt the pressure slowly building as his impatient father was on the lookout for an opening to broach the subject. Nasrollah could only hold him off for so long, until one day, Salar Moazaz had waited long enough.

"Son, you have had enough time to settle in, and now it is time for you to join me in my work. These past seven years, you have completed all the music studies necessary to help me transform music education in this country. It is your duty to your family and your homeland!"

Nasrollah, having anticipated this conversation, tried to remain calm and convincing. "My esteemed father, I sincerely believe that I could be of better service to my country by continuing my studies and having the opportunity such as my peers in St. Petersburg to write, conduct, and perform symphonies. Especially where there is an audience that understands such things. You know full well, there are only a few in our whole country who can even appreciate this art when they hear it."

Nasrollah delicately cleared his throat. "Was it not you, dear Father, who in despondence wrote to me that some Persians enjoy hearing the tuning of instruments more than the performance itself, only because it sounds more like traditional Persian music to them? I would rather not spend my time teaching at this point in my life, especially to people who do not have a yearning for the beauty of this new music. Instead, I want to compose for those who already have an evolved taste for it. That is why I must be in St. Petersburg."

Salar Moazaz was shocked at this unexpected and arrogant response his son had offered. He tried reasoning with Nasrollah. "There are many talented students right here at home who need guidance and direction to be taught an appreciation for this new music."

Noticing that his son was not convinced, Salar Moazaz wondered why Nasrollah rejected this opportunity, in light of all he had done for him. He raised his voice in frustration. "You are extremely selfish! Why do you only think of your own fame? This is the height of arrogance to regard your own countrymen as unworthy of your attention but to think that foreigners are. Try to be humble. Humility provides a certain clarity, whereby arrogance clouds one's mind."

Nasrollah, who was not expecting his father to get so agitated, remained silent. Salar Moazaz caught himself, realizing he needed to convince his son rather than scold him. Trying to sound calmer, he offered Nasrollah a more persuasive reason to stay in Persia. "Where would you even study now that Russia is going through political tumult, with the demands of constitutional reform and all the chaos? No one knows when the conservatory will accept students again, so you should put these thoughts out of your mind!"

Nasrollah had expected that his father would ask him this obvious question and had a prepared response. "Some of my fellow students from the conservatory were taking private lessons from Professor Korsakov since his dismissal, and even if the conservatory does not reopen, I plan to do the same."

Sensing his son's fierce determination, an exasperated Salar Moazaz temporarily relented but made a request of Nasrollah that he stay in Persia for at least one year. He suggested that during this time, his son assist him with his ambitious but complicated plan.

As his final pronouncement on the issue, Salar Moazaz told Nasrollah, "After that, then go and pursue your own dreams," to which his son reluctantly agreed.

When Nasrollah left the room, Salar Moazaz turned to his wife and said, "Khanoom"—Madame—"you will immediately begin searching for an appropriate girl from a respectable family to become his wife. We need to tether him to his homeland, for he is like a boat with no anchor, being swayed by every wind that blows." Unbeknownst to Nasrollah, the search for a wife had begun.

Nasrollah retreated from this confrontation feeling defeated and depressed. After the initial excitement of seeing his family, the reality of what he had given up by coming home became apparent.

As the days went by, his family and servants treated him with extra attention as a sign of respect, but also with deferential awe, for he was like a foreigner to them. He dressed differently, and his personal habits reflected the many years he had lived abroad. He had become used to conducting most of his own affairs with the help of just a few attendants in St. Petersburg. But now, he was always uncomfortable with the many people and servants surrounding him. Where he had the freedom to come and go as he pleased before, now his family was curious whenever he left the house.

In Russia, Nasrollah was used to spending his days amongst other talented musicians and having a steady stream of exciting ideas and creative pursuits in the company of his elite cadre of friends. But here in Persia, there was no one to share his views, and he was especially disappointed that his father, who had been his closest confidant in St. Petersburg, was now not in agreement with him.

Nasrollah carried on as best as possible, following Salar Moazaz's directive to introduce modern music to Persia. This was no small task, and when he was not met with outright resistance, the sheer challenge of bringing an entirely new music method to an ancient, tradition-bound culture was sometimes overwhelming. However, there were moments when he found teaching music personally rewarding, especially when his students caught on to the new methods he introduced.

The year passed quickly, and in 1906, Nasrollah was officially recognized when the new king, Mozaffar Ad-Din Shah, appointed him as director of one of the military band's divisions. Along with this appointment, the king also bestowed upon Nasrollah the honorary title of *Nasrosoltan*.

This was a joyous occasion for Salar Moazaz, who had been decorated by the shah's late father, and now his own son was awarded such an honor. This event validated Salar Moazaz's plan for Nasrollah as he had envisioned to continue the family's legacy. Salar Moazaz now saw himself as the head of what was becoming an influential family in the musical history of Persia, the Minbashians.

Nasrollah was incredibly proud of his new title and, from then on, preferred to be called Nasrosoltan, at least in public. These titles were akin to medals pinned on a chest, but they were better in the sense that unlike a medal, which would be shed with the uniform's removal, this title became a part of a new identity. Every time he was addressed, this honor reinforced and elevated not only his status but also respect for the entire Minbashian family.

Nasrosoltan had also become aware of his mother's efforts to find him a wife, and he was displeased. As he had told his friend Rustam back in Moscow, he did not want to be a passive spectator in life but wanted to create his own destiny. Therefore, Nasrosoltan never took the idea of marrying seriously, rejecting the anchor of matrimony his parents planned to use to hold him in place. To his family's disappointment, their match-making efforts were futile.

Nasrosoltan was also feeling overshadowed by his father in Tehran, with Salar Moazaz maintaining a firm grip on his affairs. Back in Russia, living with his father as a teenager, Nasrosoltan had appreciated Salar Moazaz's total control and had no issue with him making all the decisions. But having returned to Tehran, he was alarmed at the level of his father's influence on his daily life, as Salar Moazaz was deeply involved and even decided the smallest of matters on his behalf.

Nasrosoltan realized he needed to make a change to set a healthy boundary between him and his strong-willed father. But Russia was still reeling from the tumultuous political events of the past year, and he was not yet prepared to return to St. Petersburg. So, Nasrosoltan quietly began to look to his friends and family acquaintances for a way out of his predicament.

At the same time, Tehran was experiencing its own quest for constitutional reform. Protestors demonstrated forcefully for more freedom, especially from foreign interference and the shah's oppressive policies. These protests led to the first significant democratic movement in Persia and in the Middle East region when Mozaffar Ad-Din Shah signed the Persian Constitution of 1906.

The signing of this document was a considerable achievement as it established a parliament and a constitutional monarchy. The constitution incorporated progressive and liberal democratic values such as freedom of the press, freedom of political parties, and separation of religion and politics.

Despite the promising beginnings of this newfound freedom, there were still ongoing protests and demonstrations resulting in deadly skirmishes between the opposing parties throughout the capital city.

Nasrosoltan's search for a way out of Tehran finally yielded the desired result when he received a generous offer from a family friend, the commander of Shiraz's garrison. The proposal was for Nasrosoltan to become the leader of the military band there. Even though the position was not as prestigious as his current one, the compensation and supporting benefits were significant, and this would allow him the independence he sought.

When Nasrosoltan shared the offer's details with his father, Salar Moazaz was disappointed that his son acted against his advice and agreed to accept the position in Shiraz.

The day before his departure, his mother, Khata Khanoom, arranged a gathering at their home for the extended family and close friends who wanted to come and personally wish him well in his new endeavor. Food preparation for such an event was always a several-day affair, and so Khata Khanoom spent most of her time in the kitchen to ensure a successful farewell feast.

A Persian kitchen is a beautiful place, at least to the eyes and nose of an Iranian. Persian food is a stunning combination of spices, meats, rice dishes, stews, and pastries, and it is rare that the food ever runs out since so much is made that it is always too much.

Nasrosoltan's mother was preparing food for about fifty people, so many cauldrons were on the fire for the rice and stews. The smell of grilling onions and eggplants and hints of saffron and other aromatic spices, with the ever-present steam rising from the cooking rice, was the perfect picture of her kitchen, and her kitchen was her domain. Here Khata Khanoom was not the quiet lady everyone knew; she was still graceful in character, but here she was in charge, giving commands where necessary to make sure the food was prepared and presented according to her high standards. Her power was the food.

Khata Khanoom was good at cooking because she paid attention to detail—an attention she paid to most things she did. That is why Nasrosoltan wanted to talk to her alone before he left. His mother had a hold on him that he could not explain, and like most mothers, she was the glue that kept the family together. But, in hindsight, a place where Khata Khanoom felt in command might not have been the best place to discuss a subject she wanted to have none of.

Nasrosoltan said, "Dear Mother, I will miss you while in Shiraz, but I do not intend to stay there long, only for a short while, and God willing, I will be back soon. But you should know that when I do come back, I plan to return to Russia soon after that. So please, do not search any longer to find me a wife. And I beg of you to not tell your friends in Shiraz that I am interested in finding someone. I am going to be extremely busy, and I will not have time for that kind of socializing."

Out of character, and to Nasrosoltan's surprise, Khata Khanoom forcefully replied, "My son, don't think so highly of yourself. I now see you have been away from us for too long; this is no way to talk to your mother the day before leaving. You do not know what you want. You do not even know what is good or bad for you. Do not worry; I think with this attitude, there will not be many women showing an interest in you anyway. Maybe your new title has gone to your head! Don't you know the path to up is down?"

Nasrosoltan tried to calm her, sensing that she was agitated, and said, "Dearest Mother, what do you mean the path to up is down? What you say does not make sense."

She replied, "My son, I will tell you, but this is for sure: life will teach you! Up is the direction everyone wants to go because up is where people think they will find fame and glory. However, if you want to build a tall building, you must first dig down to lay a deep foundation. If not, at the sign of any trembling, the building will crack and eventually fall. Humble yourself under God's mighty hand, and don't embarrass yourself any further with this kind of talk!"

Khata Khanoom may not have said these things if she were not in her kitchen, but that is where she felt comfortable enough to say them. And she believed in what she had said. Now that the words were out, she was relieved. From the moment of Nasrosoltan's return from Russia, she had been harboring an intense dislike of her son's love affair for St. Petersburg, as if his own country were not good enough and everything in Russia was better.

Her words reminded Nasrosoltan that his mother still had much power to affect his mood. Recalling Khata Khanoom's temperament from his childhood, he knew she had always been his faithful looking glass. She would tell him off when necessary, if he was doing or saying something he should not, and then she would give him an ice-cold shoulder that nothing could melt. Through trial and error, he had learned that only time could end these one-sided standoffs. But he was leaving the next morning, so he did not have time, and he needed to finish it right there. So he tried to salvage the situation by appealing to her superstitious side, pleading, "Dearest Mother, forgive me. I did not mean for you to get upset. Please, do not be hurt. I am leaving tomorrow, and if you are angry, it will not bring good fortune for my trip!"

From her body language and brandishing of a half smile, he could sense that she relented. He then kissed her face on both cheeks, as a sign of his love and respect, after which she hurried him out of the kitchen, saying, "All right, I am not upset anymore, but now go, my son; a man should not smell of the kitchen!"

CHAPTER 6

THE LEADER OF THE BAND

Shiraz, Persia, 1907

Shiraz holds a special place in all Persian hearts, for it is the birth-place and resting place of two of the country's most revered poets, Hafez and Sa'adi. In addition to being famous for its beautiful gardens, Shiraz is also the capital of the province of Fars, the seat of the first-ever world empire in nearby Persepolis.

Salar Moazaz was not happy with his son's decision to accept this position in Shiraz. He felt the capital city was where his son had a future for introducing the new music. A more disturbing thought to him was about the position itself since Salar Moazaz was not keen on Nasrosoltan becoming involved with the family of the garrison's commander.

The commander was the son of the famous and powerful governor of the province, Qavam Al-Molk Shirazi, a wealthy landowner and a member of one of the region's most prominent families. He had publicly declared his allegiance to the new constitutional monarchy; however, there was a feeling that, in fact, he was just paying lip service to the desires of the democratic reformers. Qavam Al-Molk had no intention of giving up or even sharing his tremendous power over the region to this new democratic idealism.

Salar Moazaz and Nasrosoltan were not only forward-thinking in their desire to bring modern music to Persia, but they were also politically progressive. It was apparent to both of them that the concentration of wealth and privilege amongst the elites had held the country back from much-needed improvements.

Father and son had traveled and lived abroad and welcomed the culture and liberal ideas of Europe, wanting to see similar thinking take root in Persia. That is why Salar Moazaz and Nasrosoltan sympathized with the constitutionalists' intentions to promote democratic reforms in their country.

Salar Moazaz's suspicion of the commander's family's true allegiance concerned him, and he did not want his son to be embroiled in any political drama. But Nasrosoltan paid no heed to his father's alarm and traveled to Shiraz in 1907. The position intrigued him, and he saw it not only as a way of regaining his independence from his overbearing father but also as an adventure to live in this enticing "city of the poets, literature, and wine." As the conductor of the military band, Nasrosoltan believed he would have the necessary autonomy to introduce his unique ideas about music without external interference.

Upon arriving in Shiraz, Nasrosoltan marveled at the pleasant weather and sculpted gardens. The commander welcomed Nasrosoltan with an outpouring of respect and the appropriate amount of pomp and circumstance, which made him feel highly esteemed as an honored guest.

Nasrosoltan had first become acquainted with the commander while they were childhood classmates in Tehran. Nasrosoltan had not seen him since then but was surprised that not much had changed in his physical appearance. The commander was still short and stocky with a round face and small eyes, but now his mouth was framed by a well-trimmed bristly black goatee covering most of his lower sunburned face. He was dressed in his military suit and cap, adorned with various medals, a small pistol at his side, and an ornate jewel-encrusted decorative dagger on his belt.

When the governor had sent his son to Tehran for his education, he was sent to the same school as Nasrosoltan, which gave comfort to the anxious new student who knew no one else. The governor and Salar Moazaz were family friends, so Salar Moazaz had asked Nasrosoltan to look out for him.

From their school days together, Nasrosoltan recalled how the commander had a boastful attitude, always bragging about something to remind others of his status. He was the only child of a wealthy and influential family and felt entitled to act in this way. But to his dismay, the other students were not impressed since they were mostly of the same social status and actually considered him provincial.

He was pugnacious, getting into arguments over the most trivial matters. His display of aggressive behavior in the school courtyard, like a bully, left him with few friends. He could also quickly change his demeanor with whomever he was trying to impress and become incredibly charming. This was especially evident when he wanted something in return. Nasrosoltan heeded his father's request by assisting the governor's son at school and even defending him on several occasions.

And now in Shiraz, the commander was paying back Nasrosoltan for his kindness years earlier. He ordered that Nasrosoltan be given all the allurements one could ask for: a house with a lovely garden inside the garrison, a manservant, a cook, and a gardener.

When he first accepted this new position, Nasrosoltan had his reservations, albeit different than his father's concerns. He was apprehensive that this remote part of the country, far from the capital, would be provincial and stifling. However, after some reflection, along with his eagerness to escape his father's influence, he had dismissed these hesitations. With the dignified welcome that he received, he became more confident in the correctness of his decision.

On the evening of his arrival, Nasrosoltan was summoned to the commander's house for a dinner in his honor. The gathering included prominent dignitaries of the city and the most influential families, including the commander's father, the powerful governor.

Though the party was in honor of Nasrosoltan, the real tribute was being paid to the governor, who presided over his son and all the significant goings-on in Shiraz. Nasrosoltan observed the spectacle with a brief sense of foreboding. As the party progressed, with delicious food and wine being served and introductions to more people than he would ever remember, Nasrosoltan soon forgot this uneasy feeling.

Living in the city of Shiraz was a welcome respite from the years of living in St. Petersburg with its frigid winters and even from the constant hustle and bustle of Tehran, which seemed to grow more crowded every day. Shiraz, by contrast, is a southern city with long, warm summers and brief, mild winters. The population of Shiraz is as sublime as the climate, and the beautiful gardens beckon families to picnic and enjoy the outside atmosphere all year round.

Although life in Shiraz had a restorative influence on Nasrosoltan, after a while, he fell into a lazy routine. His position as leader of the band afforded him great respect in the community, and he was regularly invited to dine with the most prominent Shirazi families.

He soon realized that the position was not as fulfilling as he initially hoped. Nasrosoltan had imagined that he would transform the band from a regular military one to a shining example of innovation for music in the country. His challenge was that the musicians were not disciplined performers. They preferred to play the music they were used to rather than the new music and methods Nasrosoltan was trying to introduce.

Undaunted, Nasrosoltan broached the subject with the commander, appealing for his support to make appropriate changes to promote the needed innovation. Every time he raised his concerns, the commander politely dismissed them. Nasrosoltan's problems seemed trivial to the commander since he was preoccupied with the tenuous political situation in Shiraz. The commander viewed the reformer movement with suspicion, believing they were trying to wrest away the power his family had held for generations.

As the months passed, Nasrosoltan became frustrated with the lack of progress with the band. Most of his energy was spent socializing and enjoying the many comforts that life in Shiraz offered. What had initially been spiritually therapeutic slowly descended into a feeling of passive complacency. However, this all changed with the arrival of a new guest.

Chapter 7

The Governor's Guest

One evening, Nasrosoltan was invited to the governor's mansion, known as the Qavam House, for dinner and entertainment in honor of the governor's birthday. This mansion, situated at the edge of a vast well-manicured garden, housed thirty-two rooms on three stories and was magnificently decorated with tiled poems from Shiraz's most notable poet, Hafez. The garden itself was adorned with an abundance of beautiful flowers, aromatic myrtles, and towering cypress trees, including several date palm trees bordering the ornamental pool.

Upon arrival at the Qavam estate, Nasrosoltan noticed a spacious tent erected in the center of the massive courtyard where the festivities were taking place. The tent floor was covered in colorful Persian carpets, and embroidered pillows decorated the large divans, where guests could lounge about. A band of choice musicians was performing, and a young boy with a magical voice sang some of the odes of Hafez, accompanied by the Persian spike fiddle, and in a chorus by the tambourines.

Many of Shiraz's high society and several foreign dignitaries and friends of the governor were in attendance. Nasrosoltan pitied the foreign guests since, from their expressions, it seemed their ears may not have been tutored to the harmonies and delicacies of traditional Persian music.

Amongst the multitude, Nasrosoltan's gaze became fixated on a beautiful woman. From her mannerisms, she seemed to possess a fiery energy that reminded him of the European women he was acquainted with when living in St. Petersburg.

Nasrosoltan noticed that she seemed to be holding her own in a conversation with several foreign men, and as he moved closer, he overheard her speaking in French. He thought to himself, *Who is this alluring woman?*

So, with much curiosity, Nasrosoltan turned to his friend, the commander of the garrison, and asked, "Who is that lady?"

The commander replied, "She is Shams-e-Zaman, a guest of my father who recently arrived from France."

Nasrosoltan said, "She seems to be a captivating character, don't you agree?"

The commander did not immediately respond to his question but instead stared back at Nasrosoltan like he was searching for the right words. "Perhaps, but now that you ask, I must say she has a certain way about her that can be annoying!"

Surprised at this blunt assessment of the lady in question, Nasrosoltan asked, "How so?"

The commander explained, "For instance, she likes to be addressed as *madame* instead of *khanoom*, as we say in our own beautiful Persian. So, to keep her contented, we call her Madame Shams-e-Zaman." And with a roll of his eyes, he added, "Not only that, but with people she feels close to, she says she prefers to be called Madame Shamsi. What is more ridiculous is that she addresses the men as *monsieur*, as if she were still in Paris!"

He then offered, "I think she suffers from *gharbzadegi*"—a pejorative term meaning "Euro-mania." "She thinks everything here is backward and everything in Europe is so much better. No doubt, she even wishes she were born a *firangi*" (the term by which all foreigners were distinguished).

Nasrosoltan, familiar with the commander's character, was not too surprised by this comment. Even though they had been childhood friends, both had grown up with vastly different worldviews. Nasrosoltan, having lived in St. Petersburg during his formative years, welcomed progressive ideas, while the commander, on the other hand, possessed a narrower view of the world. He had never left the environs of Shiraz, except for having lived in Tehran for a short while during his early childhood. The commander was quite satisfied with the status quo and admired all things Persian, even the traditionally accepted roles for men and women.

Nasrosoltan sensed from his friend's words that everything about Madame Shams-e-Zaman's being, from her style of dress to the manner with which she spoke, ran counter to these local customs of etiquette that the commander believed women should uphold.

The commander's comment about everything being better in Europe did strike a chord with Nasrosoltan. Even though he could have taken his friend's utterance as an insult due to his own affinity toward things European, he was not offended. He decided the commander's mindset about Madame Shams-e-Zaman had more to do with her being a woman rather than her being a Europhile.

Changing the subject back to what he was more interested in discussing, he pressed his friend further. "And is she married?"

"No, she is a widow. She had been married at a young age, from a not-so-glamorous family to my father's close friend, who was appointed the ambassador to France. They lived in Paris for close to seven years until her husband's untimely death. Since her return, she has been staying here at the mansion."

Nasrosoltan then asked, "So how is it that she is staying with the governor?"

The commander replied, "Her husband has left her a great fortune in properties in Shiraz. When she returned to Persia, my father, out of respect for his late friend, requested that she spend her time as a guest at the mansion while arrangements are being made to settle her husband's affairs."

Then he added with a cunning smile, "Dear Nasrosoltan, as a musician yourself, you might find it of interest that she says she plays the piano and the violin. Of course, I have not had a chance to hear her perform, so she might just be bragging!"

Nasrosoltan did not know what to make of this frivolous comment, but this was more in line with the commander's thoughts about women; that for a man, a woman's purpose is to be pleasing to the eye and have a talent that delights his ear.

The commander then quickly suggested, "Why don't we go over, and I will introduce you?"

Nasrosoltan agreed, and they both walked over to where she was in deep conversation with a group of gentlemen.

Her back was toward them, so to draw Madame Shams-e-Zaman's attention, the commander interrupted their conversation by saying, "Pardon me, Madame Shamsi ... "

To Nasrosoltan's surprise, she turned abruptly with a disagreeable face, as if she were startled when she realized who was addressing her. This alerted Nasrosoltan to a sense of animus toward his friend, realizing that their feelings of distaste for one another may be mutual.

However, when she fully turned around and noticed Nasrosoltan also in the commander's company, her demeanor changed, and she quickly composed herself by displaying a pleasant smile for them both.

The commander continued, "I would like to introduce you to my friend that I had told you about, the composer Nasrosoltan Minbashian, son of the esteemed Salar Moazaz."

They made acquaintances. After this brief introduction, where Madame Shams-e-Zaman greeted Nasrosoltan kindly, she started to turn back around to continue the conversation she was having with the other guests before being interrupted.

But Nasrosoltan wanted to continue talking with her, so he tried to think of something to say to keep her interest and blurted out, "Madame Shams-e-Zaman, I understand from the commander that you are a student of music, especially piano and violin."

She turned back toward Nasrosoltan and said, "That is correct, Monsieur."

Nasrosoltan took advantage of the opportunity and added, "The reason I mentioned it is that these two are also my favorite musical instruments; it is encouraging to see such a love of music."

Then, to keep her from walking off, he hurriedly asked, "So tell me, if you had to choose, which of these two instruments would you say is your favorite?"

She responded with surprise, "What an amusing first question to ask someone you barely know. The answer is neither!"

A puzzled Nasrosoltan was taken aback by her forwardness and dismissive attitude, and he asked, "Neither? But how can that be?"

She replied, "As someone who likes to sing, I also consider my voice an instrument, and that is the one I would pick as my favorite!"

The self-assurance she displayed gave Nasrosoltan the sudden feeling of being off-balance and in over his head. He was not sure if he should abandon this uncomfortable conversation and move on or continue. After a brief pause in which he considered a gracious exit, he decided to remain to see where the conversation might lead. She was a challenge, and he determined he was up for one—partly because he sensed she was cultivating an air of aloofness to keep him at a distance.

The commander then suddenly interjected, "Madame Shamsi, Nasrosoltan is also well versed in the French language; you should converse!" as if to test Nasrosoltan's prowess or lack thereof. Or it could have just been a well-intentioned but mistimed pronouncement on his part. Nasrosoltan preferred to see this as a sign of his friend's ignorance rather than his wickedness.

The two grudgingly agreed to demonstrate their command of French, attempting to satisfy what they thought was the commander's curiosity. Even though the commander himself did not speak the language, he stood uncomfortably between them like a chaperone with an awkward smile on his face, acting as if he was a party to the conversation.

While they spoke, Nasrosoltan sensed from Madame Shamsi's reaction toward the commander that she did not want him there. But she did seem delighted knowing that he could not understand their conversation.

They continued speaking in French, and Madame Shams-e-Zaman said to Nasrosoltan, "You know, the commander had earlier mentioned to me that you had lived in St. Petersburg. It must have been wonderful."

He replied, "Yes, Madame Shams-e-Zaman—"

But she cut him off and said, "Please, call me Shamsi if you don't mind; Shams-e-Zaman is too formal."

Nasrosoltan appreciated her request that she be addressed more casually. He saw it as a sign of a potential thaw in her initial stance, and it pleased him that she seemed to want to be on a less formal footing.

Unlike the commander, Nasrosoltan considered Madame Shamsi a breath of fresh air, and he replied, "Yes, I miss St. Petersburg dearly and look forward to getting back soon. Have you ever been there?"

She answered with a sigh as if recalling a magical experience. "Yes, with my late husband when he was ambassador to France, we took a trip to Russia. St. Petersburg is a beautiful city, but if you miss a city so enchanting, think about how I feel having lived in the loveliest city in the world, Paris, for seven years myself. I am glad to see another person who also misses Europe and does not think it a sin to want to live there instead of here. You, who feel the same way, can perhaps understand why my desire to return to Europe burns that much deeper, especially for a woman with my many interests."

Nasrosoltan was curious to know what interests she meant and was about to ask as a ruse to continue their conversation. But instead, Madame Shamsi herself continued to explain, "Even though I love Persia and missed it when I was away, it is difficult for me to pursue my passions while living here compared to living in Europe. I have come home only to put my late husband's affairs in order so I can move back to Paris permanently." And then, with a laugh, she added, "I was born a few years too early for Persia, and it seems a few years too late for Paris! I miss Europe very much and will be going back at the earliest opportunity."

Nasrosoltan felt as she did; he also wanted a quick return to St. Petersburg, which seemed to some not as glamorous as Paris, but it was a city he had come to love.

After this brief but intriguing conversation, they parted company as dinner was being served, and she went to join the governor at his table. Nasrosoltan and the commander were seated at another, with a group of decorated military officers.

After dinner, and as the night wore on, Nasrosoltan kept watch of Madame Shamsi from across the tent, and as he followed her with his eyes, he became more spellbound by this beguiling woman.

CHAPTER 8

THE WAGER

Later that evening, Nasrosoltan, with feverish impatience, decided to approach Madame Shamsi to engage in further conversation. But no matter how much he searched, he could not locate her. When he finally found her, she was surrounded by several men who were watching her play *takhte-nard,* backgammon. She was the only single woman Nasrosoltan had ever seen in Persia sitting amongst men, smoking a water pipe, and playing the game.

Witnessing the desperate looks on the faces of her dispatched opponents, Nasrosoltan could sense their embarrassment at having lost. No player of this ancient game likes to lose, but Madame Shamsi's challengers seemed to especially hate losing to a woman. She, on the other hand, seemed to be enjoying herself, laughing merrily at the expressions of gloom on their faces.

She momentarily raised her head and noticed Nasrosoltan intently studying her every move on the board (for he considered himself a connoisseur of the game). After she defeated her last opponent, Madame Shamsi turned to Nasrosoltan, revealing a victorious smile, and asked, "Monsieur Minbashian, would you care to play?"

He responded in jest, "Madame, after seeing how you wounded these other masterful adversaries, I fear sitting across you with only this wooden board as a shield between us, for I do not wish to be the last in the line of those you have vanquished."

Madame Shamsi looked up from the board she had been arranging in preparation for the next bout, and with a flirtatious smile, responded, "You give me too much credit, Monsieur; this was all the luck of the dice, and it has very little to do with my skill. But as you have heard, nothing ventured, nothing gained, so let us then make a friendly wager. If I win, you will promise to play the piano for me, which you mentioned is one of your favorite instruments. And if I lose, I will promise to sing you a chanson, using my favorite instrument! What do you say? Are you up for the challenge?"

Nasrosoltan eagerly accepted her offer, and he sat down to begin playing. He reminded himself not to underestimate Madame Shamsi as he assumed the other men had, by losing to her in an amateurish fashion.

She played with a relish and concentration he had not seen a woman play with up to this point. He had hoped for an elegant match, where he believed his skill would be enough to get the upper hand. But to his dismay, she countered his every move, and he soon realized he needed to put all his energy into the game. What he thought would be a playful *pas de deux* turned out to be a hard-fought duel instead.

Before he knew it, they were tied two games apiece, and in this last encounter, which was to decide the winner, she had the advantage. Nasrosoltan recognized that if he did not think of some course of action, he was soon to be added to the long list of dishonored men she had bested. He began to engage her in idle conversation to affect her concentration since, as she had jokingly suggested, the dice were indeed on her side. He especially did not want to lose and have to perform like a *motreb*, a hired street performer.

He asked his formidable opponent, "Madame, do you know the origins of this game that you so skillfully play?"

While her eyes were still fixed on the board, with a hint of curiosity, Madame Shamsi responded, "I seem to recall it is from India, isn't it?"

Nasrosoltan continued, "No, not really, but by no means do I wish to distract you. Maybe I should wait until this final game has ended to pursue this conversation."

She asked him to continue, even seeming a bit surprised that he would assume trivial discourse could derail her from her ultimate objective, which appeared to be within reach.

Nasrosoltan determined that with every sentence he uttered, he would hold the dice in the palm of his hand and twirl them around to slow down the game's pace as a ploy to buy time while distracting her from her purpose.

He continued, "In the sixth century, an Indian king sent his minister to Persia with the game of *shatranj* (chess) as a gift for the Persian King Khosrow. Accompanying this offering was a letter describing that this was a game of strategy that pits two armies against one another. The Indian king had added that since there is no other game like it in all the world, he was humbly offering this gift to the Persian court in honor of the friendship between the two empires."

At this point, Madame Shamsi, who was not expecting a lecture on the origins of the game, politely interrupted him with a gentle reminder that it was his turn to roll the dice.

As Nasrosoltan continued to tease the dice in his hand, he asked her forgiveness and responded, "I apologize; I feel I may be unintentionally distracting you. If you permit, I will continue later."

Madame Shamsi was perturbed and impatiently signaled for him to continue the story. He nodded his head in acknowledgment and added, "King Khosrow understood the inherent beauty within this newly created game but was also quite displeased with this gift from the Indian king. In those days, whenever a kingdom offered a gift that was more unique or priceless to another, it was considered an act of braggadocio. Khosrow, in turn, asked his prime minister to devise a game better than the gifted one, so he could send it as his return offering to the Indian king, to humble him and put him in his place."

Once again, Nasrosoltan paused for a moment, asking her forgiveness for disturbing the flow of the game, which had precisely been his plan.

She curtly responded, "Not at all, Monsieur, please continue."

Nasrosoltan pushed on with his lengthy story. "At this point, King Khosrow's prime minister devises this game we are now playing, takhte-nard, and presents it to his king, who immediately sends it back with the envoy as a gift to the Indian ruler.

"When the Indian king first sees the game, he laughs out loud at the Persians' lack of genius, and he says to his court, 'The Persians have just copied our game of two battling armies but without any of the magnificent military pieces. Instead, they have just made each piece in the shape of a wooden coin, with opposing armies only differentiated by color. Where is the strategy in that?'"

Nasrosoltan continued, "His minister tells him, 'The Persian king thought that upon initial inspection you may think little of his gift, but he commanded that I ask you to read the letter that accompanies it.'"

At this point, Madame Shamsi, who was at first slightly irritated by Nasrosoltan's long-windedness, had now become engulfed in the story. She asked curiously, "So what did his letter say?"

Nasrosoltan found her sudden interest in his tale amusing, and as he looked around, he noticed many of the bystanders were also listening to their conversation.

With an ever-expanding audience, Nasrosoltan continued, "The Persian king wrote, 'Most gracious king of the empire of India, we are truly grateful for your wonderful gift to our court; however, there was one slight flaw that we have corrected with our gift to you. In your game, there is no provision for chance; everything depends on strategy. But as you are aware, great king, just as in life, chance plays a major role in the outcome of events.

Therefore, we have included dice, which makes the battle between two armies more realistic. There is always something unforeseen and not planned for that can derail a campaign no matter how well strategized. Hence, the dice adds this element of chance missing in your gift of shatranj!'"

The audience laughed and clapped with pride at the tale of a Persian king outsmarting an Indian one. Nasrosoltan then threw the sweaty dice down upon the inlaid wood board of the backgammon to reveal a double six. This was considered quite lucky and the best roll to have since it afforded the player many options. Slowly climbing out of the abyss of defeat, Nasrosoltan proceeded to battle his way back one fortuitous roll after another. He finally managed to win the game against his now thoroughly distracted and unsettled opponent.

Even though he was grateful for his triumph over Madame Shamsi, Nasrosoltan hoped that this would not be a Pyrrhic victory, to have won at too high a cost. He did not want her to despise him in the process. Madame Shamsi quickly collected herself, realizing perfectly well what he had done, and acted as if the loss did not bother her in the least.

She congratulated him, as did the men who had lost to her before this encounter, supposing that their stained honor had now been somehow restored by Nasrosoltan's hard-fought victory.

She rose at once, and with the most gracious smile, said, "So, Monsieur, per our wager, I must sing a chanson for you, but I hope you accept my promise for a deferred performance. I am sure there will be many such opportunities, so for now, I bid you good night."

Nasrosoltan thanked her for a game well played and replied, "It will be an honor to hear you perform; I am eagerly looking forward to it."

The hour was late, and Nasrosoltan decided to leave with the commander to go back to the garrison by carriage ride. It was a glorious evening in Shiraz, a full moon flooding the sky and beaming down upon the city, with a gentle breeze blowing down from the Zagros mountains, carrying with it the scent of jasmine flowers.

During the ride, the commander said to him, "My friend, you found Madame Shamsi enticing, didn't you?"

Nasrosoltan, unsure how to respond, answered him with a question. "How so?"

The commander replied, "It was obvious; I remember you from our elementary school days in Tehran before you went to Russia. Even as a child, you could not contain your excitement when confronted with something pleasing to your eyes. I see I can still read you like an open book! I am sure you admire her European flair. But you have also witnessed this evening how un-ashamedly opinionated she is. Perhaps that is something you enjoy in a woman? In just a few short hours, she seems to have bewitched you, but I do not blame you; she can have that effect on men. I think I may have also briefly come under her spell when she first arrived. My friend, if you will not be offended, may I give you some advice?"

Nasrosoltan, eager to hear his unsolicited counsel, said, "Please do!"

The commander, pointing his finger at Nasrosoltan, with a warning tone, exclaimed, "*Faghat movazeb bash dari ba atash bazi meekoni!*" ("Be forewarned, if you pursue her, you will be playing with fire!")

He then added, "She is to be fled from, not flirted with."

Nasrosoltan asked, "Why do you say that? Is it because she is much more assertive than most men in Persia are accustomed to?"

The commander told him bluntly, "Even though she out-wardly presents a bold face to assure us of her significance, in reality, she is a hothouse flower; turn the heat on her too much, and she will wilt!"

And then, as his eyes began to widen with excitement at the thought of what he was going to say next, the commander declared, "Also, even though I cannot put my finger on it, she seems to have a peculiar fascination with the forbidden! I know this from what our manservant tells me. She spends more time with my father than I think appropriate. When I asked my father about it, he said it is business-related, but I think she has some ulterior motive."

Nasrosoltan sensed a hint of jealousy when the son spoke of his father and the young woman's attention toward him. The commander had unintentionally, in his warning to Nasrosoltan, let it slip that he had also been enamored with Madame Shamsi. This made Nasrosoltan wonder if the commander was still infatuated with her.

The commander continued, "You see, my father was appointed the executor of her husband's estate before they left for France. Now that he has passed, she has come back from Europe to take possession of her inheritance. My father believes she has not shown the ability to take matters into her own hands, and he still has not decided what to do about it. He worries that someone may take advantage of her, especially if she has full control over the properties, but I have no such concerns. In the short time that she has been here, I have seen her shrewdness up close. I tell you in great confidence, my friend, I want her gone as soon as possible. Forgive me if I have disabused you of your illusion concerning this *zanike* (a rude way of addressing a woman), Shamsi!"

The commander dishonored her by using an offensive insult instead of saying madame or *khanoom*. It was not the excess of drink talking but his way of belittling her, and he seemed to find extreme pleasure in referring to her in this callous manner.

Nasrosoltan was surprised at hearing all this and felt there was something left unsaid in his friend's diatribe against her, particularly Madame Shamsi's side of the story. Nasrosoltan recalled how she seemed uncomfortable with the commander when he had introduced them, and he was now even more curious to find out why.

He found it ironic that if the commander spoke any French, while he stood clumsily between them during their conversation, he would have known there was nothing to fear from Madame Shamsi overstaying her welcome. She was more eager to leave Shiraz than he was for her to go. Nasrosoltan decided to keep this bit of information to himself for now.

The commander noticed that Nasrosoltan was perplexed and said, "This is the last I will talk of her tonight. In your mind, you may anoint her how you wish, but if you pull away the façade she so masterfully covers her true intentions with, you will see what I mean! She is all talk and lacks imagination, even though she thinks she knows better than everyone. So, tell me, why would you be interested in someone like that?"

Nasrosoltan had not come away with a feeling that Madame Shamsi was deceitful, as the commander had insinuated. He was now shocked at the level of the commander's disdain toward her and wanted to delve deeper into the mystery of this woman. He tried to ask the commander what he meant when he said Madame Shamsi was shrewd while at the same time declaring she had little imagination.

Finally, after multiple attempts by Nasrosoltan of asking and not receiving a straight answer, the commander hinted at why their relationship had gotten off on the wrong foot when he was first introduced to Madame Shamsi.

"I was just making small talk when I asked this ambitious and arrogant girl where she preferred to live, Europe or Persia. But instead of answering my question, she offered me a rude and dismissive reply, stating she prefers the decadence of the west to that of the east! What does that even mean?"

When the commander shared the details of his initial interaction with Madame Shamsi, Nasrosoltan realized that her frivolous comment had genuinely offended him. He wondered if this was the reason the commander was still holding a grudge.

Nasrosoltan understood how Madame Shamsi's European mannerisms and bold pronouncements could give the impression that she was overly ambitious. But he did not think that she was ambitious in the usual way, furthering her position at every opportunity for the sake of moving up in the world. Instead, Nasrosoltan saw her ultimate goal to live where she was free to do what she wanted. For a single Persian woman in a male-chauvinistic society, this was an improbable desire.

When they arrived at the garrison and disembarked from the carriage, the commander turned to Nasrosoltan and said, "I may have had too much to drink this evening; please do not take seriously anything I have spoken. Just keep our conversation about her between us."

Nasrosoltan assured him that this was just friends talking and to have no worries, and he thanked the commander for his company that evening. As he lay down to rest, thoughts of Madame Shamsi consumed him. The mystery of the commander's words also plagued him, as he impatiently hoped for another opportunity to spend time with her.

As the days passed and Nasrosoltan heard nothing more from her, he began to settle into his daily routine of instructing the band. He now viewed his dallying encounter with Madame Shamsi as just a stretch of his imagination. However, an unexpected turn of events afforded him the opportunity he desperately sought.

CHAPTER 9

AN EXCURSION TO MARGOON

It had been several weeks since the party, and one evening while dining, the commander said to Nasrosoltan, "So you must do me a great favor; I know I can count on you!"

Nasrosoltan inquired, "What do you need?"

The commander continued, "The wife of the French envoy to Tehran, Maximilien de La Martinière, has asked to visit Shiraz with her two children. They are eager to take an excursion to the Margoon waterfalls in the mountains outside the city."

He chuckled, adding, " I am told the children at first thought the place was full of snakes and were scared to visit" (the name *Margoon* means "snakelike" in Persian, from the way the water crosses through the furrows of the rock).

But then the commander's face turned sour as he relayed the rest of his story. "Once the children were made aware it was just a name, they insisted upon seeing it before returning to France after the ambassador's appointment. I wish no one had told them the truth, and they would have decided not to come. I do not have time for such entertainment!"

Wondering the commander's purpose in telling him this story, Nasrosoltan asked, "And so what does this have to do with me?"

The commander replied, "Madame de La Martinière is a friend of Shamsi from diplomatic circles in Paris, and so they will stay at the governor's mansion. My father requested that I escort

Shamsi, Madame de La Martinière, and her children to Margoon to assure their comfort and safety. This is the last thing I want to do: babysit two women and a couple of children for several days while they gossip in a language I do not understand. I told my father that this was a burdensome task, and I do not have the time for such nonsense! He became outraged over my refusal and only calmed down when I mentioned that you would take my place instead. At least you speak their language, and now that it is a done deal in the governor's eyes, you cannot deny me this favor."

Nasrosoltan was delighted at the thought of spending time with Madame Shamsi, especially away from the curious eyes of those in the garrison and the governor's mansion. However, he did not feel that the commander was asking a favor but rather demanding one.

Nasrosoltan decided to take advantage of the circumstance, fully aware of how much the commander needed his assistance. So, he initially feigned disinterest and agreed that this was nothing more than being an attendant in waiting for the traveling party. Nasrosoltan did not appreciate the commander's *fait accompli* without having beforehand consulted him, but he did not mind his friend feeling obligated to him. He reasoned, the more he sounded indifferent to the request, the larger the commander's debt of gratitude if he acquiesced.

As it turned out, after a few more glasses of wine and amicable negotiation on the issue, Nasrosoltan's calculation was a correct one. The commander's demanding tone slowly changed to one of gracious cajoling instead.

It was getting late, so Nasrosoltan finally agreed to the commander's request. The commander excitedly told him, "My dear friend, thank you for doing this for me. I will never forget it!"

That evening, it was difficult for Nasrosoltan to settle down to sleep, being so enlivened by the thought of spending time with Madame Shamsi once again.

A fortnight later, the French guests, having arrived from Tehran, were now rested and ready to begin the excursion to Margoon. They decided to leave early in the morning to avoid the heat of the day under the famed Shiraz sun. The commander provided a letter with the governor's seal to Nasrosoltan, directing that certain privileges and attention be extended to them on their journey.

He counseled Nasrosoltan, "Do not worry; your trip should not take too long. From what I gather, both women are experienced horse riders, as are the children, so you will be able to make the journey and return within several days."

The commander was ignorant of Nasrosoltan's eagerness to spend as much time as he could with Madame Shamsi, so a quick return was not high on his list of priorities.

The next day before sunrise, the traveling party, including three guards and several servants, left en route to the falls. The commander had been right about Nasrosoltan's companions as they turned out to be accomplished riders. They rode at a brisk pace and covered twenty miles that day. By nightfall, they made their way to a hamlet halfway between Shiraz and their destination, where they spent an uneventful evening, as everyone was exhausted from the hard day's ride.

Toward the second evening, after another day of good-paced riding, they finally reached the alpine village of Sepidan, on the outskirts of the waterfall. They were promptly greeted by the lord of the town, called *kadkhoda* in Persian, and they presented him the letter of convoy from the governor.

The kadkhoda extended a kind welcome in the Persian fashion and provided a guest house for their stay that night. After they cleaned up from their long journey, he invited the travel-weary guests to a hearty meal of mutton, which was too fatty for the children's liking but was a pleasant and well-received dinner by Nasrosoltan and the ladies.

Once they finished dining, the remains from the meal and the traditional tea and sweets were sent out for the accompanying guards and servants. As the kadkhoda bid them goodnight, Nasrosoltan indicated that he would walk out with him to check on the others. After thanking him for his hospitality, Nasrosoltan spent some time chatting with him outside. Nasrosoltan asked him whether there was a different route for returning to Shiraz after their planned visit to Margoon the next day.

The kadkhoda replied, "The other roads leading back to Shiraz may give you a shorter distance to travel but are not as safe. There had been bandits on the surrounding roads until a few weeks ago when I took care of the issue once and for all!" He drew a line across his own throat to depict how he had solved the problem and then added with a laugh, "So why tempt fate? Just go as you came with God's protection!"

With Nasrosoltan still outside, and the children already asleep in the other room, Madame de La Martinière had a few moments to speak freely to Madame Shamsi about what was on her mind.

"Shamsi, you have been surprisingly quiet about what you think of our companion, Monsieur Minbashian! He is an attractive man, and I know you favor good-looking men. So, unless you already have made some attempt that I am not aware of, why have you not found an opportunity to get closer to him?"

They were close friends from their days together in Paris, so Shamsi was not surprised by this direct question, and she replied, "Yes, he is a fascinating man. He does not think like most of the men here in Shiraz; he has a European mindset that is appealing. But as you know, I came back to Persia for one reason only, and that is to collect my inheritance. I have no need for attachments of this sort."

After a momentary pause, Madame Shamsi revealed, "Though, now that you mention it, he may be useful in helping me reacquire what is rightfully mine."

Madame de La Martinière's ears perked up, as she was curious to know the details of what Madame Shamsi alluded to, but Nasrosoltan returned, so they had to cut their conversation short.

As he joined the ladies comfortably sitting on the floor near the fireplace, Nasrosoltan apologized for leaving them unattended for so long. After a short while of talking and drinking tea, Madame de La Martinière reached into her handbag and removed a small package, asking, "Would you like to join me in smoking some opium? My physician in Tehran prescribed it to alleviate my headaches." As opium in Persia was consumed in a manner like wine in southern Europe, the others accepted the offer without pause.

The relaxed state of euphoria that followed their smoking led to Madame Shamsi addressing Nasrosoltan with a sultry voice. "Monsieur, I never forget a debt that I owe, and my obligation to you is a chanson."

She slowly got up and situated herself in the middle of the room as if on a stage. She then began singing a lost-love lament in French with the most captivating voice. As Madame Shamsi sang, she kept looking into Nasrosoltan's eyes, mesmerizing him like a snake charmer, with gentle sways of her head and hands outstretched invitingly toward him.

Nasrosoltan had never felt such an intense desire for any woman before this, wishing the moment would never end. Perhaps it was the effect of the opium, or maybe it was genuine affection, but whatever it was, the feeling crept into his heart and ensnared his soul as he succumbed to her siren song. The sound of her voice seductively beckoned him with a hint of furtive lust, and he wanted to jump up and embrace her. But instead, an infatuated Nasrosoltan remained in place in a trance, with his heart thundering.

Madame de La Martinière, also affected by the opium, lay in a daze, not saying a word, watching this scene unfold and wondering to herself if this was part of Madame Shamsi's unrevealed plan.

When Madame Shamsi finished her impromptu performance, both Nasrosoltan and Madame de La Martinière
applauded, and then she sat down very close to Nasrosoltan.
Without giving it a thought, he reached out and grabbed her
hand, kissing it in appreciation of what he had just heard.

Holding on to her hand, he said, "Madame Shamsi, that was
divine! I am delighted to have won our backgammon match. If
not, I would have never had the pleasure of enjoying your magnificent voice. I am sincerely grateful."

But rather than reciprocate his affection, Madame Shamsi
quickly pulled her hand from his grasp, and abruptly arose and
sternly exclaimed, "We have a long day ahead of us tomorrow;
we should get some sleep now that all bets have been paid!"

She then gestured to Madame de La Martinière that it was
time to go to their room. As Nasrosoltan also got up and bid them
both a good night, he suddenly worried that his impulsive gesture
of grabbing and kissing her hand may have given her offense.

Early the next morning, after a breakfast of fresh eggs, goat
cheese, and tea, they departed for the Margoon waterfalls. They
rode until the narrowing path forced them to disembark and
traverse the remainder of the way on foot. The trail threaded over
and between rocky outcrops that skirted the bottom of the falls,
passing stunning viewpoints along the way. Nasrosoltan welcomed the walk and hoped for some private time to talk with
Madame Shamsi. Fortunately, he ended up alone with her, behind the eager children, who rushed up ahead with Madame de
La Martinière and the guides.

After a while of marveling at the beauty of the surrounding
nature, the two shared some small talk to break the ice from the
last evening's unexpected ending. Feeling the time was right,
Nasrosoltan casually asked her, "Madame Shamsi, I have been
curious about something and have for some time wanted to
broach the subject with you. I hope you do not consider it as
being too forward if I ask you a question?"

Madame Shamsi, who had earlier asked her friend to take the children ahead of them for the same reason of wanting to be alone with Nasrosoltan, replied nonchalantly with a smile, "Monsieur, ask what you wish; I do not offend easily."

He continued earnestly, "I have sensed an animosity between you and the commander, and I am puzzled by this. Is there a particular reason?"

Madame Shamsi replied, "It is really not too complicated, but I do not want to disparage a friend of yours, especially when I am a guest of his father. Let me just say, it results from a misunderstanding on his part."

Nasrosoltan pried further, not satisfied with this half answer. He then confessed that the commander was not as close a friend as she perceived, enticing her to divulge more. "You know I have known the commander since childhood, and I am keenly aware of his reactionary mindset and, at times, disagreeable demeanor."

After a brief silence, where Nasrosoltan wondered if a response was forthcoming, Madame Shamsi began to slowly tell him what happened when she first met the commander.

"When I first arrived in Shiraz from France, the commander paid me an extraordinary amount of attention. I was grateful at first, having been away from Persia for so long and with no husband to take care of everything. I was a little lost."

As if reliving the moment, Madame Shamsi paused to collect herself before she continued. "Then one day, when we were alone, he admitted his attraction to me. I brushed him off as if it were a joke. But another time, he found me alone again in the sitting room, and he approached me, smelling of sweat and alcohol. He leaned in close, breathing on me with his terrible stench, and told me if I were 'friendly' with him, he would see to it that all my business affairs would be arranged in my favor."

Nasrosoltan was shocked to hear this and asked, "How could he do such a thing? So what did you do?"

Madame Shamsi took a deep breath before relaying the rest of her painful tale. "I thanked him for his offer and tried to defuse the situation by telling him that I thought we were already friends. However, he persisted, saying he wanted more from the friendship."

Madame Shamsi stopped walking and turned away from Nasrosoltan, with her head bowed as if shamed as to what she was going to reveal. Nasrosoltan stopped as well, and he gently touched Madame Shamsi's elbow to comfort and steady her, hoping that she would continue.

She appreciated his show of concern and slowly lifted her head and lowered her voice, saying, "Then he physically tried to become too familiar with me, which I immediately repelled."

Looking directly into Nasrosoltan's eyes, she continued, "He seemed to enjoy that I felt powerless. The look in his eyes frightened me. I got a glimpse into the depths of his deviant behavior when he grunted, 'Don't worry, no need to cause a scene, you will enjoy it!'"

Nasrosoltan was beside himself with anger and hit his fist into his other open hand as if he was punching the commander. Seeing Nasrosoltan's reaction, Madame Shamsi continued breathlessly, "Fortunately, I was able to push the brute off me, and I frantically told him to get away and leave me alone, and I threatened to scream!"

Nasrosoltan was totally on edge, with a thousand questions—impatient to hear the outcome. "What happened then? Did anyone come to help you? What a beast!"

Madame Shamsi turned and began walking on the path again. "He became extremely offended, collected himself, and walked to the door, mocking me, saying, 'So, from now on, should I stand over here and talk to you?'

"But then, he immediately returned to sit down next to me, grabbed my hand forcefully, and gave it a slobbery kiss, as if marking his territory, like a wild animal. Then without saying another word, he got up and left the room."

Madame Shamsi threw a sideways glance toward Nasrosoltan to gauge his reaction. His mind was racing, and he was furious with the commander. But before he could say anything, she went on. "It was disgusting, and I felt unclean, so the instant he left, I washed my hands repeatedly, not wanting any trace of him on me. I was frightened and did not want to tell anyone because of my precarious position with his father. I have done everything since then to avoid him, or at least make sure there are other people around to discourage his dreadful behavior."

Nasrosoltan, who was now craving to know all that happened, asked, "What has been the situation since then?"

Madame Shamsi replied, "After that day, even though we never discussed the incident, at every opportunity, he exhibits the most awkward behavior in my presence as if he is a jealous lover of mine. This small-minded man questions all my actions and is possessive over whom I socialize with. Of course, I have not given him any impression of mutual interest!"

Before Nasrosoltan could ask another question, Madame Shamsi continued, "But obviously, he was embarrassed and angry over my rejection and tried to influence his father's opinion of me with untruths and innuendos. Thankfully, the governor has not fallen prey to such nonsense. Unfortunately, the more time I spend in the company of his father, the more the commander finds this awkward, as if it is an affront to his own masculinity."

Madame Shamsi finished her tale with a fiery statement. "The commander is a lewd and ignorant man, lacking any sense of propriety. I actually pity him since he is a prisoner of his appetites!"

Not only did Madame Shamsi's harrowing tale tantalize Nasrosoltan's ear, but it also confirmed his suspicion that the commander was infatuated with her. An infatuation that had only grown more potent by her rebuff and air of unavailability. After a few moments of silence to let all of what he had heard sink in, Nasrosoltan replied, "I'm so sorry that you had to experience this shameful and clumsy attempt by the commander for your affections."

Even though Nasrosoltan felt that the commander clearly acted like a lecherous brute, he sensed that Madame Shamsi's assessment of herself as a scared, helpless victim did not add up. In the back of his mind, Nasrosoltan had a passing thought that this passionate woman, who was clearly skilled in the art of love and intrigue, may have had more control of the situation than she let on. He had witnessed her holding her own amongst a throng of powerful and entitled men at his first meeting with her. In fact, she seemed to relish being the center of attention. Even on this very excursion, she had shown herself to be immensely capable.

After hearing her story, Nasrosoltan was also concerned that his hurried kiss of her hand the night before might hint at his own potential for aggression in her eyes. He needed to distance himself from any comparison with the commander, but he could not help wanting to delve deeper, so he tried to show as much empathy as possible.

Nasrosoltan added, "I can now see why the commander acts uncomfortable in your presence. It is refreshing to see that you know how to take care of yourself when in a difficult situation."

Madame Shamsi gave him a welcoming smile but said nothing in return, so Nasrosoltan continued questioning her. "But if you do not mind me asking, why then do you spend so much time with the governor? Is it to rub salt in the commander's wound?"

Madame Shamsi laughed, acknowledging that she would enjoy the commander suffering at the thought, and replied, "No, that man is really not that important for me to want to think of ways to disturb his peace. The truth is that his father has power of attorney from my late husband and thereby control over all my inherited properties, and he does not relinquish the title to me. He says I am a respected guest, but I feel more like a prisoner. The decision my husband made a few years ago has now come back to haunt me. Especially troublesome is that the apple has not fallen far from the tree. I sense the governor, like his son, sees me as more than just the wife of his late friend. He is subtler than his son, but I believe it is only because he feels he can afford to be."

Nasrosoltan understood what she alluded to and added, "I am sorry to hear that you are being kept here against your will. So, do you have a plan to free yourself from your gilded cage?"

The mention of a plan made her uneasy, and Madame Shamsi responded defensively, "I have no plan! If I did, I would not stay here one day longer than need be. You know what I speak of: why be stuck here when I could be in Paris, or you could be in St. Petersburg? This makes me wonder, why are you here? You have nothing tethering you; why not just follow your heart and go back to the place you love?"

Before this unexpected reaction of hers, Nasrosoltan had felt he was making some progress in connecting with Madame Shamsi. But she appeared to be too masterful for Nasrosoltan, who did not have much experience with worldly women, and he struggled to keep pace with her. When she became agitated, Nasrosoltan thought to rebalance their interaction with a confession, admitting, "Just as your late husband has unknowingly anchored you here, I am also bound by a promise to my father. You could say I am also a prisoner of my word to him."

She then gently touched his arm and, with an inviting smile, looked directly into his eyes and said, "Then it seems we are both passengers stuck on a ship going nowhere; maybe we should both jump out together and swim to our freedom. But you must promise to save my life if I appear to be drowning. Then we can both be free: you from the obligation to your father and me from the governor's curious overtures."

Just as her voice mesmerized Nasrosoltan the night before, these words also seemed to cast a spell over his thoughts and feelings. The commander may have been right in calling her shrewd, for she knew exactly what to say to lead Nasrosoltan further into an obsession over her, without ever making a clear pronouncement of how she felt in return.

Overwhelmed with the hope that he and Madame Shamsi might have a future, Nasrosoltan turned his attention to deal with the potential obstacles to his yearning. The biggest problem was the governor. As he thought about it, he recalled her mentioning the governor's overtures and curiously asked, "Has the governor also made an indecent proposal of some sort?"

Madame Shamsi replied, "No, not indecent, and yes, a proposal perhaps, but not in so many words. I think he is using control over my inheritance to keep me close to him. He is a proud man and extremely suspicious. I think he was even envious of the commander at first, but it is amusing now to see that instead, it is the commander who is jealous of his father's attention to me. Honestly, I am surprised the governor ever permitted you to escort us here to Margoon—unless, of course, he does not know!"

Nasrosoltan assured her that, in fact, the governor did know, saying, "The commander himself had been tasked with the duty by his father, but could not, and therefore he asked me to accompany you on the expedition. The governor had agreed that I escort the group. Believe me, I was not happy that the commander had already promised the governor that I would do it before he even asked me. Don't misunderstand me; I am delighted with the outcome since I was looking forward to spending time with you away from the others."

Madame Shamsi sensed an innocence in Nasrosoltan that was endearing but recognized that the commander had not been truthful to his friend.

She said, "I am surprised to hear this. It seems much happens in the governor's mansion that goes unnoticed in the garrison only a short distance away."

A puzzled Nasrosoltan inquired what she meant. She replied, "My dear Monsieur Minbashian, the governor has been visiting his family at their ancestral home in Qazvin for the past month and is not expected to return for at least another ten days. When do you think the commander even had a chance to ask him?"

As the thunderous sounds of the waterfall crashing down upon the rocks two hundred feet below came into their earshot, this tidbit of information Madame Shamsi had revealed also delivered a deafening blow to his ego. He now saw himself as a pawn in a game he did not even know he was playing.

He stopped for a moment on the path, turned to her, and attempting to save face, said, "Well, now that I know the bad blood between you, I can see why the commander acted this way. He had to obey his father's order so the envoy's wife and children could see Margoon. But understandably, he did not want to accompany you, so he used this untruth to lure me into doing the job."

Nasrosoltan almost stopped there but thought to make clear his feelings on the matter. "I do not mind, and come to think of it, I am even grateful to him! Whatever his demented reason, it is me who is walking with an elegant lady on a delightful excursion, while he sits in the stifling, hot afternoon sun of the garrison."

When they reached the others up ahead, Madame Shamsi left Nasrosoltan's side to join her friend to thank her for allowing them some private time. Madame de La Martinière asked if she had enjoyed her talk with Nasrosoltan, to which Madame Shamsi simply replied with a nod of her head and an affirmative wink.

The party spent a few hours exploring the surrounding area, and after lunch beside one of the small natural pools near the falls, they made their way back to the horses to begin their return journey to Shiraz.

Along the way back, Nasrosoltan kept hearing in his head Madame Shamsi asking him to promise to save her life if he noticed her drowning. He wondered, did they have a pact? As Nasrosoltan reflected upon their conversation, he convinced himself that they did. He could hardly believe how rewarding this adventure had been, and he fell deeper into his affection for her. He desperately wanted to be her savior.

During the next week, back in Shiraz, Madame Shamsi sent Nasrosoltan an urgent message asking if they could meet someplace where they would have some privacy.

Desire, opportunity, and temptation are a combination that does not happen often, but when it does, it is hard to escape. And so, an eager and titillated Nasrosoltan acted quickly and invited her to a friend's house on a quiet, tree-shaded side street near the bazaar. He could barely contain his excitement and canceled his engagements for the whole day, and then struggled to endure the slow passage of time until their meeting.

When it was finally time to depart to meet her, he had to stop himself from hurrying and arriving too early, so he purposely took a longer route to get there. As he traveled toward their meeting place, Nasrosoltan noticed a street-tough man he had seen earlier in the day when he had retrieved the house key from his friend. The man was quite recognizable since he had a distinctive scar running down the left side of his face, which Nasrosoltan attributed to a knife fight gone bad. This unnerved him since he thought to see the man once again, within the span of a few hours, was probably not a coincidence.

It was not unusual for the governor or commander to have people such as criminals and political opponents followed, but he did not know why he would be. As a precaution, he realized he needed to lose the tail, in light of his rendezvous with Madame Shamsi.

He started walking faster and headed straight into the bazaar through one of the grand doors. The man also started to increase his pace and followed him inside. Nasrosoltan finally evaded the man through the labyrinth passages of the bazaar, with time enough not to miss his appointment with Madame Shamsi.

After they met up at the house in the early afternoon, they spent a few passion-filled hours laughing, talking about the future, and making dreamy plans of meeting one day in Europe, in either Paris or St. Petersburg.

As evening approached, they left the house and neared the bazaar where they were to part. To Nasrosoltan's utter surprise, Madame Shamsi did not follow etiquette protocol of how men and women were expected to act in public. Instead, upon bidding him farewell, she unexpectedly kissed him on the cheek and embraced him tightly in front of curious onlookers. This show of her intimacy toward him was welcome, but he was concerned that her outward display of affection would invite gossip when they needed to be careful and discreet.

Nasrosoltan was enamored with her, and maybe he even liked it that she was so bold and unconventional. So, he did not waste this special moment by giving the matter another thought. After such a glorious afternoon, he was consumed with thoughts of Madame Shamsi, and he excitedly looked forward to sharing many more such afternoons with her in the days to come.

CHAPTER 10

THE SONNETEER OF SHIRAZ

Two days later, while Nasrosoltan was still living in the fantasy world inside his head, he was awakened by someone furiously banging on his door. When he opened it, he found an agitated commander pushing Nasrosoltan back into the room while closing the door behind him.

He angrily asked Nasrosoltan, "What have you done? The governor is terribly upset that you escorted Shamsi to Margoon and were alone with her for two nights. Just a few days ago, she was seen in public embracing you! My father is a jealous man; beware of his wrath and stay out of his way, understood?"

Nasrosoltan, who was startled and dumbfounded, tried to catch his breath, wondering if it was the commander who had been spying on him. If so, he now worried that the commander knew about his amorous rendezvous with Madame Shamsi.

Thinking to protect her honor, he chivalrously but defiantly replied, "You were the one who asked me to escort the guests. I did not even want to go and initially rebuffed you, as you must surely recall. You should have told the governor that your misrepresentation of the truth was why I thought I had his blessing in escorting them. What happened to your vow to never forget the favor I did for you? Think of that instead of barging in here and threatening me!"

The commander was taken aback by Nasrosoltan's forceful reply. He softened his tone slightly as he asked, "Do you dispute proposing to her that you both jump off together from the ship that is Shiraz, which is going nowhere? And how comical that you think in this way you would be saving her life!"

Nasrosoltan was shocked to hear the exact same words Madame Shamsi had spoken to him at Margoon and accusingly asked the commander, "Are you spying on me?"

The commander replied, "You know, while you sit at the piano all day and tickle the ivory, we have more important things to take care of. By now, you must realize that not much happens in Shiraz without us knowing. This is not St. Petersburg; here, secrets do not remain so! But to answer your question, no spy told us this. Shamsi told my father what you said to her, and he is furious that you were trying to steal her away!"

Nasrosoltan was aghast and felt betrayed, just when he was about to fall on his sword for her. He found himself standing amidst the ruins of a relationship that had fallen apart before it had even begun. And this, with only a few words from the commander's lips. What the man offered of Madame Shamsi's revelation shook him to his core, and he became worried for his own safety.

Hearing of her treachery, instead of defending her honor, he understood his need to protect his own and replied, "No, no, I did not say those things to her! It was she who mentioned these things. And you are telling me, she told the governor that it was I?"

The commander may have been provincial, but he had played his hand wondrously, using Nasrosoltan to get Madame Shamsi in trouble with the governor. But just as she was a skilled backgammon player, Madame Shamsi had also upstaged the commander in his game. Her story to the governor, repeating everything she had said to Nasrosoltan as his words to her instead, made the governor jealous enough to do whatever she wanted—to stop her from sneaking away with Nasrosoltan.

Now that Madame Shamsi had gotten what she wanted, Nasrosoltan became disposable to her. The governor saw Nasrosoltan's action as an unpardonable insult, and for that, he wanted him gone in a disgraceful fashion.

The frustrated commander, unsure whether to believe Nasrosoltan or Madame Shamsi, asked, "Have you gone mad? I cannot believe how naive you are! Do you not remember, I warned you about her, that you must flee her and not flirt with her. Well, in any case, I do not think it matters anymore. I believe you should leave Shiraz. If not, I am afraid my father will order the guards to remove you, which will bring you much dishonor. I will try to buy time until you leave on your own volition before he has a chance to heap abuse on you."

It was then, in the depths of his despair, and emptied of his delusions of strength, that Nasrosoltan reflected with hopelessness upon all that had transpired. Recognizing that he had been played by those he thought he could trust, with a hint of surrender in his voice, Nasrosoltan told the commander, "No need to complicate matters; I will go on my own accord tomorrow morning."

The commander reached out to shake his hand, and Nasrosoltan wanted nothing more than to spit in it. Instead, even though the duplicity devastated him, he made the gentleman's choice, offering his own hand in return.

Madame Shamsi's deception rattled Nasrosoltan, but what especially hurt him was that her last kiss on his cheek was nothing more than a Judas kiss. What he thought was a seal confirming their love turned out to be the final play of her well-executed plan and her ultimate betrayal of him.

He could not sleep that night except for a few precious moments, when suddenly toward daybreak, a loud commotion of shouts and the firing of shots outside awakened him. A sense of lurking tumult engulfed him, and he feared it was the governor's guards coming to remove him, as the commander had warned. When he ran outside to see what was happening, his manservant rushed to tell him the governor had been shot four times and assassinated by a supporter of the constitutionalists. Chaos ensued within the garrison, and soldiers quickly took positions to protect the commander and others in charge. Nasrosoltan was ushered back into his house, and he retreated to his bedroom to contemplate his next move.

Qavam Al-Molk's assassination led to much unrest and created a power vacuum in the city. Days came and went, and supporters of the shah used the occasion to wage savage attacks on civilians suspected of being a part of the assassination plot. The once calm and almost idyllic life in Shiraz suddenly turned hostile and dangerous.

Nasrosoltan felt as if the winds of violence had followed him from St. Petersburg to Shiraz. Just a short while back, in Russia, he had witnessed the same sort of savagery against civilians demanding similar constitutional reforms.

In the aftermath of the governor's assassination, the commander forbade Nasrosoltan to leave Shiraz until things quieted down. Nasrosoltan had a prominent position as a recognized sympathizer of the reform movement, which suddenly had become a severe liability. His futile attempts to pay respects to the commander over his father's assassination were rebuffed, and he was met with wary faces from even the most junior guards. They were protecting the commander, but Nasrosoltan's rank and friendship should have allowed him some level of access, and he became alarmed at this abrupt shift in attitudes toward him. After a few weeks of feeling trapped in Shiraz, Nasrosoltan finally met with the commander and pleaded for his return to Tehran.

The commander granted Nasrosoltan's request to return to the capital, and when he agreed, Nasrosoltan thanked God that he had not spat in the man's hand rather than shake it, the last time they had seen each other.

On the day of his departure, Nasrosoltan decided to spend the few remaining hours in Shiraz at a public place for his own safety, not wanting to become another victim of the swift chaos that followed the governor's assassination.

He visited the poet Hafez's tomb, as many Persians did, hoping that spending time in the beautiful gardens and reading the *Divan of Hafez* would deliver him from his fear.

As he walked around the gardens, listening to the soft singing of the birds, his anxiety gave way to a sense of peacefulness. He looked around, wondering how he had willingly been lured into this at first deceptively comfortable, yet unsatisfying and intrigue-filled existence in Shiraz.

Tired of his own bad decisions, he vowed to himself at that moment, in the presence of the great poet's spirit, to alter his trajectory and get back to his passions, wherever that may take him.

In the Persian tradition, whenever one faced a dilemma or a difficult decision, one consulted the *Divan* for guidance on a course of action. This was known by the Persians as *fale-Hafez*, which involved fortune-telling by randomly opening a page of the *Divan* and then interpreting the verse in response to the person's query.

Nasrosoltan wondered what his future would hold with his impending return to Tehran. He opened a page, and the sonnet read:

> *"Love," I cried, "a little pity*
> *Show to me, a hapless stranger,*
> *Poor and lonely in Love's City."*
> *But she answered:*
> *"Foolish stranger,*
> *Yours the fault, not mine, for losing*
> *Thus, your way; 't is your own choosing*
> *Blame not me, O tiresome stranger."*
> *Once more, O HAFIZ, dawns the morning cup,*
> *Another day in which to seek her face!*
> *Patience! The day will come, in some strange place,*
> *When thy strong hands her veil at last lift up.*

Nasrosoltan was disappointed to not receive the answer he was seeking, even though he did not know what answer he was looking for. However, he did know it was not this. The talk of love was the furthest thing from his mind. Love, after what Madame Shamsi had just done? *Never,* he said to himself, blaming all women for the sins of one.

Nasrosoltan dismissed the sonnet and this so-called fortune-telling as another superstitious tradition and therefore reflected no further upon its meaning. Of course, this was a sign of his own youthful arrogance, since the great sonneteer, Hafez, always expressed the opposite in his poetry: that one should fight superstition. Although, there was one truth Hafez had offered him, a recognition that he had lost his way, which he now clearly realized he had.

But patience was not the advice he wanted to hear, for what he desired was a quick return to St. Petersburg. He could not wait to reacquaint himself with what he loved most, composing music, reasoning that only music would deliver him from this inescapable yearning that he could not satisfy. He thought, *At least this I know for sure; music will never betray me!*

CHAPTER 11

A LETTER FROM A FRIEND

Tehran, Persia, 1908

By June of 1908, with the ill-fated Shiraz adventure behind him, Nasrosoltan began planning his return to Russia. Tehran was now embroiled in political turmoil as Mozaffar Ad-Din Shah, who had signed the new constitution, had died, and his son, Mohammad Ali Shah, had inherited the throne.

With the help of both the British and the Russians, Mohammad Ali Shah tried to subdue and eliminate the new parliament elected during his father's rule. Ironically, this move was a rare show of unity between these two European powers that had divided Persia into two separate zones of influence. The young shah attempted to cut short this democratic movement with the help of the Persian Cossack Brigade—the only capable military unit available to the king at the time.

The Cossack Brigade was the elite cavalry unit modeled after the Caucasian Cossack regiments of the Imperial Russian Army. The brigade was independent of the regular Persian army, and even though the rank and file of the squad were Persian, the troops were commanded by Russian officers.

This did not sit well with many of the Persian recruits, who felt they had no opportunity for career advancement. Even more galling to them was that the brigade was effectively under the control of the Imperial Russian Legation in Tehran. Since it was the brigade that had kept Mohammad Ali Shah on the throne after his father's death, the new king was considered a Russian puppet.

In late June, under the command of Colonel Vladimir Liakhov, the brigade shelled the parliament building, directly attacking the core of Persia's nascent democracy. And the colonel's atrocities did not stop there, as he then ordered the execution of several leaders of the constitutionalists. Liakhov's show of support to the shah led the king to appoint the Russian as military governor of Tehran.

It amazed Nasrosoltan that wherever he went, from St. Petersburg to Shiraz and now back to Tehran, there was such violence being unleashed. He had no intention of staying any longer in a city that had effectively become a military garrison, frantically trying to get his paperwork ready for a quick return to Russia.

He wrote to his friend Rustam, with whom he had been in regular correspondence since his return to Persia, inquiring if he deemed the situation in St. Petersburg now suitable for his return. Seven weeks later, he received a reply letter from Rustam, but the contents caused him much consternation, for it bore some news Nasrosoltan was not expecting.

> *21 August 1908*
> *My Dear and Respected Friend, Nasrollah,*
>
> *Greetings from St. Petersburg. I wonder if I should now address you as Nasrosoltan instead? I derived much pleasure reading about your prestigious title awarded by the king. I congratulate you. However, I will wait until we meet again to toast to each other's health, as you promised we would do, to see by which name you wish a friend to call you.*
>
> *In any case, I eagerly await your return to Russia, for you have already been away longer than you had initially anticipated. It will be a pleasure to see you once*

again. As you must be aware, much has happened here in Russia, especially in St. Petersburg, since your departure.

Even as people go on about their business, there is much anxiety in the air, with those demanding constitutional reforms getting bolder by the day. There is the fear of another Bloody Sunday. There are strikes and political demonstrations, and the revolutionaries are causing social unrest. What is especially alarming is the political assassination of civil servants and police.

I have read in the Petersburg Gazeta-Kopeika *that your country is going through similar times. I pray that you stay safe and that these events will not further delay your return.*

For my part, I thank God that he has blessed me with good fortune concerning my business ventures. Since Russia's loss in the war with the Japanese a few years ago, the tsar demanded that the Trans-Siberian Railway be upgraded from a single track. Many here blame the single track for supply difficulties and eventually defeat. This new directive of the tsar increased the need for iron products, and my business prospects have soared as a result. Consequently, I have also made many friends in high society in St. Petersburg, some of them with significant influence in the royal court.

Not all the news is good news, though, as just a few months ago, I contracted typhoid from eating bad oysters, and I was confined to a nursing home for several weeks. What you may find of interest is that after my recuperation, I received an invitation to a private performance by the St. Petersburg Court Orchestra. They performed the new work of your fellow student at the conservatory, Stravinsky.

I did enjoy the piece, even though I am no connoisseur of the symphony. The program notes mentioned his dedication "to my dear teacher, N.A. Rimsky-Korsakov," which made me think of you and how you desired to return to apprentice under his tutelage. This Stravinsky has caused quite a stir in St. Petersburg music society, and some critics have even gone as far as to state that "he is breathing new life into what is considered a moribund Russian music scene."

Upon reading these last few sentences, Nasrosoltan suddenly felt a tremendous disappointment in the course his own life had taken, as he had not created any music of significance since he left Russia. He wondered if he had been wasting his time directing military bands in the middle of nowhere when he could have followed in the footsteps of the likes of Stravinsky, in the center for the arts, St. Petersburg.

Nasrosoltan became so despondent that he almost did not finish reading the final paragraph of Rustam's letter, which bore the news that would change the direction of his own life:

Hopefully, you will soon return to further your music studies and write similar music; however, I am sorry to inform you, if you have not yet heard, that in June of this year, Professor Korsakov died after a long illness. The music community here is deeply saddened, as I am sure you are also when reading this. I never like to finish a letter to a dear friend on a sad note, so please forgive me if this is the first you have heard of this news.

I am considering permanently moving to St. Petersburg from Georgia since my business now demands it. If I do, upon your return, it will allow us to see each other more often. I look forward to hearing from you soon.

With great respect, your friend,
Rustam

Nasrosoltan could not believe that Professor Rimsky-Korsakov was dead. He now realized he would never have the chance to study with him and cursed himself out loud for having obeyed his father's command to return. Nasrosoltan regretted not following his heart and staying in St. Petersburg, as the opportunity he desperately sought had now slipped through his fingers.

Salar Moazaz was curious to know what was in the letter from St. Petersburg, and when he asked Nasrosoltan, a wave of despair descended over his son's face.

Nasrosoltan's voice was tinged with sadness as he told him, "Father, I am sorry to tell you that your teacher Professor Rimsky-Korsakov passed away a few months ago, after a long illness."

Nasrosoltan let out a sigh as he fell into self-pity and continued hopelessly, "Now my dream of working with him is finished!"

Salar Moazaz, who was also distraught by this news, gave Nasrosoltan a gentle pat on the back and tried to console him. "My son, in Persian, we have a saying, that death is a camel that kneels before every door! So we should have expected that at some point, we would hear this news. The professor was a kind and decent man, and he never treated the foreign students any different than the Russians. I do owe him much gratitude for his unique gift of teaching me the intricate details of harmony. *Khoda-beeamorzatesh.*" ("May God bless his soul.")

Salar Moazaz continued by asking, "So can I assume you will be postponing your return until a more favorable time, or better yet, not go back at all, since your whole purpose for returning to Russia was to work with the maestro, wasn't it?"

Nasrosoltan, who was still in deep anguish over the unexpected news, said nothing in response, so Salar Moazaz continued, "Although this is unfortunate news, it is a sign that you should stay and, as I have said before, serve your country. I need your help in educating the next generation of musicians, and who better to assist me in this endeavor than you?"

Nasrosoltan was disturbed that his father wanted him to now stay even longer and responded defiantly, "Dear Father, no one understands better than you that, as a composer, I want to write music and have it performed for receptive ears. There are only a handful of people here in Persia who can even read the notes I put to paper, let alone appreciate the work once it is performed. I am already so far behind my peers. My friend Rustam, in his letter, mentioned that another conservatory student, Stravinsky, has already written and had a symphony performed in St. Petersburg. He has even received great praise in all reviews!"

Salar Moazaz replied as if it was apparent, "Who stops you from writing the music you so wish to express? Is the ink or paper any different here than it is in St. Petersburg?

"Can it be that you are using this as an excuse for the fact that you have not produced anything? It is natural, for I also have had moments where my writing is blocked. But as you can see, I have been able to write great music after many attempts and failures. It is the nature of artists to feel repressed, but then some event, such as was the case for me with the Constitutional Revolution, opens the channel of creativity. Even the recent travesty committed by Liakhov, shelling our treasured parliament building, has stirred up feelings in me that I use to write. I participate in the rebellion against what I feel is injustice through writing inspiring music.

"You should use this time, right here and right now, to compose, and you will start seeing results. The same Professor Korsakov you so wished to have worked with wrote nationalistic music. You, too, can write *soroods*"—national and patriotic marches—"which our country is in dire need of!"

Nasrosoltan became defensive and interjected, "But, Father, it is difficult to work where the culture does not value this new music and the musicians who perform it. I just heard from a friend who lives in southern Tehran that he has to carry his violin underneath his cloak whenever he leaves the house. Do you know why? It is for fear of the reactionaries taking it and breaking it since they despise music for their own demented reasons."

Salar Moazaz, displeased at being interrupted, replied, "Son, this is the exact reason I am asking for your assistance! We must change the culture that sees music as a threat or a vice but should instead see it as a vehicle for lifting the spirit. People are now divided in how they think of these matters.

"Ours is a country that needs a unified identity. When someone comes to Tehran from Shiraz, that person feels he is in a different country, for he only considers his *vatan*"—homeland—"as the place he was born. However, in ancient Persia, one would travel thousands of miles and proudly still feel a part of the same great empire. You think that being written up in a St. Petersburg newspaper is the ultimate sign of success? But I believe being able, through the gift of music, to make that same Shirazi feel like he is part of a greater nation-state wherever he goes in this beautiful land of ours is the pinnacle of success. And yes, even though no newspaper will write your praise, your reward will truly be greater than that. This is where you should search for your legacy!"

Nasrosoltan's father went on with added fervor, "It was these same soroods and not the symphonies that you so desire to compose that were part of Persian culture before the Arab invasion centuries ago."

Nasrosoltan sat speechless, deep in thought, listening to his father ramble on. Salar Moazaz took advantage of the silence and continued by reminding his son of the proud history of Persia. "The victorious armies of Cyrus and Darius fought and conquered the known world at the time, with military musicians at their side in the field of battle, giving them courage through hearing these anthems."

Nasrosoltan countered, "Dear Father, I can see the role marches may have had in the history of our country, but we live in different times now. I want to write symphonies because I do not believe there is a great demand for ordinary marches."

Salar Moazaz took offense at his son's belittling the writing of marches, which was his own specialty. He defended his argument, trying to convince Nasrosoltan one last time by adding passionately, "Even great European composers wrote and performed grand marches. The famous Austrian Strauss composed one such march, of all things, called 'Persischer Marsch.'" ("Persian March.") "Isn't it a shame that instead of a Persian, a European had to write a Persian march?"

As he made this last comment, Salar Moazaz was visibly exasperated with trying to change his son's mind, and he signaled that the conversation was over.

A disheartened Nasrosoltan realized he was almost disrespecting his father with the continuous back-and-forth arguments, as he returned to his room to reflect upon their uncomfortable conversation.

When he calmed down, he thought that his father was right; now that the professor had died, there was no immediate rush to return to St. Petersburg. Nasrosoltan decided that he would tell his father what he wanted to hear: that he would stay a bit longer. At the same time, he continued to plan for an eventual return to Russia to make his own mark as a composer.

Nasrosoltan reluctantly agreed to his father's request to teach at the Dar al-Funun music school. The school had been closed due to the conflict between the constitutionalists and the shah but was now set to reopen. Nasrosoltan spent the next year teaching and slowly realized that through instructing, he had redeveloped the desire to write music.

As his pupils showed signs of progress in their understanding of the music, he derived a sense of real satisfaction. He recognized that his father was correct about the influence he could wield, especially with young, fresh, and fertile minds starting to develop the same passion he had for music. To Salar Moazaz's delight, Nasrosoltan did what his father had suggested and began work on several marches.

The one thing Nasrosoltan still missed, however, was the atmosphere of the cafés in St. Petersburg. There he would sit for hours drinking and discussing music with other conservatory students, debating the new music evolving right before their eyes. But in Persia, there were only a few with whom he could discuss such ideas, and this thirst to share his passion for music with like-minded composers deepened his longing to return to St. Petersburg.

The longer he stayed in Persia, he worried he would lose the dream St. Petersburg represented. For him, this meant the freedom to create and thrive independently from his family obligations. Nasrosoltan was left suffering from this inner conflict, unsure of what to do next.

At the same time, the volatile situation between his two beloved countries was also moving toward a climax. As neighboring countries, Russia and Persia had a long, complicated, and frequently competitive history.

The recent Russian influence to support the shah finally resulted in a violent backlash by the Persian people. In July of 1909, with the help of resistance fighters from the north of Iran, the constitutionalists finally defeated Colonel Liakhov's Russian-backed forces and conquered Tehran. Mohammad Ali Shah was able to escape to exile in Russia, and the Second Parliament, in an extraordinary meeting, replaced the fleeing shah with his eleven-year-old son, Ahmad Shah.

This was welcome news for Salar Moazaz and Nasrosoltan, for they had both sided with the constitutionalists in spirit and despised Liakhov. Since the Russian colonel was the Cossack Brigade's commander and Salar Moazaz had to report directly to him, his political feelings about Liakhov had created friction between them. Salar Moazaz finally felt relieved, personally, and for his country's hope of reform, that Liakhov would be out of the picture once and for all.

In honor of the liberation of Tehran, Salar Moazaz was inspired and wrote what was to become the first Persian national anthem. As his crowning achievement, Salar Moazaz was honored to have this piece performed at the new shah's coronation and again during the shah's visit to Great Britain. This further intertwined nationalism and music, as the elder Minbashian had always wished.

CHAPTER 12

A MAN OF THE CLOTH

During the summer of 1912, as was the custom with many well-to-do Persians, Nasrosoltan's family moved from their home in Tehran to their summer garden in the foothills of the Alborz mountains. They did this to spend the hottest months of the season in a more favorable climate. The setting of this garden, with its simple cottage and surrounding wooded areas, including a creek of ice-cold water flowing down from the mountains, was a welcome relief from the hubbub of the capital city.

The Minbashians were welcoming to guests on day trips from Tehran. They always made sure plenty of kababs were served alongside wine or the favorite *arak* (an anise-flavored, distilled alcoholic beverage). On many occasions, guests would bring along friends and family without prior notice, for Salar Moazaz enjoyed meeting new people and was known to be a gracious host.

On Fridays, for entertainment, there would be many activities after lunch, such as reciting poetry and playing card games and backgammon. Most of these activities would take place on large wooden bedframes, covered in Persian carpets and lined with pillows. The guests could lean back or lie down as they wished, enjoying tea from the samovar or the cold watermelon and salted cucumber slices by their side.

One such Friday, a cousin of Nasrosoltan named Abbasgholi Khan, who worked in the newly created Government Gendarmerie, came to the outing accompanied by a young and rather peculiar-looking man. When he introduced this man, Abbasgholi Khan announced, "Our guest today is also known to some as a man of the cloth!"

Nasrosoltan, who was quite close with his cousin, inquired privately, "Dear cousin, why did you bring this man that no one knows to our gathering—and a cleric at that?"

Abbasgholi Khan let out a hearty laugh, and to alleviate Nasrosoltan's concern, he said, "This man is the furthest thing from a cleric. I met him at another gathering and thought to bring him to add to the after-lunch entertainment today. He is, in fact, a *falgir*"—fortune-teller—"and everyone will soon see why he is known as a man of the cloth!"

Nasrosoltan was not pleased, as he did not believe in this type of superstition. He was always surprised how people could so readily rely on a cup of coffee or a deck of cards to divulge an unknown future and how they could even pay large sums for such a ridiculous pastime.

In Russia, Nasrosoltan had seen the vast popularity and cultural impact fortune-telling had on the people and how it had also found acceptance among the most educated strata of St. Petersburg society. In fact, some people would not make any decision without consulting such seers for guidance.

In Persia, this was one of the instances where Nasrosoltan agreed with the clerics who opposed fortune-telling. But his reason for not appreciating divination was different than theirs. Nasrosoltan believed fortune-tellers were plainly hoaxers and charlatans looking to fleece the uninformed. However, he did not attach any religious prohibition against this fascination, as the pious did while quoting their sacred texts.

Abbasgholi Khan said, "Don't worry; it's all in good fun, but I have to admit I was so surprised at this man's abilities and what he revealed about my own future that I just had to bring him."

Abbasgholi Khan moved closer to Nasrosoltan and lowered his voice to a whisper. " The man is both deaf and mute, from birth, I believe."

Since the fortune-teller could not speak, he used an oversized piece of cloth with all kinds of words and numbers written on it. He would point to them when wanting to express what he foresaw in someone's future. There were also several sizable rectangular dice that did not have numbers but instead had unintelligible symbols that only the falgir could decipher. He used these by rolling them and then writing out on a piece of paper, in formulaic fashion, a calculated final number which directed him to the word or number he would point to on the cloth.

Nasrosoltan decided he was not going to partake in this charade. So, he sat by as several of the women had their fortunes told, with the falgir gesticulating wildly and grunting unintelligibly to get his point across. The ladies were bewildered and could not believe what they were witnessing.

From their expressions, it seemed the man was reading right through them with his accurate portrayals, leaving them in a state of both shock and amazement.

One of the women turned to another to ask, "How can he know this?" Some laughed nervously, and others feigned anger, attempting to dispel the information his dice and cloth provided, which they did not want broadcast publicly. It pained Nasrosoltan's conscience to see the fortune-teller deceiving these inquisitive women.

Sensing Nasrosoltan's disdain, the fortune-teller then turned to him and gestured to have his future told. Nasrosoltan shook his head to say no, but the man pointed to a word on his cloth in response. Nasrosoltan looked closer to see what word he alluded to, and it read *fear*.

Nasrosoltan broke out in laughter and turned to Abbasgholi Khan and asked, "Is he trying to say I am afraid of him?"

His cousin replied, "No, I think he means you fear hearing your fortune told."

Nasrosoltan dismissed the idea that he was fearful of a few words on a piece of cloth and the absurd formulas of a fraud. But after his cousin's repeated insistence, Nasrosoltan finally agreed to have his fortune told in the spirit of some afternoon fun.

In the weeks leading up to this Friday gathering, Nasrosoltan had been preoccupied with the plans for his desired return to Russia. He had determined that even though Rimsky-Korsakov had died, he still wanted to pursue his music career in St. Petersburg.

Nasrosoltan was finding it difficult to enjoy this get-together with friends and family. The source of his anxiety was a letter he had received a few days earlier from Rustam, replying to his inquiry as to whether the conservatory would readmit him for the next session. Rustam wrote:

> *I have met with the conservatory director through the introduction of a good friend. As fortune would have it, the new director is none other than your music professor when you had first come to St. Petersburg, Alexander Glazunov!*
>
> *Glazunov says he remembers you fondly, as he does your father, and he seemed eager for you to continue your studies here. He mentioned that there are now specific new regulations that have been instituted after the reopening of the conservatory. One is that foreign students now need a letter of introduction from the Russian legation in their home country.*
>
> *Glazunov has reassured me that since you have already been an alumnus of good academic standing at the conservatory, you are sure to be welcomed. Still, his hands are tied with this new decree, which is now a necessary requirement of readmittance, albeit a formality due to your prior relationship. He emphasized that the*

new session would begin in late September, so the con-
servatory would need your letter no later than the first
week of September to reserve you a place.

This news caused Nasrosoltan much trepidation as the tim-
ing was tricky, leaving him only a few weeks to get the letter and
send it on to St. Petersburg. But what disturbed him further was
that when he went to the legation to get the letter, they told him
that this was under the purview of the man he and his father both
despised—Colonel Liakhov.

Liakhov was the barbaric man who ordered the shelling of
their sacred parliament building and hunted down and executed
several constitutionalist leaders. He was a man who believed
blood spilled for his cause was blood well spilled, and he always
told his troops that the constitution was their enemy. Everything
about the man ran counter to the beliefs of the Minbashians.

Liakhov was pardoned by the constitutionalists after his surrender and the liberation of Tehran, as the Persian government
feared retribution from the tsar if any harm came to him. After a
while serving in the capital, the Russian colonel was now summoned back to St. Petersburg.

Nasrosoltan was engulfed in an internal battle between his
burning desire to go back to St. Petersburg and his revulsion at
asking Liakhov for the necessary letter. He did not pursue the
matter any further once he realized the hated Russian would need
to be involved. However, Nasrosoltan also recognized another
year of work at the conservatory would be missed if he did not
seek the colonel's help.

Time was now of the essence, and in the days leading up to
this Friday gathering, Nasrosoltan was slowly losing bits of his
resolve. He came close to succumbing and almost made an appeal to his father for help, but he knew Salar Moazaz did not
want the Russian's name even brought up, let alone requesting
any kind of assistance from him.

Nasrosoltan was lost deep in thought as to what to do about his situation when the falgir suddenly let out a shriek to get his attention. He then rolled the dice in his hand and let them loose on the carpet-covered wooden bed frame.

The fortune-teller looked at the dice with a hint of surprise, raising a quizzical eyebrow as if questioning the result, and quickly made some calculations that seemed to be for show. The falgir then wrote down something and pointed to the word *love* on his cloth. With a strange smile on his face, he showed Nasrosoltan what he had written on a scrap of paper.

It read, *You do not believe in fortunes, not even those that poets tell you from the grave.* Then he pointed to the word *love* again, signaling what topic he meant.

Nasrosoltan was startled since he had told no one of the *fal-e Hafez* he had read at the poet's tomb in Shiraz. That sonnet had also spoken of love, but Nasrosoltan had quickly dismissed it.

Like the women who were shocked at hearing their fortunes told, Nasrosoltan also wondered, *How could this man have known such a thing? This is more than just a mere coincidence!*

Once again, he was pulled out of his thoughts when the fortune-teller waved his hand vigorously in front of Nasrosoltan's eyes, alerting him to the next revelation.

The falgir pointed to the word *safar* (journey) on the cloth, and with wild movements of his hands, he gestured that there was a long journey in Nasrosoltan's near future. Then he pointed to the word *love* again, which Nasrosoltan took as maybe a good omen for his return to St. Petersburg in pursuit of the music he loved.

Suddenly, the man shook his head as if to indicate he saw something unpleasant. He immediately pointed to the word *khanevadeh*, meaning "family," and with his hands, he made a tearing gesture, implying a falling apart.

Nasrosoltan laughed at the ridiculousness of this prediction, for he wondered how it could be that he would ever break with his family.

"Never!" he exclaimed, and the fortune-teller displayed a sly smile and directed his attention to a final word on the cloth, which read *pride*, and then he pointed directly at Nasrosoltan.

The falgir wrote on the paper, as his final pronouncement, *It is pride that is the enemy of love.* Then he made the tearing gesture with his hands one last time and bowed his head, signaling he was done.

What Nasrosoltan expected to be an entertaining afternoon turned into a not-so-pleasant one, and he became anxious.

He thought, *What did the man mean, that pride is the enemy of love?*

He reasoned that the falgir was evidently mistaken, and it was hate, not pride, that was the enemy of love.

After the falgir finished reading Nasrosoltan's fortune, Abbasgholi Khan noticed the sudden change in his cousin's demeanor and suggested that they take a walk in the woods.

All along the way, Nasrosoltan was quiet and still buried in his thoughts. Assuming it was the fortune-teller's words that were haunting him, Abbasgholi Khan tried to lift Nasrosoltan's spirits. "Dear cousin, in your face, I read that you are troubled. If it was something he said, don't worry. In his readings, the falgir throws out many things to see what sticks, and sometimes he gets lucky. He is just an entertainer, so don't let him ruin the rest of your day with his ramblings."

Nasrosoltan hid his true feelings from Abbasgholi Khan, assuring him that it wasn't the fortune-teller's words but the uncertainty about his return to Russia that distracted him.

Later that week, the Russian legation planned a ceremony in honor of Liakhov before his return to St. Petersburg. High-ranking officers of the Cossack Brigade, including Salar Moazaz, were expected to attend as a formality, though no one found a reason to celebrate anything about this man.

On the evening of the event, Nasrosoltan, who was not invited, said to his father, "If you permit, I would like to join you in attending the ceremony."

A surprised Salar Moazaz asked, "Why would you want to come when I don't even want to attend myself, especially that you have no such obligation?"

Nasrosoltan answered, "Dear Father, after many weeks of internal conflict about what I should do, I have finally decided to swallow my pride and ask Liakhov to write a letter of introduction for me. This is the only way a place can be reserved for me at the conservatory in time for the next session."

Salar Moazaz was shocked, and he angrily responded, "You say you are swallowing your pride, but it is your pride that is making you want to do such a thing! It is your pride that is deceiving you into thinking that St. Petersburg has a better future for you than staying in your homeland and composing music here. For the hope of this fame and fortune, are you willing to prostrate yourself before this Russian?"

Nasrosoltan quickly tried to console his father and confessed, "Father, I mean no disrespect, but how many national anthems does Persia need? You have already written one, which will last for a long time, and another is not needed."

This comment seemed to have the desired effect. Salar Moazaz, who was about to erupt, began to listen carefully and visibly became less agitated as his son pleaded his case.

Nasrosoltan continued softly in a respectful tone, "You are also a composer; why can you not understand what I am feeling? I have within me this burning desire to compose, but the environment is not suitable for me here. If I stay any longer, I will end up contributing nothing of significance."

Nasrosoltan paused briefly to let this last admission sink in before he went on with his most profound confession, pouring his heart out. "Every moment I am away from the conservatory, I feel I am falling far behind, and I fear I will lose this final opportunity to realize my dreams. I have already stayed much longer than I had intended and promised to you. Now, I am begging you, allow me to ask for Liakhov's assistance so that I can return to St. Petersburg."

Salar Moazaz became dejected but felt powerless in the face of his son's steadfastness and despair. "You are your own man, so I will not stand in your way. But make sure Liakhov does not think I will be indebted to him if he agrees to your request. This is between you and him; I want no part of whatever arrangement you set up for yourself. I will also pray to the Almighty for your sake since it seems it is only God that can help you control your pride!"

As he lingered on this thought, Salar Moazaz then continued with the assurance of a father with many years of experience. "Pride's nature is to consume. My son, from ancient times, they have said that pride is the chief cause of misery in every family since the world began!"

Nasrosoltan kissed his father's hand in gratitude for his acquiescence and replied, "Dear Father, you shall see, I will make you proud!" as if he had not heard one word his father or the falgir had cautioned him about this vice.

CHAPTER 13

AN UNUSUAL REQUEST

With his father's halfhearted blessing, Nasrosoltan was finally able to acquire the needed letter from Liakhov. The Russian even offered to personally deliver it to the conservatory director, Glazunov, since he was departing for St. Petersburg soon. With a sly smile, he told Nasrosoltan, "I will gladly do this as a special favor for your father!"

The Russian knew Salar Moazaz did not like him, and the feeling was mutual, so this was not a gesture of goodwill toward him. Liakhov even took it a step further by offering to deliver the letter himself to provoke Salar Moazaz even more. Even though Nasrosoltan understood Liakhov said it that way, intending to hurt his father, Nasrosoltan said nothing. He didn't care if Liakhov felt his father was now indebted to him since the colonel was leaving for Russia and would not be returning to Persia. How ironic that the man who had held thousands in the capital city captive as military governor of Tehran was now instrumental in providing independence to one of its citizens.

Nasrosoltan telegraphed Rustam, asking him to inform Glazunov's office that the letter would soon arrive by personal delivery. He also added the date when he would be in St. Petersburg and requested that, if possible, Rustam find him suitable accommodations.

The day before Nasrosoltan was to leave for Russia, he received a reply telegram from Rustam:

25 August 1912
Dear Friend,
Congratulations! The conservatory is informed of your imminent arrival. Accommodations located. Please bring pistachios. Looking forward to your return.
Respectfully, Rustam

Nasrosoltan found the request for pistachios peculiar, but did as his friend asked, knowing that Rustam had a soft spot for this Persian delicacy as a cocktail nibble.

The next day with bags packed and after the lengthy Persian goodbyes, Nasrosoltan finally departed for St. Petersburg, seven years after leaving for what he had thought would be a short visit home.

Nasrosoltan arrived in St. Petersburg in mid-September with a week to spare before conservatory classes resumed. It was the beginning of the short fall season that would see St. Petersburg getting back to work to prepare for the long winter ahead, after the summer's excesses. As he remembered, this month was the most enjoyable time in the city.

Nasrosoltan was fondly reminded of the glorious autumnal colors in the surrounding parks and gardens, highlighting the city's unique beauty. He arrived in time for what was known to the locals as *babe leto*, or "grandmother's summer," those rare days that summer's comforts extended well into the fall.

On the day of his return in the late afternoon, he was met at the train station by Rustam. His friend had hired a private carriage to take Nasrosoltan to his new place of residence.

On the way there, after catching up on the latest news, Nasrosoltan said with a laugh, "By the way, even though you probably wrote the request for pistachios in jest, I did bring some as you requested, so we can enjoy them tonight when we drink to new beginnings!"

Rustam chuckled and said, "I knew you must have thought what an unusual request, with all that was going on in your life. But you should know, I did not ask you to bring the pistachios for me, but for your new landlady.

"She is an elegant woman by the name of Madame Lazar. She is of Armenian descent and was eager to tell me her whole life story in just one short visit. I have a suspicion that she fancies me; it happens to me quite often with tenderhearted women. She owns a handsome building south of Nevsky, near the conservatory, with four apartments, where she lives in one and leases the rest. The price is reasonable for its location and amenities.

"Knowing you, I am sure you will like it. Madame Lazar had only one apartment left and was about to lease it until I met with her and mentioned that it was for my noble Persian friend, a graduate of the conservatory."

Rustam continued as the carriage made its way through the city, "Talk of Persia led to remembrances of her early childhood, as her family emigrated from Persia many years ago when she was a young child. She mentioned her love of your country's pistachio nuts as one of the snacks she really misses. Her father would bring her some each day when he would return home from work.

"When I heard this, I looked for an advantage, so I promised that you would bring her some pistachios if she decided to lease the apartment to you, to which she jokingly agreed. So you see, it was not such an unusual request after all!"

Nasrosoltan laughed heartily and felt grateful for his friendship with this capable and resourceful man. He was drawn into the life story of his prospective landlady, and he asked his friend, "Is this charming woman married?"

Rustam replied, "Madame Lazar is a widow now. Her husband was a lieutenant general in the Imperial Russian Army who died tragically, but as a hero, in the Russo-Japanese War a few years ago. Another aspect that you may find interesting is that she is a piano tutor to a couple of high-society families in St. Petersburg.

"I noticed that in a boastful manner, and for special emphasis, she left her most impressive pupil for last, informing me that it was the tsar's niece. She made a point to mention it was not out of financial need, since with the rents she collects and her husband's pension, she lives quite comfortably.

"Even though she told me she tutors for the love of music, I believe it is mostly to keep her connection with the royal family in this way. Once I mentioned to her that you are also well versed in the art of playing the piano and that you are a composer, her eyes lit up. So, expect an invite for tea from her occasionally, my friend."

Nasrosoltan was surprised by this last comment from Rustam since he did not appreciate being obligated to have tea with someone with whom he would rather just have a professional relationship.

The next few months were busy times for Nasrosoltan as he settled in and began his curriculum at the conservatory, studying to the late hours of the evening. But whenever Rustam was not on travel for business, the two would go out on the town.

Despite his initial reluctance, Nasrosoltan had met Madame Lazar for tea at her apartment a few times during the past several months. The first time, to formally introduce himself and deliver the pistachios that were part of the terms of the lease, and the other times, just to pay his respects.

Madame Lazar always enjoyed speaking broken Persian with him, and he would flatteringly tell her she spoke the language beautifully. But she knew he was saying it out of kindness, and after a few sentences, they would continue to converse more comfortably in Russian.

On one visit for tea, she had asked Nasrosoltan to play something for her on the well-tuned piano she had in her apartment. He had agreed, and he was especially delighted when she praised his performance and told him he could use her piano whenever he needed to.

In late December, when Nasrosoltan visited with her again, he noticed that her right hand was bandaged, and she seemed to be in low spirits. He asked her, "Madame, what happened to your hand?"

Madame Lazar, who was visibly distressed, replied, "Monsieur, what can I say? I am so upset. Two days ago, I was tutoring the spoiled child of one of my clients, and he kept being silly and refused to pay attention to the right notes, so I slapped his hand lightly. He, in turn, bit my index finger with such ferocity that I now have a broken bone, and the wound needed several stitches!"

Madame Lazar continued with tears welling up in her eyes as she worked herself into a frenzy at recalling the event, "The doctor told me it might be six months before I can play the piano like before, and I am absolutely beside myself with despair. In anger, I told his parents I would not be returning to teach such an ill-mannered child!"

As Madame Lazar recalled how terrible she felt that day, she continued indignantly, "They seemed less shocked at what their child had done to me than at my natural reaction."

Nasrosoltan, feeling her pain, said, "Madame, I am so sorry to hear of this; a lady of your stature and talent should never have been treated with such disrespect! However, it seems it is worth the loss of income to not be treated as such, and I pray that hopefully, all will be better soon."

Madame Lazar appreciated his kind words of sympathy and replied, "But Monsieur Minbashian, my despair was never for the loss of income, for I am quite comfortable financially." This, of course, he already knew since Rustam had earlier mentioned it.

She continued, "My worry is not for money but for the weekly piano lessons for Princess Irina. Now that my finger is damaged, I am afraid I will be of no use, and her mother, Grand Duchess Xenia, will be looking to replace me. Once someone replaces me, even when my condition improves to where I can play again, who is to say they would want me back? I have developed a special bond with this sweet girl, and she with me. It would be a pity for me to lose such an opportunity due to this unfortunate mishap!"

Nasrosoltan, attempting to console the distraught woman, said, "If you wish, I can ask at the conservatory if one of the students would like to sit in for you while you get better."

Madame Lazar replied, "I thank you for your kindness, Monsieur Minbashian. The family is now on vacation at their Crimean estate for the new year. The next lesson we have scheduled is in a month, thanks be to God, or else I would not have time to find a suitable replacement. And I appreciate your offer of assistance in searching for another piano tutor; however, the grand duke and duchess are quite particular about whom they let meet their daughter. This is because, as you must understand, she is a shy and reserved girl, and I must add that she is also quite beautiful, so they want to keep her protected."

Nasrosoltan responded, "I totally understand; perhaps then we can ask for a female student, so there will be no misgivings. If you agree, I shall begin inquiries on your behalf when I get back to the conservatory."

Upon hearing this, an exasperated Madame Lazar replied, "My dear Monsieur Minbashian, I already know that altogether there are only a handful of female students at the conservatory, and only one studies the piano. But, in any case, the family would not want a young girl of the same age tutoring their daughter."

Then suddenly, and without any warning, Madame Lazar stunned an unsuspecting Nasrosoltan. "Please forgive my forwardness, Monsieur Minbashian, but I have heard you perform the piano in this very apartment, and you have an exceptional gift. You are already a graduate of the conservatory and have studied under the most impressive musical minds of our country. Again, forgive me for being so bold in what I am about to ask, but I humbly request that if her family accepts, you agree to tutor the princess in my stead until I recover from my injury."

Madame Lazar rattled off the string of compliments about him so rapidly that it took Nasrosoltan a moment to register the implication of the request.

However, before he could say anything, she continued persuasively, "In this way, I will be able to retain the position, and you will be doing me a great service. I have known this family since this girl was ten years old, and they trust my judgment concerning her musical studies. The grand duchess will understand that a cultured gentleman such as yourself, with an impressive musical heritage, will be a great addition to the other talented tutors for her daughter."

The last thing Nasrosoltan expected was such an unwelcome request, which took him completely by surprise. Even though he did not want to show it, especially to someone who was a tutor, he considered the task of individually tutoring this girl, who was probably not serious in her music study, quite beneath him.

He saw himself as an accomplished composer who had studied for years in the conservatory alongside the most successful composers of the day. He had taught music to military officers and had conducted military bands. Still, most importantly, the king of Persia had bestowed upon him the title of Nasrosoltan for his service to his homeland in music education. A favor that the Madame considered an honor, the tutoring of a grand duke's daughter, Nasrosoltan saw merely as an inconvenience he wanted no part of.

A routine social visit to Madame Lazar for tea turned into an uncomfortable encounter. Nasrosoltan tried to diplomatically defuse a problematic situation in which this request was thrust upon him.

Trying to hide his palpable unease, he offered a brusque reply. "I am indeed flattered that you considered me; however, as you are aware, the conservatory demands all of my attention. Unfortunately, I do not have the time to tutor the princess."

Madame Lazar sensed Nasrosoltan's displeasure but also did not want to dampen their newly developed relationship. Even though she was visibly distressed at his refusal to even consider tutoring the princess, she said, "My dear Monsieur, I understand how demanding the conservatory coursework is. Thank you for listening to me ramble on; I appreciate your kindness. I am sure I will think of some other way in the next few weeks. Hopefully, God will answer my prayers."

They both saved face and agreed to meet up again during the second week of January, after the Russian Orthodox Christmas.

CHAPTER 14

A MOST UNFORTUNATE TURN OF THE WHEEL

Rustam invited Nasrosoltan for New Year's Eve celebrations at the newly built Astoria Hotel, which had just opened a month earlier but already was a landmark at the heart of St. Isaac's Square. The Astoria had been commissioned a few years back, so it would be ready in time for May 1913 to celebrate the Romanov dynasty's tercentenary anniversary.

The hotel had more than two hundred bedrooms and fifty-two private suites, the fanciest restaurants, and elegant ballrooms. The Astoria was where the high society of St. Petersburg was gathered in the hotel's Winter Garden ballroom to attend the most lavish party of the year.

Rustam had become a wealthy iron magnate through his business ventures with the company building and extending the Trans-Siberian Railway. He decided that whenever he was in the capital city, he would stay in a private suite at the Astoria. He was a man who liked to be served, and service was this hotel's specialty.

The evening's cuisine, amongst other culinary delights, included Russian delicacies of black and red caviar, beef stroganoff, and the ever-present chilled vodkas. The more gratuities one gave, the better the service. Rustam had developed a reputation for easily parting with his money, especially after being served one too many rounds of his favorite drink. He enjoyed being treated like aristocracy. The attention shown to him by the servers and attendants made other revelers at the party murmur amongst themselves, wondering who he might be in terms of rank and station in life.

Nasrosoltan, through association with Rustam, also received much attention, especially from the young ladies looking for wealthy potential suitors, mistaking him for one.

Around two o'clock in the morning on New Year's Day, inebriated and fatigued from the party's excesses, the two left the festivities by carriage. But instead of taking Nasrosoltan to his apartment, Rustam instructed the driver to go to an address on the other side of the city. It was a frigid evening with occasional snow showers, and the biting-cold wind chills through the imperial capital were enough to wake them from their drunken stupor.

When Nasrosoltan inquired where they were going, Rustam answered, "To visit a lady!"

A surprised Nasrosoltan then asked, "Dear friend, please tell me, why in heaven's name would we leave a venue with the most beautiful women in St. Petersburg to go across the city in the snow and the cold to visit another lady?"

Rustam laughed and said, "This lady is different, for if she smiles upon you tonight, you will leave happier than you were when the ladies at the Astoria were smiling at you. However, if she does not favor you, you will wish you had never come along."

Nasrosoltan asked, "What are you speaking about?"

Rustam replied, "I am speaking of Lady Luck, for we are going to a *vokzal*."

Nasrosoltan thought Rustam had too much to drink, for *vokzal* in Russian is the word for the train station. When he inquired further, Rustam chuckled and said, "No, we are not taking a train ride in the early hours of the morning. *Vokzal* is what they call a gaming house here since it is how the Russians pronounce the word *Vauxhall.* I am told in London, Vauxhall is where they have a pleasure garden with all kinds of entertainment. However, at this vokzal, we shall play the game of chance, roulette. I remember you telling me you enjoy gambling, so let us bring in the new year together with some good fortune!"

No matter what it was called, the gaming house was in an impressive building, and from the outside, one would never know what was going on inside.

Even though many Russians liked to gamble, games of chance were not looked upon kindly by the authorities. However, if these kinds of establishments did not openly flaunt their existence, they were free to operate—if the policemen were bought off to turn a blind eye. A small slot in the front door allowed the proprietor to identify the potential patron and decide whether to open the door or not. But from the welcome Rustam received, it seemed he was no stranger to this vokzal.

Inside, the décor included beautiful wooden furniture and walls covered by colorful paintings. Fine vodka was being offered by well-attired servers as if it were water, which no doubt was intended to make it easier for patrons to part with their money.

Sitting in the center of the room was the main attraction, the roulette wheel. The game was quite simple: choose a number or a series of numbers or pick a color of red or black and ask the croupier to place the bet. The room was filled with tobacco smoke from cigars and cigarettes as the men at the foot of the wheel calmed their nerves with every puff. One could see the extremes of emotion, from fear to greed and from dejection to elation, written across their faces with each winning number announced aloud by the croupier.

Rustam and Nasrosoltan took their seats, and the croupier tipped his head to Rustam in greeting, and for this gesture, he received a ten-ruble note before Rustam had even made one wager.

Nasrosoltan asked him, "Why did you give the croupier a gratuity now?"

Rustam leaned in close to Nasrosoltan, and in a confiding tone, replied, "Once he calls out 'no more bets,' you have to wait until the next turn of the wheel if you have not yet placed a bet. However, when he notices I have not decided upon a number or color, he gives me extra time before making the announcement. So in a sense, you can say it is not a gratuity but that I am literally buying myself some time!"

Rustam asked Nasrosoltan, "Do you have enough money with you since I know you did not expect to be at a gaming house this morning?"

Nasrosoltan replied that he did. When he had left for Russia, he had brought with him enough money for six months of study and living expenses. After that, for the remaining six months of his stay, his father was supposed to wire additional funds through the Russo-Persian bank branch in Tehran to the head office in St. Petersburg.

Nasrosoltan had a habit of carrying most of the currency with him always, thinking it was a safer option to have his money at his disposal whenever he needed it. He left only a small amount in his bank account for an emergency.

Even though this gaming house also offered *chemin-de-fer* and faro card games, Nasrosoltan was happy to see the roulette wheel. Back in Persia, while playing cards, some of those whom he considered friends had cheated him and produced hidden cards when needed with the discreet sleight of hand.

Although Nasrosoltan had caught them at it, he ended up leaving a large sum of money on the table because of his pride. His reaction to that event was to just get up from the table, and instead of making a fuss to get his money back, pronouncing to those still seated, "Keep the money if you need it so bad as to cheat a friend!"

After that incident, Nasrosoltan decided he would rather not gamble with cards, so he preferred games of chance that did not employ them. He naively thought the possibility of cheating was less with dice or the roll of a roulette ball than with cards.

Rustam decided to only play the red and black colors that New Year's morning. Nasrosoltan proceeded to bet upon the number seven exclusively since this number had always been his favorite.

This was not because of the typical seven days in a week or the Persian belief in seven heavens, but because, as a musician, he viewed most things through the prism of music. He had studied Western music for most of his life, and the heptatonic scale consisted of seven notes. Nasrosoltan appreciated that many timeless works had been created with a simple reshuffling of these seven notes.

Having stayed in Russia for seven years during his first trip, and having lived in Persia for seven years before returning to St. Petersburg, certainly had something to do with his affinity for this particular number. So, he assumed this could not just be a coincidence.

What an unexpected twist. Nasrosoltan, who so easily dismissed superstition in every other phase of his life, embraced it so passionately when playing a game of fortune, for superstition is an ever-present companion of the gambler.

As Rustam wished, the new year did bring them good fortune, and they both won. Nasrosoltan's number seven came up many times in those few hours, and he managed to increase his impressive winnings. Witnessing this, the other patrons slowly gathered around him and started to bet on the same lucky number seven whenever he did.

By around seven o'clock in the morning, Nasrosoltan had won so much that he doubled all the money he had brought with him for his initial six months of stay in St. Petersburg. Seven being his lucky number this visit, it also seemed to him to be the right time to get up and leave.

Nasrosoltan turned to Rustam and said, "We had better leave before Lady Luck decides to stop smiling upon us, my friend!"

The unexpected windfall made Nasrosoltan feel extremely generous. His largesse was on display as he gave extravagant gratuities to the croupier, the servers, and even the doorman at the gaming house. Winning that much money induced a sense of power in him. Nasrosoltan considered his tremendous luck as a good omen since the Persians believe that if the first day of the year begins with good fortune, it bodes well for the remainder of the year.

The next few weeks passed by quickly as Nasrosoltan prepared for the stringent examination requirements of his orchestration course. Totally immersed in his studies, some days, he would even forget to eat, but Madame Lazar's kindness kept him fed. Every so often, she would check up on him with offerings of her specially baked *pirozhkis*, stuffed with mashed potatoes, mushrooms, onions, and eggs. Even though he appreciated Madame's cooking, her thoughtfulness made him feel even more guilty for refusing her request to teach the young princess.

Madame Lazar had one week left to find a suitable replacement before the princess and her family returned from vacation. She tried hard not to show her despair, aware that Nasrosoltan felt terrible about his unwillingness to assist her with her predicament. He did, in a small way, repay her kindness and assuage his guilty feelings by tuning her piano, which had gone out of tune due to the sudden temperature change in the weather. But it made little difference to her, for she could not use the piano these days because of her injury.

The day after New Year's Day, Rustam had departed for a several-month business trip to the eastern provinces of Russia, where the railway construction was in high gear. Consequently, Nasrosoltan spent many evenings alone. One such evening, with the pressures of the upcoming examinations bearing down upon him, he decided to go out on the town for some much-needed entertainment and rejuvenation.

After dinner with some conservatory friends, Nasrosoltan left the restaurant and recalled with excitement the evening a few weeks earlier when he visited the gaming house with Rustam. Remembering vividly how they both left victorious, he decided to visit the vokzal once again.

Upon entering the establishment this night, he was immediately recognized as the generous gratuity giver from a few weeks back. The croupier tipped his head to Nasrosoltan, just as he had to Rustam that magnificent evening a short while ago. As was the case that night, the croupier quickly received a ten-ruble note in return. Nasrosoltan had just purchased the few precious extra seconds he would need to decide upon his bets this evening.

Initially, Lady Luck was sitting at Nasrosoltan's side as if she had never left him from the last time he visited, and his winnings kept growing. His confidence grew to the point that he doubled and sometimes tripled the amount he placed on each number.

At some point during the evening, when it looked as if Nasrosoltan would once again leave the gaming house with a small fortune, he caught the attention of the gaming-house manager. The manager noticed the excessive gratuities the croupier was receiving and decided upon a change. He called in a replacement croupier, which they often do to change a winning patron's luck. Nasrosoltan did not think much of the move, for hope springs eternal when one is winning.

Perhaps it was the different way the new croupier flung the ball along the circular roulette-wheel track, or maybe the way he spun the wheel itself in the opposite direction, but whatever the reason, Nasrosoltan began to lose.

With every loss, he grew more defiant in the face of defeat, and he began to battle misfortune by increasing the amount he wagered. It was as if time stood still, and he was the only player at the table, with his eyes fixated on the spinning wheel and where the ivory ball would fall.

There was something macabre about losing, and the more he lost, the more he wagered, to either win it all back in an instant or just to lose everything and be done with it.

A pleasant evening had turned into misery, for he lost all he had won the last time he visited, and some. He could not decide whether to just get up and leave or to play a few more rounds in hopes that his luck might change.

The odds are that a gambler usually stays, as did Nasrosoltan. He downed the remaining vodka in his glass in one swallow, and on the spur of the moment, placed all his remaining money—the money he needed for his rent to Madame Lazar for the rest of his stay—on one single bet.

The number seven had brought him great fortune a few weeks back, and he hoped that by chance, just one last time, it would be his lucky number once again.

Before the croupier could call out, "No more bets," Nasrosoltan took all he had and gave it to him and said, "*Chislo sem pozhaluysta!*" ("Number seven, please!")

Everyone at the table was amazed at the amount he wagered, and all on just one number, leaving everything to chance. Nasrosoltan's attention was focused on the croupier's hand, which in slow motion dropped the ball on the wheel's track as it spun for what seemed to be an eternity. Nasrosoltan knew much depended on where the ball would come to rest.

Finally, when the ball finished circling the wheel, it fell into where the frets separate the numbers, jumping wildly from one number to the next, as if unsure where it was supposed to go. The ball fell into his number seven with some momentum as Nasrosoltan, who displayed a tranquil countenance, was but a nervous wreck within.

He silently prayed to Lady Luck that the ball would just give up and remain there. However, it was not meant to be, for it was as if the ball used the little life it had left to fling itself across the fret separating the number seven from number twenty-eight on the wheel, and it finally rested there in a quiet calm.

The wheel itself continued to spin in perpetual motion, with the ball sitting comfortably on number twenty-eight, just a few millimeters away from what could have been a totally different night for Nasrosoltan.

The croupier called out the winning number, "*Dvadtsat vosem,*" and began to pay the winning wagers. A collective sigh from the onlookers would have let Nasrosoltan know the disastrous outcome even if he had not been looking. But of course, his eyes had been fastened on the ball, following every movement of its wicked dance.

He got up from the table, took the last ten-ruble note he had left in his pocket to pay the carriage driver to go back home, but instead gave it as a gratuity to the croupier. With no outward show of emotion, he said goodnight and wandered outside to begin his long walk home.

CHAPTER 15

TWO ANSWERED PRAYERS

It was quite a distance from the gaming house to his apartment, and Nasrosoltan finally made it back home just as people in the city began to emerge to start their morning. He was cold, fatigued, and in terrible spirits, for during the lengthy walk, he wondered how he would manage his finances, but he found no answer.

He had lost everything except for a small amount he kept at his bank for an emergency, and this month's rent was due to Madame Lazar the day after next. Luckily, his conservatory tuition had been paid, but the modest sum that remained would only suffice for food and sundries, and that was only until his father wired more money to him in a couple of months.

Under no circumstance was he going to ask his father to send the funds sooner. By doing so, he would have to divulge the shameful reason for the request, and he did not want the reputation of being a wastrel son.

In the same vein, even if Rustam was not away on business, Nasrosoltan's pride would not have allowed him to borrow from his well-to-do friend. In fact, he decided he did not want to reveal to anyone what had transpired.

He hoped to avoid seeing Madame Lazar until he could figure some way of paying his rent in the next week. Nasrosoltan was not a religious man, yet he prayed to God that he may find a way out of his predicament. Unbeknownst to him, Madame Lazar was also praying for an answer to her problem in finding an acceptable replacement to tutor the princess.

As Nasrosoltan turned the key and entered the building, he noticed Madame Lazar on the other side of the door. She was searching for her cat, which had a habit of wandering the hallway in the early hours of the morning. From Nasrosoltan's appearance, she noticed he had not slept and asked, "Monsieur Minbashian, have you been studying for your examinations all night?"

Feeling relieved that she had suggested a better reason for his coming home so early in the morning than what had really occurred, he nodded his head and mentioned that he was exhausted.

In a gesture of politeness, he asked, "Madame, how are you today?"

This was apparently the wrong question, for almost immediately, she became emotional and began to weep uncontrollably, so Nasrosoltan asked her why she was distraught. Madame Lazar could not speak as she continued to sob.

Nasrosoltan suggested, "Why don't we go and sit down someplace. We don't want to disturb the other tenants so early in the morning."

She agreed and offered that they go back to her apartment. They went in and settled on her couch as Nasrosoltan tried to console her.

Precisely what he hoped would not happen did happen. Nasrosoltan aimed to have a plan to cover his expenses, but he did not even have a moment to himself before he came face-to-face with Madame Lazar. Seeing her in this condition worsened his own dilemma of what to do.

He thought to himself that there was no way he would now add to the Madame's burden by telling her about a delay in his rent payment. He decided to just listen to see what was troubling her, even though he had a suspicion it was related to tutoring the princess.

She calmed herself a bit and addressed him. "Monsieur Minbashian, I am beside myself. No matter how I have tried, I cannot find a suitable replacement to tutor the tsar's niece. The family will return the day after tomorrow, and my first lesson is planned for next Monday. I could not sleep all night and spent the whole evening praying to our Lord to answer my prayers. When I came looking for my cat, and the first person I saw was you so early in the morning, I knew our Lord had answered my prayers. What are the chances of meeting this way if it was not meant to be?"

She continued, as she wiped away her tears, "I feel obliged to ask you one last time, for I will be remiss if I remain silent. I beg of you, please help me, for I have nowhere else to turn!"

And then, with the few broken Persian words she remembered from her childhood, Madame Lazar pleaded, saying the same in his native tongue—"*Jenab Minbashian, tamana meekonam, khahesh meekonam!*"— in a final attempt of appealing to his heart, to win his cooperation.

Then Madame Lazar reverted to speaking Russian and mentioned something that drew his attention. "I am quite aware that you have no need, but the tutoring also commands generous compensation."

It may have been that he was exhausted and wanted a quick end to the conversation, so he did not think carefully before he blurted out, "Madame, do not despair. It pains me to see you so disillusioned this morning. Do not worry any longer; I will do what you ask!"

Undoubtedly, the mention of generous compensation at such a time of financial woe had much to do with his change of heart. Upon hearing himself say those words and witnessing the sudden look of surprise on Madame Lazar's face, he paused briefly, thinking about what he had just done.

Realizing that he could not call back the words from her eager ears, Nasrosoltan thought to perhaps light two candles with one flame by helping himself through helping her.

Before Madame Lazar could say anything, he quickly added, "But there is one condition!"

Madame Lazar, who was not expecting him to relent so quickly, was in awe at how soon her fortunes had changed. Where just a few minutes before, she had been so lost, now she had optimism and hope for the future.

She enthusiastically exclaimed, "Monsieur Minbashian, yes, yes, please tell me, what is the condition, for I will do anything you ask!"

Feeling a twinge of guilt at the sign of Madame Lazar's unbridled excitement, Nasrosoltan replied, "Madame, I do not wish to be involved in any financial transactions between the family of the princess and myself. I just want to go to the palace at the specified time to tutor her and leave, and I would like for you to still collect whatever compensation yourself. You can instead consider my once-a-week tutoring for the next few months my payment of rent. In this way, I also will feel much better about the situation."

Without hesitation, she agreed, understanding his request to be in line with the kind of man he was. Madame Lazar knew he did not want to be considered as hired help, even if it was to one of the longest reigning royal families of Europe. Believing that her prayers were now answered, Madame Lazar had no idea she, too, was the answer to Nasrosoltan's prayers this same day.

At this point, Nasrosoltan was so spent that he told her he had to go and rest. They agreed that the Madame would seek an audience with Grand Duchess Xenia, mother of Princess Irina, for a meeting on Monday, an hour before she was to be tutored. She suggested that they travel together by carriage to the palace on the Moyka River Embankment. Madame Lazar planned at that time to introduce Nasrosoltan to the family and hopefully agree upon the temporary arrangement she had in mind.

The following Monday, Nasrosoltan met Madame Lazar outside the building at the appointed time and joined her in the troika carriage she had hired for their short trip to the palace.

Whenever visiting the royal family, the Madame always paid for expensive transport with a hefty charioteer. She was a woman who liked to make an entrance. As appearance was everything in St. Petersburg society, the station and wealth of the master or mistress were reflected in the grandeur of the carriage and driver.

It was the middle of winter, so the carriage drivers looked even more stupendous with their splendid furs. Madame Lazar did not mind spending the extra money on the weekly spectacle, for she wished to separate her station from the other help and tutors at the palace. She made a point to let everyone know she tutored for the love of music and not for compensation.

Nasrosoltan had dressed immaculately for this afternoon's audience since, after all, he was visiting the palace. He was to meet Russian royalty, even though meeting royalty was not something new to him, for his family had been close to the Persian royal family. However, under the circumstances, he wanted to make an excellent first impression. Madame Lazar herself always dressed up for the occasion, and all the neighbors knew just by seeing her in such formal attire that she was on her way to visit the palace.

The Madame used the short carriage ride to impart as much information about the princess and her family to Nasrosoltan as she had time for. He could not get a word in edgewise, for the Madame spoke without pause, so he just decided to enjoy the view and listen to every detail she offered.

Madame Lazar mentioned that the grand duke and duchess were second cousins and had seven children: six boys and one girl, Princess Irina, their eldest child.

Madame Lazar added this tidbit about the princess: "Her parents use the anglicized form of her name at home, and instead of Irina, they call her Irene. Irina is more fluent in English and French than in Russian, as most royal children are."

As she was about to ramble on, she stopped for a moment and turned to Nasrosoltan, urgently asking, "Do you, by chance, speak any English or French?"

Nasrosoltan was startled by the sudden question and responded, "Yes, I speak a bit of English, but I am much more fluent in French—" But before he could go on any further, Madame Lazar cut him off mid-sentence, once she had heard what was needed, and proceeded with her own chatter.

The fascinating thing Nasrosoltan had noticed in his prior teatime conversations with Madame Lazar was in her description of people. She always noted if she thought they were attractive, as was the case in her portrayal of the grand duke's family.

She continued without taking a breath, "Princess Irina is beautiful, with piercing blue eyes, and is shy and timid but sensitive and intelligent. The grand duchess is quite involved in the children's education and sees that they are well tutored in languages, music, and the arts. That is why it is so important to gain her approval for you to sit in as the princess's temporary piano tutor.

"The Grand Duke Alexander Mikhailovich himself is a kind and handsome man, a naval officer, and an acquaintance of my late husband. He personally offered me condolences upon my husband's untimely death in the Russo-Japanese War!"

Hinting that she was closer to the royal family than she really was, she added, "By his close friends and family, the grand duke is called by the nickname Sandro instead of his given name, Alexander."

The Madame continued her narrative of the inner workings of the palace, even in the absence of any encouragement from Nasrosoltan. "The household staff consists of three nurses, an English and French tutor, five maids, four butlers, the grand duchess's lady-in-waiting, and the grand duke's aide-de-camp, in addition to three cooks." Displaying a tinge of envy, she added, "The family always takes all the help on their summer trips to France."

Then she moved in closer to him, lowering her voice to a whisper, as though she were divulging a state secret, and added, "The grand duchess and the tsar are quite close, and he visits his sister for dinner on the last Friday of every month."

As she went on and on, Nasrosoltan thought, *How long must I endure this inconvenience and pay for the mistake I made one evening at the gaming house so that I now have to tutor this girl?*

His lack of judgment had cost him not only the money he lost but, most of all, the precious time he needed to study. But now, he had an obligation to spend at least some time in this fashion, and he was troubled for putting himself in this unfortunate position.

As they approached the palace grounds, Nasrosoltan took advantage of Madame Lazar's need for breath and interjected a query before she could continue on, "Madame, how do you know so many intimate details of this family's inner life?"

He quickly regretted asking this question because she immediately responded with her incurable verbosity, "Well, even though I have tutored Princess Irina from the age of ten and have been involved in their household for many years, I garner most of these details from my late husband's sister, who is the princess's governess, Nadezhda Nazarov.

"My husband's family were upper class but impoverished, what one would call 'landless nobles.' He and Nadezhda were orphaned at a young age, and their uncle took care of them for a while, but he ended up mismanaging and losing the properties they owned. My husband, God rest his soul, provided for his sister throughout his life. He sent Nadezhda to France for her primary education, and upon her return, enrolled her in the Bestuzhev Courses, where she earned her degree in nursing.

"Before the war with the Japanese, the royal family had contracted a British governess solely for Irina's upbringing. However, before she could arrive, the war began, and the British took the Japanese side. That is when her appointment was terminated, and she was asked not to come."

Madame Lazar continued offering Nasrosoltan information he found irrelevant. "You know, Monsieur, sadly, Nadezhda did not inherit the same good looks of my husband, which may have something to do with her being a spinster. But what she did inherit was a delightful demeanor and a pleasant character, well suited to working with children."

Nasrosoltan pitied himself now, even more, having to listen to the life story of a governess that he had no interest in hearing about.

But Madame Lazar, who was enjoying talking with her captive audience of one, hurriedly continued, "Unfortunately, when my husband died, Nadezhda had nowhere to turn, so I mentioned her situation to the grand duchess. After careful consideration, the royal family graciously employed her as Irina's governess. The family love my sweet sister-in-law and is happy how things turned out, that the British governess was asked not to come.

"Between you and me, they should be grateful. Nadezhda speaks several languages, and as I mentioned, she is a nurse, and above all, is from noble birth, so she had nothing less than that Englishwoman."

Madame Lazar continued her story energetically while a thoroughly subdued Nasrosoltan quietly listened. "After my husband's death, Nadezhda had a need to belong, and the royal family has shown her their utmost kindness. They appreciate that she is fiercely loyal to them, especially to Irina. I can attest that she is genuinely like a family member now!"

And then, with a sense of pride, the Madame exclaimed, "I believe I have a unique talent in making appropriate introductions, so let us pray that today is no different for you."

Nasrosoltan's thoughts had wandered off by this time, but he appreciated the few moments she ceased talking. However, Madame Lazar was not done yet.

After a few moments of quiet, she continued with new details. "When Nadezhda first started working at the palace many years ago, the youngest of the children could not pronounce her name correctly, so he started calling her Nana, and the name has stuck so that now all call her by that name. At first, it was in jest, but she does not mind and considers it quite endearing. However, the one thing I must warn you about Nana is that she has a rather loose tongue and will divulge the most private information in detail!"

Nasrosoltan found it amusing that a lady who had just recited the grand duke's whole household's life portrayed another as having a loose tongue. Hearing Madame Lazar saying such a thing made him recall a Persian saying: *Seer be piaz meege boo meedee.* ("The garlic tells the onion, it is you that smells.")

When they arrived at the palace entrance and disembarked, they were met by one of the butlers and Princess Irina's governess, Nana, who had come to see Madame Lazar. But truthfully, Nana wanted to give a quick and subtle look at the potential piano tutor Madame Lazar had told her about.

The staff promptly escorted Madame Lazar and Nasrosoltan to the elegantly decorated sitting room and offered them tea until the grand duchess made her entrance. Nasrosoltan especially admired this room's décor, which was adorned with Persian carpets, reminding him of his own family home in Tehran.

After what seemed to be a much longer wait than the thirty minutes they spent sipping their tea, Grand Duchess Xenia entered the room, and they both rose to formally greet her.

She apologized for having kept them waiting and turned to address Madame Lazar. "Nana already told me about the injury to your hand. I hope you feel better soon. I appreciate that you care so dearly for the princess's pursuit of her music studies that you went to the trouble of thinking of a replacement." The grand duchess appeared unenthusiastic about the situation. She even seemed a bit anxious as if she were unsure how to proceed with the new arrangement thrust upon her.

Madame Lazar quickly thanked the grand duchess and added with an elegant flair, "Your Imperial Highness, it is my pleasure to introduce to you Monsieur Nasrosoltan Minbashian, a graduate of the conservatory. Monsieur Minbashian's father also studied here and was one of the students of Professor Nikolai Rimsky-Korsakov.

"I can attest that he is an outstanding pianist who has graciously agreed to tutor Princess Irina if Your Highness so decides. If approval is given for this new arrangement, I have also consented to accompany the Monsieur, at least for the first few sessions, to afford the princess a smooth transition in her course of study." Madame Lazar offered up the information in a rapid-fire and confident manner as if to ward off any doubt about Nasrosoltan's suitability as a tutor.

Grand Duchess Xenia looked at Nasrosoltan directly for the first time and thanked him for coming, adding, "May God bless the soul of that dear man, Professor Rimsky-Korsakov." She seemed visibly calmed by her fond recollection of a beloved national figure; however, she still seemed undecided about a course of action.

The grand duchess added, "Monsieur Minbashian, even though your credentials are praiseworthy and quite impressive, I would still like to discuss the matter with the grand duke before making a final decision. I hope you understand."

Nasrosoltan sensed the hesitancy in her voice. He was taken aback that the decision was not final upon having met him in person, mostly since the position was just for tutoring a young girl to play the piano. He suddenly became anxious that the arrangement he had so nonchalantly taken for granted just a few moments earlier may not be afforded him.

Nasrosoltan wondered if he should try to say something to further interest the grand duchess in his services. But he worried anything he may say at this point would be interpreted as a sign of desperation. Therefore, he decided to say nothing further except to thank the grand duchess for the audience and await her husband's decision.

As he and Madame Lazar got up to leave, the Madame was more concerned than Nasrosoltan was about the grand duchess's noncommittal response. She already knew he was a proud man, and she worried that he may change his mind if he felt disrespected.

Thinking to salvage the situation, she blurted out, "Your Imperial Highness, I forgot to mention in my introduction of Monsieur Minbashian that his given name is really not Nasrosoltan. This is actually a title bestowed upon him by the Persian king for his services to the advancement of music in his homeland!"

Nasrosoltan was surprised by her proclamation. He was embarrassed and disturbed that she would offer this information just to procure the position she so desperately wanted him to receive. He was astonished that she even knew this fact about him since he had never discussed it with her.

Even though Nasrosoltan detested this desperate move by the Madame, he got the impression that this added information had an influence. He noticed a slight shift to a more pleasant demeanor in the grand duchess. It seemed that this incidental detail about his station appeased the grand duchess, and Nasrosoltan became hopeful that there would no longer be a need for her to discuss the issue with her husband.

As fate would have it, Grand Duke Alexander returned to the palace earlier than he usually would have. Seeing them gathered in the sitting room, the grand duke joined them and was first greeted by his wife. She introduced Nasrosoltan and mentioned all that they had discussed, from his heritage to being a graduate of the St. Petersburg Conservatory.

The grand duchess explained, "I have asked for Monsieur Minbashian's patience so we could have a chance to discuss the possibility of him replacing Madame Lazar until she recovers from her injury."

Nasrosoltan welcomed the fact that another man was now present. He appreciated the direct way in which men communicated. He felt more comfortable speaking with the grand duke considering the grand duchess's indecisiveness in offering him the position just moments before.

The grand duke, who had shown up at the most opportune time for Nasrosoltan, did not have the same hesitancy his wife initially had about him. He greeted Nasrosoltan pleasantly and curiously asked, "So, you are Persian, but your surname, Min-bashian, sounds Armenian. Are you of Armenian descent?"

Nasrosoltan replied, "No, Your Imperial Highness, my ancestors hail from Georgia. My great-grandfather was born in Tbilisi, in what we Persians call Gorjestan."

The grand duke replied with a smile, "What a coincidence. I was also born in the capital, Tiflis"—the Russianized form of Tbilisi—"but in what we Russians call Gruziya. But no matter what we call that land, all can agree it is truly the most beautiful!"

Nasrosoltan took advantage of the talk of Georgia to inject some needed levity into their discourse. He retold Rustam's story about how the Georgians were resourcefully able to have God bestow upon them the most beautiful place in the whole world.

Everyone laughed at the story, and his quick wit convinced the grand duke of the correctness of his first impression of Nasrosoltan. Grand Duke Alexander, unlike his wife, did not think his daughter's piano lessons were of such importance that any further discussion on the matter was necessary.

So, he said to Nasrosoltan, "Monsieur Minbashian, I would like to welcome you as the princess's piano tutor until the Madame recovers. I thank you for coming here today, and I also thank you, dear Madame Lazar, for your show of kindness to our daughter and for introducing the Monsieur to us."

Grand Duchess Xenia, who was delighted that her husband had saved her from the awkward situation, agreed and said, "I am glad that we settled the matter. We can now continue the regular schedule for her lessons, so give me a moment to tell her what has transpired. As you well know, Madame Lazar, the princess is not fond of sudden changes."

Chapter 16

Beauty Is in the Eye of the Beholder

Nasrosoltan and Madame Lazar waited while the grand duchess informed Princess Irina that she would temporarily have a new piano tutor. The Madame took this moment to apologize to Nasrosoltan for having divulged his title to gain favor with the grand duchess. With her apologies, she added, "I hope that you will consider this water under the bridge, especially since it resulted in an agreeable outcome for all."

Nasrosoltan, realizing there was no benefit to be gained by showing his displeasure, responded, "My dear Madame, you did catch me off guard."

Relieved to see Nasrosoltan was not upset, Madame Lazar replied with a smile, "If you are wondering how I knew about your title, Monsieur Somkhishvili confided in me when he secured the apartment for you."

Nasrosoltan jokingly cursed his friend under his breath as Nana appeared and escorted them to the music room, where Princess Irina was waiting for her lesson. Upon entering the room, Nasrosoltan could not believe his eyes and was momentarily stunned. The stories he had heard did not do justice to what his eyes were witnessing. How could it be that a simple request from his landlady had now put him in the presence of such magnificence?

After all these years, Nasrosoltan had finally come face-to-face with such beauty, a Tischner. This was a spectacular Beethoven-era pianoforte built by Johann August Tischner in St. Petersburg in 1826, based on the Broadwood model Beethoven owned and wrote for.

At the conservatory, Nasrosoltan learned that there were only twenty-four of these pianos made. The piano gifted to Tsar Nicholas I was the only one with an inlay of the Russian imperial crest, while the others bore an attached plaque instead. When Nasrosoltan inspected the piano further, he noticed the embedded crest. He immediately realized this was the same piano that must have been passed down to the grand duchess from her great-grandfather.

Since Nasrosoltan, in his excitement, was so focused on the piano, he had not yet been introduced to Princess Irina. Attempting to salvage this awkward moment, Madame Lazar nervously interjected, "Your Serene Highness Princess Irina Alexandrovna, I would like to introduce Monsieur Minbashian."

Nasrosoltan suddenly came to himself, recognizing his blunder in etiquette. He bowed slightly with his hand on his heart. "I pray Your Serene Highness does not mistake my deep admiration for such a wonderful work of art as a sign of my disrespect. On the contrary, I am truly honored to have the opportunity of tutoring Your Highness, especially on such a glorious instrument!"

In return, the princess, tongue-tied and diffident, smiled in silence, avoiding his eye. At the request of Madame Lazar, Princess Irina then sat at the piano bench alongside her. The Madame wanted to show Nasrosoltan what piece she had last worked on with Irina to give him a baseline from which to proceed in his upcoming lessons.

Nasrosoltan sat at an adjacent chair and studied her form for proper posture, for he believed that to play the piano correctly, it was important how the body was placed in front of it. He took advantage of his seating position to observe the whole scene instead of just watching the placement of the fingers and hands.

He noted how wonderful the piano itself sounded, with its leather-covered hammers and wool dampers. It was the perfect instrument to play Beethoven's piano sonata no. 27, which the Madame had been teaching the princess to play. Nasrosoltan was fond of this piece and considered the main melody exquisite, containing both passion and energy.

Beethoven himself had indicated in German regarding the final movement of the work, "*Nicht zu geschwind und sehr singbar vorgetragen.*" ("Not too swiftly and conveyed in a singing manner.") But in the little time Nasrosoltan observed Irina playing it, he noticed that the Madame had unfortunately not communicated this nuance in her tutoring.

It seemed to Nasrosoltan that the princess had talent at playing and was also good at taking instruction, even though she appeared nervous. He attributed this to her being uncomfortable with a stranger looking over her shoulder. Having taught music to many students in Tehran and Shiraz, he understood that with practice and familiarity, this nervousness would pass.

Every so often, Irina tried to steal a glance at Nasrosoltan to see if she could detect whether he approved of her playing. However, her effort was to no avail, for he showed no sign, at least none that she could decipher.

Nasrosoltan was quite enamored by the piano and eagerly awaited a moment when he could sit and play. Still, he did not want to seem overly enthusiastic, especially on this first visit to the palace.

The princess, who was having trouble playing a section of the piece, asked Madame Lazar to show her how to correctly perform the part. The Madame, due to her injury, and as if reading Nasrosoltan's mind, turned to him and asked, "Monsieur Minbashian, would you do us the honor?" She got up and offered him her place on the piano bench.

Princess Irina became flustered at the suggestion, for she did not expect that he would sit in such proximity to her, and she proceeded to get up in a gesture of presenting the whole bench to him. However, Madame Lazar motioned for her to remain seated, which she did with some hesitation.

Nasrosoltan first asked Irina's permission to sit beside her, and once again, with a shy nod, she gave her approval and he sat down. He pointed to the sheet music and said, "Your Highness, as you can see, Beethoven himself has notated on this composition that it should be played not too swiftly and conveyed in a singing manner." Then he proceeded to play the part as intended by the composer.

Nasrosoltan could not believe how beautiful this instrument sounded as he played. He felt a unique bond between each finger and the ivory keys they were placed on. In what seemed an effortless manner, Beethoven's music filled the room with an elegance that left Madame Lazar and Irina awestruck. He performed as if he were on a concert stage, oblivious to his surroundings. Nasrosoltan found it surprising that in the span of a few hours, what at first seemed to him a tedious weekly chore had suddenly transformed into a time he would look forward to, just to sit at this noble piano.

He played with such passion that, unbeknownst to him, both the grand duke and duchess had entered the music room, standing in silence at the doorway, not wanting to disturb his performance.

When he finished, the grand duchess began to applaud, and Nasrosoltan felt a hint of embarrassment as he had completely lost himself in his playing, almost forgetting where he was.

Nasrosoltan attempted to get up from the piano to stand in respect for the grand duke and duchess, but the grand duchess signaled for him to stay seated to continue with his lesson.

As Irina's parents left the room, Nasrosoltan sat back on the bench and turned to address the princess. "This piece is one of only a few of Beethoven's compositions that carry such instruction of playing in a singing manner, in place of the traditional

Italian tempo markings. That is why I admire it so much; when performed properly, it is as if the piano itself has come to life and is singing the maestro's creation!"

His playing moved Irina. She had never had a tutor with such charisma and confidence. She found something charming about his self-assuredness, which reminded her of her own father, yet his sense of confidence also unsettled her.

Nana, who heard the applause emanating from the music room, rushed in, not wanting to be left out of the happenings. With a smile, she winked at Madame Lazar, signaling her approval of the man she had proposed to become Irina's tutor.

Madame Lazar hinted that it was time to conclude the day's lesson. When they got up from the piano bench, Nasrosoltan told Irina, "Your Serene Highness should continue practicing this piece so that we can work on it next week."

As they were leaving the palace, the grand duchess thanked Madame Lazar again for having introduced Nasrosoltan, which made the Madame think that it was good he would be going back to Persia by the end of the year. For if not, she supposed, she would not have the opportunity to reclaim her position, considering the surprisingly pleasant reception Nasrosoltan had received at the palace this day.

CHAPTER 17

SOWING THE SEEDS OF DOUBT

The winter months passed swiftly as Nasrosoltan kept busy with his music coursework and accompanying auditions, in addition to tutoring the princess every week. He found it gratifying that the sessions were proceeding better than he initially expected. In fact, for the first time in a long while, Nasrosoltan felt everything was going his way.

In the beginning, Madame Lazar's tagging along each week had irritated him, but he now saw the benefit of her attendance. She spent the time chatting over tea with Nana in the kitchen, and this allowed him to be more at ease in teaching the princess without the Madame's ever-curious eyes looking over his shoulder.

The visits to the palace had become an enjoyable pastime for him. He began looking forward to the weekly appointment, especially when he had the opportunity to play the Tischner. Nasrosoltan was also pleased that on some occasions, after the conclusion of the lesson, the grand duke would invite him into his study to enjoy a brandy.

Grand Duke Alexander had a curious nature. Initially, he mostly inquired about the conservatory students' views on the political situation in the country. As an advisor to the tsar, the grand duke knew he must have his ear to the ground for any rumblings amongst the students, believing that radical ideas and protests usually first took root among them.

In their first couple of meetings, Nasrosoltan was unsure if this was the real reason for the grand duke's interest in him. But as the weeks went by, and they spent more time together discussing many topics of mutual interest, a feeling of respect developed between the two men. Most of the time, there was light conversation centering around music, history, or archaeology, a topic the grand duke had a fascination with. He was curious to learn more about the ancient Persian capital of Persepolis once he became aware that Nasrosoltan had visited the historical ruins when he lived in nearby Shiraz.

But during their last meeting, the grand duke seemed distracted, and their conversation turned heavy. When Nasrosoltan asked him the reason, a gloom fell over the grand duke as he unexpectedly shared his personal feelings about an impending European war. "Unfortunately, very few agree with my prediction, but I believe such a war will happen within a few years, and I worry that Russia is ill-prepared for such an event." He confided in Nasrosoltan that he was preoccupied with how to militarily make his country ready for what was to come.

Even though Nasrosoltan appreciated the grand duke's feeling close enough to divulge his private concerns, this comment surprised and worried him. Russia had now mostly recovered from the upheavals of several years ago: the humiliating Russo-Japanese War, the massacre of Bloody Sunday, and the continuous strikes and unrest. The grim view the grand duke had offered did not correspond to the spirit of optimism and the unprecedented prosperity the country was experiencing in 1913.

***

Meanwhile, Rustam had returned to St. Petersburg from his long trip to Siberia. As usual, he was staying at the Astoria, where Nasrosoltan had come to meet him one evening. Over dinner, as they discussed the political situation and the rumbling social unrest, Rustam mentioned, "Russia is now in its prime, and the next few years will probably be the best years for the country and consequently for my business." Nasrosoltan understood the implication that Rustam's already impressive fortune would rise along with the country's projected growth.

Rustam confessed, "The only concern I have is with the pesky Balkan States. What really worries me is that they will not be able to settle their differences on the share of the spoils of their victory over the Ottoman Empire." After a few more sips of his drink, with flushed cheeks, he said to Nasrosoltan, "If they are not careful, they could even lead Russia into a broader war with the Austro-Hungarian Empire, and that, my friend, would be a major catastrophe."

Nasrosoltan replied, "But I thought war is always good for business, isn't it?"

Rustam nodded in agreement. "I meant catastrophic in terms of the destruction that would be unleashed, but of course, we businessmen always make money during times of conflict. I just have a sense we could make even more with just a few extra years of peace and prosperity." Nasrosoltan found it interesting that Rustam echoed the grand duke's speculation of an impending regional conflict.

In return, Nasrosoltan shared what he had been up to while his friend had been away but made no mention of the gaming house fiasco. Then he casually added, "And in addition to all my work at the conservatory, I am now tutoring Princess Irina."

Nasrosoltan displayed an air of fulfillment, especially when he mentioned in a subtle but bragging manner, "The grand duke sometimes even invites me to drink brandy with him after the conclusion of his daughter's lessons."

A surprised Rustam asked him, "I know it is not for the compensation or having an occasional brandy with a grand duke, so it must probably be to get close to the princess! I have heard she is quite beautiful and is considered one of the most eligible women in all of Russia. Is that the real reason, my ingenious friend?"

Nasrosoltan was taken aback and immediately refuted the notion. "No, no, not at all! I am doing this as a favor for poor Madame Lazar. Remember, I told you how she begged me for weeks to sit in for her while she recovered from that unfortunate injury to her hand?"

He continued defensively, stammering out unnecessary details a little more urgently than he intended, "I felt so sorry for her a few days before the grand duke's family came back from vacation since she did not know where else to turn. So I decided to offer her my assistance."

Nasrosoltan paused for a moment to calm himself down and then added, "For your information, the princess is timid and does not engage in conversation, except for asking short questions concerning the lesson. Mostly she avoids my eye, but I attribute this to her youth and inexperience."

Rustam, sensing he had touched a nerve, replied jokingly, "Or perhaps you could attribute it to your seriousness; maybe she is afraid to talk to you. You must know you can be intimidating."

Nasrosoltan defiantly answered, "Nonsense. I am quite agreeable, and as you know, I have a healthy sense of humor. I always enjoy a good laugh at the appropriate time!"

As Nasrosoltan responded, he felt a twinge of irritation at his friend's suggestion that he had anything but honorable intentions in tutoring the princess. In his attempt to conceal the real reason he had accepted the position, he wanted to be sure not to expose himself to embarrassment for something he considered worse.

Rustam, sensing his friend's uneasiness, changed the subject and asked, "Would you like to go to the gaming house after dinner?"

Nasrosoltan tried to quickly think of a plausible reason to decline the invitation, never wanting to set foot in that wretched place again. Before he could think of an excuse, Rustam added, "The manager asked about you; he said you are the type of customer they love to see more often. I asked him why, and he mentioned you visited one evening while I was on travel, and you made quite an impression. He told me he had never seen someone lose so much on one single wager with such dignity."

Nasrosoltan, while trying to escape his ignominy, said with a laugh, "Yes, it seems that when we went together, Lady Luck was actually at your side and not mine since when I visited without you, she was nowhere to be seen. You must have taken her with you to Siberia. It appears so from what you tell me of the successful outcome of your business."

Nasrosoltan did not divulge that he lost all his money and was now tutoring the princess to pay his rent. He gave Rustam the pretext of needing to get up early in the morning to finish working on a composition and graciously declined his offer.

On the carriage ride back to his apartment, he could not stop thinking of Rustam's insinuation over why he agreed to tutor the princess. His friend had unknowingly planted a seed of doubt by questioning his motives. During the dinner, he was tempted to tell his friend the real reason he was tutoring. Instead, he chose to defend himself from Rustam's innuendo rather than admit his gambling weakness and feeble decision-making, which he considered a more severe fault to confess.

As it so often happens, when a man finds himself confident, at a point where he feels he can do no wrong and the stars are all aligned in his favor, just a hint of skepticism from someone begins the process of self-doubt, creeping up like weeds in the garden of the mind. This is when each wavering thought feeds the tangled web of incertitude. In a few short hours, Nasrosoltan's attitude shifted from one of self-confidence before dinner to one of uncertainty afterward, as he started to question whether others also saw his tutoring the princess as his way of gaining favor with her.

He debated with himself whether he should have ever accepted the position in the first place. These thoughts disturbed him, so he looked forward to a good night's sleep, believing it to be the best remedy for his confused state.

The next day after attending a conservatory seminar, he went back to his apartment to join Madame Lazar to travel to the palace. When he knocked on her door, she opened it halfway, looking quite ill. "My apologies, Monsieur. I must have eaten something that did not sit well with me last night, and I feel terrible. As you can see, I will not be able to accompany you to the lesson today."

Nasrosoltan had grown accustomed to her company during the carriage rides to the palace, even though, at times, he could do without her incessant chatter. However, today of all days, after what Rustam had suggested and the idle thoughts he had allowed to take root in his mind, he did not want to go alone. He did not want it to seem as if he had planned the Madame's absence to get closer to the princess.

Nasrosoltan suggested that Madame Lazar get some rest and quickly left for the palace, not wanting to be late to his appointment.

As the carriage approached the palace gates, Nasrosoltan did not know why he was in a panic. He tried to console himself but instead ended up cursing the roulette ball for finding a home in an unfortunate spot on the wheel.

When he exited the carriage, the butler, as usual, was there to escort him into the palace, but for some reason, Nasrosoltan did not like the way he looked at him. The same with Nana: when she saw him, he perceived a distinct change in how she greeted him. Of course, they were just surprised that Madame Lazar was not with him, nothing else, but he had let his imagination run wild, thinking that they also questioned his motives for teaching the princess.

All this made Nasrosoltan act more formal and reserved than usual. When the time came for the princess's lesson, without the customary greeting and small talk, he abruptly sat at the piano and began the instruction.

***

The princess was surprised at his unusual behavior, for even though she knew Nasrosoltan was a stern man, she had noticed a softening in his demeanor over the past few weeks. She attributed this change to the occasional after-lesson meetings with her father or a sign of her own progress in playing. In any case, she had valued the gradual change in his comportment; however, today, she noted that he seemed to be in a foul mood.

At one point during the lesson, an already anxious Nasrosoltan became agitated that after repeated attempts, Irina could not correctly play a specific section of the piece. He came close to scolding her when he raised his voice and told her, "You have not prepared as I had suggested, and I ask that next time you practice more seriously!"

Irina, who was not used to being addressed in this manner, became quiet and began to fight back the tears. She valiantly continued to try to perform the part; however, being so nervous now, she stumbled even further.

***

Sensing Irina's uneasiness, Nasrosoltan suddenly caught himself and tried to soften his stance by suggesting they take a short break. This gave him time to gather his thoughts and allowed Irina a moment to regain her composure.

In a bid at being more pleasant, he pointed to her ever-present French bulldog pup, who slept in the corner of the room under the window during their lessons, and asked, "What is your dog's name?"

His unexpected question seemed to surprise Irina. This was the first time he had ever talked to her about anything other than the lesson. Nasrosoltan noticed her face suddenly beaming with excitement as she eagerly replied, "Her name is Bijou. We brought her back from our sojourn in southern France last summer."

Irina continued after a brief pause, "She loves to sit under the window in the sun and listen to me play the piano. She has an ear, or should I say, great ears for music!" Of course, this was her attempt at humor, pointing to the French bulldog's most prominent feature, her adorable bat-like ears.

The puppy, hearing her name mentioned, rose and made her way toward the piano, seeking additional attention. Irina reached down and brought Bijou onto the bench, assuming Nasrosoltan may want to pet her. Nasrosoltan, trying to be more cordial than his usual self, pet the puppy with a few quick taps on the back.

An excited Irina asked, "Monsieur, would you like to hold Bijou?"

Even though Nasrosoltan did not really want to, he agreed anyway, to prolong this rare moment of bonding, so she placed the puppy onto his lap. He was unfamiliar with how to correctly hold a puppy, and Bijou seemed uncomfortable from the onset of Nasrosoltan's attempt. He struggled to return the puppy to the princess, but during this exchange, he must have either frightened or squeezed the sorry dog too hard, at which point Bijou relieved herself by raining a shower all over Nasrosoltan.

This unforeseen event caused them both to drop the puppy mid-transfer, and Nasrosoltan, with his shirt now soaked, jumped up in anger. He cursed the dog in Persian, blurting out "*Pedarsag*," which amusingly in Persian means, "Your father is a dog." Bijou, absolutely terrified by the fall and the ensuing ruckus, scampered away to the corner of the room, accompanied by a continuous whimper.

The princess, who at first was in shock at the unfolding scene, suddenly burst into laughter, all the while trying to catch herself by putting her hand over her mouth. Every time she succeeded in quieting her laugh, she would take one look at Nasrosoltan and could not help herself, and once again would unleash a flurry of giggles.

Nasrosoltan, who was red in the face with anger at what Bijou had done, was even more embarrassed by Irina's uncontrolled laughter. He was about to unfurl a tirade upon her when he turned and looked at his own reflection in the mirrored wall on the side of the room. Nasrosoltan realized that he did look quite comical and in that instant recalled what he told Rustam about his sense of humor; that he could "enjoy a good laugh at the appropriate time."

He suddenly realized the sincere innocence in Irina's laughter, for she was not mocking him; this was just her natural reaction to a sequence of unanticipated events. It was then that Nasrosoltan also began to laugh at himself.

Once she witnessed Nasrosoltan also laughing, Irina began to laugh harder, to the point that Nana rushed into the room to see what had happened. When she saw Nasrosoltan and the princess both laughing at his predicament and Bijou still shivering and whining in the corner of the room, she realized what had occurred. Nana immediately offered to have Nasrosoltan's shirt cleaned if he waited in the sitting room, temporarily wearing a borrowed shirt.

While Nana rushed to retrieve a shirt for him, Nasrosoltan and Princess Irina had a few moments to reflect upon what had just happened, and he said to her with a chuckle, "At least Bijou did not grace the sheet music as she did my shirt; therefore, hopefully, next week we can continue where we left off!"

The princess appreciated his sense of humor and, with a captivating smile, assured him that she would be better prepared. Nasrosoltan, for the first time, saw a sweet, blossoming woman with a delightful laugh rather than just a student he was tutoring. As fate would have it, an anxious puppy had sparked an unreserved connection between the two souls.

Nana rushed back in with a clean shirt and escorted Nasrosoltan to the sitting room, offering him tea while he waited. He spent some time perusing the grand duke's elegantly framed family photographs situated on the fireplace mantel. Nasrosoltan seemed to solely focus on the images of Irina amongst the other family members, as he started to notice her sparkling eyes and her gentle elegance, which he had somehow been indifferent to until now.

Later that day, upon returning to his apartment, Nasrosoltan found a note Madame Lazar had left under his door, inquiring how the lesson had gone. He thought, *She will have a good laugh at my expense when I tell her about it the next time I see her.*

That evening, Nasrosoltan had trouble sleeping, and he tossed and turned, but he did not know why. The afternoon's events consumed his thoughts as he recalled each scene in what seemed like slow motion. Nasrosoltan wondered why he had been so anxious when he got to the palace and why he had almost scolded the princess just because she could not correctly perform a part. It was not like him to be swayed emotionally, as if a willow in the wind, from nervousness to anger to uncontrollable laughter, and he did not understand the reason.

He decided, since he could not sleep, to attempt working on a composition, but that was also to no avail. He tried to read some poetry to rest his mind but could not concentrate, and his mind kept wandering in an excited state. As morning approached, his restless thoughts gave way to a few precious moments of calm, and he finally fell asleep.

CHAPTER 18

BLACK EYES

Princess Irina entrusted everything to her closest confidant, a friend she could share every detail of her life with—her diary. It was only with this diary that Irina could reveal her fears, her hopes, and her dreams.

Lately, Irina was intrigued by stories she would hear about the goings-on in St. Petersburg; in the parts of the city a grand duke's daughter would not likely visit. Even though Nana did not leave the palace much, occasionally, on her time off, she would meet with friends from her nursing school days, and Irina was curious to hear all about her outings.

One such evening, a friend of Nana, who was married to an artist, invited her to a café for dinner and music. Nana was careful not to divulge too much to the sheltered princess, but Irina would write everything Nana would share in her diary.

Nana told Irina, "That evening, in the stuffy tobacco-fumed air of the café, a man performed one of the most beautiful songs I ever heard! I asked someone at our table the name of the song, and he said it was called '*Ochi chyornye.*'" ("Black Eyes.")

Nana continued excitedly, "The man told me he was a Ukrainian and that this romantic Gypsy song is popular where he comes from. He even boasted that he knew all the words by heart."

Irina, who was captivated by Nana's story, inquired, "How do you know if he really knew all the words by heart, dear Nana? Could it be that he was just bragging?"

Nana grinned with pride as she explained how she had found out if he was truthful, "Well, I was bold enough to ask him to write the words down on a piece of paper, which he did."

An enthralled Irina laughed along with Nana at her telling the story. Irina then insisted on seeing the paper. When Nana retrieved it for her, Irina recorded the words in her diary:

> *Black eyes, passionate eyes*
> *Burning and beautiful eyes!*
> *How I love you, how I fear you,*
> *It seems I met you in an unlucky hour*
> *Oh, not for nothing are you darker than the deep!*
> *I see mourning for my soul in you,*
> *I see a triumphant flame in you:*
> *A poor heart immolated in it.*
> *But I am not sad, I am not sorrowful,*
> *My fate is soothing to me:*
> *All that is best in life that God gave us,*
> *In sacrifice, I returned to the fiery eyes!*

Nana confided to Irina, "Every time I see your piano tutor, Monsieur Minbashian, with his beautiful, fiery dark eyes, it reminds me of this song!"

Irina added her own observation in her diary:

> *Nana has undoubtedly taken a liking to Monsieur Minbashian. I have noticed that lately, her dress is a little more elegant, and her face is somewhat more made up. Even her hair is given a touch more attention on the days he shows up for my piano lessons.*

Irina also wrote how Bijou had sullied the Monsieur's shirt and that at first, she felt terrible for him, but that everything had ended in laughter. She noted how surprised she was at her own sudden shift in demeanor, from being almost in tears from his mild scolding to being in tears from laughter. As if reminding herself to practice more during the week, Irina wrote and underlined several times, *I will make sure to be prepared to impress him during my next lesson!*

And practice she did, many hours each day to the amazement of her mother, for the grand duchess had never seen her daughter so eager to master a lesson. Grand Duchess Xenia was so impressed that she mentioned it to the grand duke, and he also expressed his satisfaction with how events had transpired.

The grand duke chuckled. "Perhaps we should thank the child who bit Madame Lazar's finger!" He paused briefly in thought and then added, "Monsieur Minbashian carries himself with a certain dignified air, as he has the right balance of respectability and self-assuredness without being immodest. I do enjoy my conversations with him. He seems to have greater experience than his years would indicate."

The grand duke then offered, "I would like to invite him to dine with us one evening. I think he would consider it an honor. You must admit, my dear Xenia, we have never seen Irene work so diligently in all the years she has been tutored by Madame Lazar." Grand Duchess Xenia concurred, and they decided to find a suitable time to formally invite him.

The day of the next lesson arrived, and an eager and well-prepared Irina waited with anticipation for Nasrosoltan at the appointed hour. However, the very punctual Monsieur Minbashian did not show up, and even after an hour of Irina waiting for him in the music room, he was nowhere to be found.

Feeling despondent, Irina called for Nana to inquire if she knew of a schedule change. But with just one glance at her governess's attire, she was reassured that this was, in fact, the day Nasrosoltan was supposed to come. Irina started to wonder if he had been embarrassed and insulted by the events of last week and even worried that he might discontinue tutoring her. As these thoughts began to upset her, the butler walked in with a note Nasrosoltan had sent by courier.

> *Your Serene Highness, forgive me for missing our appointed lesson today and the lateness with which this note is delivered. Director Glazunov suddenly asked that I audition for him this afternoon, and I had no time to spare except to send you this message. With sincere apologies, until our lesson next week, Minbashian.*

Although displeased that she would not see him, Irina was instantly relieved that he had sent a note of apology and found his reason for an excuse to be a valid one. She caught herself missing his presence, as opposed to all the other times when if he had not shown up, she would not have given it a second thought. Evidently, the events of last week had also left an impression on Irina. Even though it was not Nasrosoltan's intention, his note this day produced acute disappointment in two women in the same household when Nana also learned of the contents.

Later that evening, Irina revisited her diary. However, instead of recording any of the day's happenings, she found herself reading again with great interest what she had written several entries ago. She looked back at the *Ochi chyornye* poem Nana shared with her, and as she went over the words, she conjured up the image of Nasrosoltan's dark eyes, and she fell asleep still clutching her diary.

CHAPTER 19

THE SECRET MEETING PLACE

Nasrosoltan's coursework at the conservatory took more of his time these days, as he pursued increasingly challenging exercises in composition and orchestration. He desired to follow the same upward trajectory of his contemporary, Igor Stravinsky. Nasrosoltan respected and envied Stravinsky for having had the opportunity to study privately with Professor Rimsky-Korsakov.

Stravinsky, who often described Rimsky-Korsakov as his second father, never had any formal music education. The professor had even dissuaded Stravinsky from entering the conservatory, instead offering him private lessons for a couple of years. Nasrosoltan was not as fortunate since his chance of being personally tutored by Rimsky-Korsakov was lost forever with the professor's death. Nevertheless, Nasrosoltan closely followed Stravinsky's career and was excited and curious to see the public reception of his latest work.

In the newspaper, he read that Stravinsky had just premiered his latest composition, "The Rite of Spring," in Paris at the Théâtre des Champs-Elysées, with dignitaries, royalty, and renowned musicians in attendance. It was Nasrosoltan's lifelong dream that he would also perform his music for an audience of this caliber at such an esteemed venue and to have glowing reviews printed in newspapers and music journals.

However, as he read on, he realized that the critics were not all kind to Stravinsky's latest creation. It seemed that some of the more vocal audience at the premiere considered his work to be harsh sounding, and they reacted to the extreme with catcalls and whistling to show their displeasure. Dueling factions tried to drown each other out—one group dismissing Stravinsky's music as grotesque, the other enamored by his avant-garde approach to laying a new world of music at the horizon, calling him a genius.

Nasrosoltan had a deep reverence for musicians such as Stravinsky, who composed path-breaking works that tested the artistic boundaries of music. He understood that even though audiences and some critics wanted music that sounded pleasing to the ear, composers, especially ingenious ones, needed to push the limits. He believed music should stir human emotions, which it seemed Stravinsky's work had succeeded in doing.

In Persia, Nasrosoltan and Salar Moazaz had experienced a similar situation in trying to modernize Persian music, where traditional musicians resisted novel ideas and the needed innovation. To the dismay of these musicians, Salar Moazaz had compared Persian music to Western music as "a camel in a hopeless race against a railroad train, only to find out that it was lagging farther behind all the time."

Some considered the Minbashian family's attempts to restructure Persian music to fit Western norms as a contemptuous disregard for traditional music. However, this family viewed it as a necessity. They felt it was imperative to break new ground and push the boundaries to bring Persian music out of what they believed had been years of stagnation. That is why Nasrosoltan had such an affinity for the groundbreaking work Stravinsky produced, and he admired the composer's boldness in the face of criticism.

Although Nasrosoltan was fascinated with Stravinsky's stylistic diversity in pushing these boundaries, he was most of all enamored with romantic musicians, with one of his favorites being Franz Schubert. Schubert was not only a romantic composer, but he was also a progressive thinker in musical terms.

Many years earlier, Professor Rimsky-Korsakov had tasked Salar Moazaz with orchestrating a Schubert piano four-hands march. In the process, Salar Moazaz developed an admiration for Schubert that also carried over to Nasrosoltan. When speaking about Schubert, Salar Moazaz would refer to the composer as the "Austrian poet of music" due to his ability to transform his feelings into musical notes with lyrical melodies. Father and son had played several of Schubert's military marches together in Tehran, as these works were scored for two people at one piano.

Nasrosoltan favored Schubert so much that he decided to tutor the princess on one of his works, the Fantasia in F minor, which he composed during the last year of his life. It was said that Schubert wrote this work in dedication to his pupil Countess Karoline Esterhazy, for whom he held a hopeless passion.

Nasrosoltan pitied Schubert's weakness in loving a woman who did not reciprocate his love. He wondered why the composer had allowed himself to experience such agony. Even though Nasrosoltan admired Schubert's ability to create a masterpiece from such personal frailty, he also found the composer's unrequited love to be his Achilles' heel. Schubert's story reminded Nasrosoltan of his own fragility while infatuated with Madame Shamsi. Recalling how terrible he felt back in Shiraz, Nasrosoltan vowed to never let a woman make him feel that way again.

At the same time, Nasrosoltan also thought Irina may enjoy knowing Schubert's inspiration for creating this piece. He believed it would allow her to understand the composer's angst as he wrote for the woman who incited such a masterful work. Nasrosoltan found it unusual that he now spent so much time thinking of the princess during the week, as opposed to in the past when Irina had barely entered his mind.

The day before his next lesson, Nasrosoltan visited Madame Lazar for tea and conversation. After they had a good laugh at his story about Irina's puppy, she unexpectedly said to him, "My dear Monsieur, I have decided not to accompany you to the palace for your weekly lessons anymore. I now find it unnecessary since you have gained the confidence of the family, and I wish to spend more time attending to other activities."

This surprised Nasrosoltan since he knew what a curious lady she was. Although she did not mention this aloud, she was now getting the details about the events at the palace from Nana, so Madame Lazar did not feel she had to be physically present. Additionally, she found comfort in the fact that the family was happy with Nasrosoltan's tutoring. Since he would be going back to Persia in several months, her position remained secure, which had been her ultimate objective all along.

Nasrosoltan replied, "Dear Madame, I respect your decision, but know that you will be missed."

As he offered these words, Nasrosoltan actually felt relieved. Even though he never considered her tagging along each week like a chaperone as becoming of his position, he had enjoyed Madame Lazar's presence. Her being there had kept the always-inquisitive Nana from showing up unexpectedly during their lessons. But he also found it ridiculous that anyone from the household would need to keep an eye on them. Of course, unbeknownst to him, Nana's curiosity had more to do with his "fiery eyes" than her need to keep tabs on them during their lessons.

The next day, with the new Schubert sheet music in tow, he came to the palace at the appointed time and, as usual, was welcomed in by the butler. He was excited to begin tutoring Irina on the piece, and she, in turn, seemed more delighted than usual to see him. He noticed she was radiant this day and was eager to show him she was well prepared through diligent practice since their last lesson.

After Irina flawlessly performed the section she had so much trouble with the previous session, Nasrosoltan said to her, "Your Serene Highness, you played that piece with a passion and emotion that I had not witnessed until today. I think it is the perfect time to begin working on the new music I have brought."

151

Princess Irina was both excited and surprised to hear a compliment since before now, he had rarely praised her playing.

Nasrosoltan continued, "It is a work of Schubert for four hands, which is different than a piano duet. Playing a two-piano duet may make one think of a struggle to compete. Playing with four hands on the same piano, however, requires harmony and balance between the two performers."

Irina was barely able to absorb the compliment he had offered moments before while Nasrosoltan raised the bar for her lessons. As she listened to the new challenge, she began to fidget and look nervous. Nasrosoltan noticed Irina's countenance and purposely softened his tone to encourage her in this new endeavor.

He continued, "This can be difficult, but also fascinating when performed with perfect execution and the requisite practice, as you just demonstrated."

Nasrosoltan proceeded to tell her the story behind the Fantasia, which she listened to with keen interest. When he finished, Irina asked, "I feel so sad for poor Schubert; did the countess know he loved her, or was she unaware?"

Nasrosoltan replied, "Not much is really known about their relationship, except that he dedicated this work to her. She was exactly Your Serene Highness's age when he tutored her, and Schubert was a man older than I. If the age difference had not been an issue, the difference in their social standing would have probably made it impossible for any romantic relationship to develop. Therefore, it seems it did not matter whether she knew or not."

This remark moved Irina, who then inquired, "But Monsieur Minbashian, when one is truly in love, why would age or social standing be an impediment?"

Nasrosoltan admired Irina's genuine innocence; her question revealed her inexperience in matters of love and life. He replied, "You are correct; it is not a crime to love someone who does not reciprocate; or to love someone who, in the eyes of society, should not be the object of one's affection. However, the lesson I take from Schubert's life is that he used those feelings, which probably brought him more sorrow than joy, to create a work of art that has endured so many years after leaving this world.

"This music will continue to be performed for ages by the likes of Your Highness and me, for he truly created an everlasting masterpiece. At least Schubert did not let those feelings go to waste. I must believe he did love her since, in my opinion, true love creates rather than devastates. That is what should be celebrated—this beautiful music! Now, let us begin since the hour is getting late."

Irina had never heard him speak in this manner, and she had never spoken of love with a man before. Evidently, she was closer to womanhood than anyone realized. She was intrigued by the new music and especially the story behind its inspiration. As they were about to sit side by side on the piano bench, for the first time, Irina seemed excited and silently hoped that he would sit closer to her than he usually sat.

Four-hand works are typically composed so that players do not get in each other's way. But because Irina was unfamiliar with the music, there were moments where her hands would inadvertently touch Nasrosoltan's as they played. Sometimes their wrists even caressed one another when their fingers raced over the piano keys.

The first time their hands crossed over, the bottom of Nasrosoltan's wrist lying on top of Irina's, it seemed as if for a moment neither wanted to move forward from that position onto the next key. That anxious encounter prompted Irina to giggle and blush while Nasrosoltan awkwardly pulled his hand away in a flash of fright, bringing it back into a safer sphere. He could feel his heart racing, a feeling that confused him.

Whenever their hands met on the keys during the lesson, the same emotions surfaced, surprising them both. She would tremble with panicked excitement at the opportunity for the next wrist-to-wrist encounter, and he could feel his heart pounding within his chest as hands moved closer to meet on the keyboard.

Even though they could not look at each other while playing four hands, their hands communicated as if they were in private, shutting out the gaze of any would-be spectator. Accidentally placed fingers brushing against each other created brief moments of contact between them, in a safe space, where such touching and nearness were permitted. Without the secret meeting place of the keyboard, this would not have been possible.

This was uncharted territory for both, and the excitement that was ignited by this closeness felt especially uncomfortable to Nasrosoltan. To Irina's surprise, he abruptly ended the lesson earlier than usual, giving her a few instructions for practice, and then departed.

That evening, Nasrosoltan once again found it difficult to sleep as he was in a state of distressed excitement. He felt anxious and apprehensive and was preoccupied with thoughts of Irina. He became fearful that the relationship was transforming from a straightforward tutor-and-pupil one to something more complicated and problematic for him. He worried that he was playing with fire, which ironically was the same warning the commander had given him back in Shiraz when he was infatuated with Madame Shamsi.

No one would blame a young princess for having such feelings, especially one so sheltered and protected. Still, his honor would inevitably be tainted and his reputation sullied if anything untoward developed between them.

Nasrosoltan decided the best course of action would be to stop tutoring Princess Irina since he needed no distraction so close to finishing his studies and returning to Persia. He thought that the next morning, he would tell Madame Lazar that he needed to concentrate on his own burdensome coursework and could not continue to tutor the princess any longer.

However, this thought lived for only that one short moment since Nasrosoltan considered retreating a show of weakness. He wanted to rise to the challenge, reasoning that he had enough control over his feelings to continue tutoring Irina without letting things get out of hand.

Nasrosoltan blamed himself for leading this sweet woman along with talk of Schubert's unrequited love for his own pupil. He realized how unaware he had been at the time of the subtle similarity between his tutoring a princess and Schubert's tutoring a countess. He supposed she may have misinterpreted his choice of music and his telling of this story as signaling that he had similar feelings for her.

Attempting to shut out such distracting thoughts, Nasrosoltan decided to put all his mental energies into his work. He spent day after day ensconced at the conservatory in serious study. This course of action seemed to work as he slowly regained his confidence. He reasoned that what had happened during the last lesson was nothing more than a passing fancy, and he would confirm this for himself the next time he tutored the princess without a hint of emotion.

The next lesson appointment soon arrived, and Nasrosoltan was once again off to the palace. He decided beforehand to exude an air of formality during his short stay, to dispel any notion of misplaced affection between the two.

As Irina sat down at the piano next to him, he noticed things about her he had not paid attention to during prior appointments. Her eyes seemed so innocent yet captivating. Her silky hair carried a subtle fragrance, and her long, slender fingers danced joyously on the piano keyboard. Everything about her seemed perfect this day. No matter how he tried, he could not be as formal as he had planned, and as soon as they performed on the piano side by side once again, the same feelings and emotions stirred up within him.

Nasrosoltan tried to calm his racing heart as uncomfortable thoughts surfaced, making him more nervous. He took a quick sideways peek at Irina as she methodically performed the piece she had practiced so carefully. Irina, in turn, stole a glance at him from the corner of her eye, with the most enchanting smile fixed upon her lips, while continuing to play.

She had indeed practiced much that week, for they played the first movement of the Fantasia in perfect harmony, not missing a beat. He was extremely impressed with her dedication to the music, which enthralled him even more.

Nana, who had come to offer tea, stood by the entrance taking in the sounds emanating from the room, and she realized this was not the time to disturb them.

When they finished performing the section, Nana entered the room, put the tea tray down, and poured them both some tea. As she left the room, she attempted to hum the beautiful melody she had just heard. Nasrosoltan and Irina both laughed, as they were totally unaware she had been listening.

Nasrosoltan was thankful Nana could only see their backs, conscious that she could have witnessed their affectionate nonverbal cues. He complimented Irina for her playing, and a grateful Irina replied, "Monsieur Minbashian, you should also be complimented for sharing with me the story behind such a work of beauty; it makes practicing more enjoyable when one knows the intent of the composer."

Nasrosoltan thanked her and then began to perform parts of the second movement, instructing Irina on what part of the piece she was to focus on for next week's lesson.

He confided, "I particularly like this second movement when Schubert opens it with a somewhat angry and turbulent theme that leads to a great deal of tension. This will then give way to a quiet, more lyrical second theme. It is a delight to perform. Your Serene Highness will surely enjoy it."

At this point, the princess turned to him and said, "Monsieur Minbashian, I know you address me as Your Serene Highness out of respect and proper decorum, but it would please me if you address me in private by my given name, Irina. I detest formalities such as these titles."

Nasrosoltan welcomed the fact that she felt at ease enough to suggest this. With a smile, he replied, "Then it is only fair that you would also call me by my name." Then he jokingly added, "However, since Nasrosoltan is actually a title, I fear you may detest using it."

Seeing her smile fondly in return made him realize that his plans to be more formal had now totally gone by the wayside. More importantly, his resolve to control his emotions was fruitless in her presence, so he decided it was time to leave. She seemed visibly disappointed at his abrupt departure, as he bade her adieu until the next week.

CHAPTER 20

A DAY AT THE MUSEUM

Another sleepless night awaited Nasrosoltan. The more he tried not to think of Irina, the more he did. He was walking on the razor's edge between the fear of jeopardizing his tutoring position and an unnerving infatuation for Irina. He had experienced this feeling before, back in Shiraz, and that memory still felt like a wound that had not healed. Nasrosoltan desperately wanted to avoid the same emotions from resurfacing to betray him once more.

His life had suddenly become too complicated, and he realized he needed to seek guidance for soothing the unrelenting turmoil within him. He knew he should stay away from Princess Irina, yet with each lesson, this had become more difficult for him to do.

In his quest for calm, Nasrosoltan decided to consult his old friend Rustam to discuss his predicament. He sent word to Rustam at the Astoria to see if he was available to meet the next day, noting that he needed to discuss something with him urgently. Rustam replied via return note that he could not meet the next day since he had a prior appointment with the minister of commerce, adding:

> *I also have some good news to share. My family is finally moving to St. Petersburg from Tbilisi in the coming weeks. I am overjoyed, and I look forward to them finally meeting you.*

Rustam ended by suggesting they have lunch the day after next, at the Astoria. Reading his friend's note made Nasrosoltan think about how much he missed his own family, and suddenly a feeling of loneliness engulfed him. In St. Petersburg, he had no friends other than Rustam. He did have acquaintances from the conservatory with whom he socialized. But with none of them did he feel close enough to discuss matters of a personal nature or to ask for their advice.

Nasrosoltan was eager to meet with Rustam to see what words of wisdom he may offer. Obviously, his friend was more experienced—not because of his years and graying hair, but because he had a unique way of recognizing solutions to problems through his keen perception of situations. This ability may have been the reason for Rustam's success as a businessman, always seeking what others may have missed. More than anything, Nasrosoltan just needed someone trustworthy with whom to share these feelings he had bottled up within himself.

The next day, to ease his cluttered mind, he planned to visit the State Hermitage Museum. Nasrosoltan hoped that art could clear his vision to find a path out of his confusion. On his way there, he noticed a crowd of people going in the same direction toward one of the government buildings, where hundreds of striking workers had already gathered and were demonstrating.

Even though the Russian economy was growing at a pace that was the envy of other European nations, there still was much discontent with the tsarist regime. There had been a massacre of striking Siberian gold miners a year earlier that had led to an eruption of protests and industrial unrest throughout the country. This mayhem had now spread to the capital city with a series of strikes and demonstrations.

Rustam had become an investor and partner in the Putilov Company, which produced railway products and supplied artillery to the Imperial Russian Army. He had mentioned to Nasrosoltan how anxious he was that his workers would follow suit and strike. He even confided to Nasrosoltan that some nights he could not sleep, consumed with such worries. Nasrosoltan understood Rustam's concerns, but he also felt sympathy with these workers. It did not seem fair to Nasrosoltan that while the owners of capital, like his own friend, were increasing their wealth several-fold a year, these workers had to fight for safe working conditions and fair compensation.

Considering how money seemed to have provided a poor pillow for Rustam, Nasrosoltan was at least grateful that his insomnia had to do with his feelings for Irina rather than for money.

When Nasrosoltan approached the gathering, the crowd was peaceful, with the strikers protesting loudly. As he strained his neck to look over the mass of people, he sensed a tension in the air. A feeling of foreboding overtook him as he witnessed government troops on guard at the building entrance, with their rifles and bayonets primed.

Suddenly without warning, a few shots rang out. Nasrosoltan initially thought the troops were firing in the air to disperse the crowd. But the gunshots seemed to come from a direction other than where the guards were standing. He had heard that agent provocateurs sometimes mixed with the demonstrators to create havoc, to entice the soldiers to respond with force. No matter who had fired the shots, it resulted in the now terrified crowd scrambling for cover.

Nasrosoltan was far away in the back of all that was happening but was immediately overwhelmed by the crowd barreling toward him. He attempted to get out of the way of the stampede when someone pushed him, knocking him down to the ground forcefully. The sound of the roaring crowd frightened him. Nasrosoltan struggled to get up off the ground, but he lost his balance and was knocked down again. He could not breathe, panicked that he would suffocate, while all around him, people were running and screaming in fear. His heart raced, and his limbs felt numb, and he thought he was going to pass out when out of nowhere, a stranger's hand reached out to grab his. If not for this helping hand, which allowed Nasrosoltan to get back to his feet, he would have certainly been trampled. He finally righted himself and was able to mix in with the crowd and run to safety.

He escaped the commotion and collapsed on a nearby street bench, still breathing heavily. While Nasrosoltan sat there catching his breath and dusting himself off, he remembered the tragic and bloody Sunday afternoon in January 1905, when thousands were killed by the tsar's Imperial Guard. It made him wonder if history may be repeating itself, a thought which greatly disturbed him.

His plan to visit the museum now seemed frivolous in light of what he had gone through, so an unsettled Nasrosoltan abandoned the idea of going altogether. Since he had lost his bearings, Nasrosoltan tried to reorient himself to find his way home and soon realized that he was actually very close to the Hermitage. Now out of danger's way and feeling much calmer, Nasrosoltan spent a few moments wondering what to do. Even though he was still unnerved, he changed his mind and decided to go to the museum after all. Nasrosoltan hoped that viewing the rare artwork on display would help settle his nerves and afford him a feeling of serenity amid the morning's chaos.

Once at the Hermitage, the first exhibit Nasrosoltan encountered included Napoleonic war era paintings, many containing scenes of gruesome death and destruction, rattling him even further. He had decided to come to the Hermitage to gain peacefulness; instead, he was confronted with blood and guts, something he was in no mood for, not even in a masterpiece. Nasrosoltan immediately recognized he had made a mistake in coming to the museum after such a harrowing morning, and he decided to leave.

On his way out, as he passed one of the cavernous rooms dedicated to French painters, Nasrosoltan found himself fixated by a Henri Matisse painting, *Harmony in Red.*

The painting had a magnetic pull, drawing him in closer. He sat down in front of this sizable oil-on-canvas masterpiece and carefully spent time studying the bright red colors and the rhythms of the foliage patterns. For some reason, this particular painting had a powerful effect on his sensibilities, distracting him from his recent troublesome thoughts.

As he studied the intricate details of this work, it was as if he could almost hear the painting. This surprised Nasrosoltan as he began to recognize similarities between music and painting. He noticed how both shared principles of rhythm, harmony, and balance. The same rhythm he used in his compositions, inviting listeners to sway to the music, was used here by Matisse, inducing Nasrosoltan's eyes to dance from one point of this painting to another. And just as Nasrosoltan used musical motifs to give his melodies their overall balance, the artist had used this same balance to add structure to *Harmony in Red*. A harmony and balance that, as of late, was missing in Nasrosoltan's life and that he was desperate to restore.

This visit to the Hermitage actually turned out to have a calming, therapeutic effect on Nasrosoltan, silencing the chatter in his mind and washing away the dust of confusion from his soul. A much-needed interruption of what had been, until today, a hectic schedule of study and tutoring, culminating in the calamitous events of the morning.

Nasrosoltan left to go back to his apartment and realized he had lost track of time, as the sun had set long ago, and it was totally dark outside. The trip to the museum had cleared his mind enough that upon returning home in the fresh evening air, he was finally able to have a good night's rest.

CHAPTER 21

THE ARROGANCE OF IGNORANCE

The next day, Nasrosoltan arrived at the Astoria to lunch with Rustam. After looking around the stately lobby, he did not see his friend, who would usually be reading the newspaper and smoking a cigarette. Nasrosoltan decided to sit down to wait for him, but after a half hour, he became concerned, as Rustam was never late for their meetings. He approached the hotel's front desk and asked the attendant to contact Rustam's room to announce his arrival.

The man asked, "Was Monsieur Somkhishvili expecting you?"

Nasrosoltan replied, "Yes, for lunch at the restaurant." The man requested that Nasrosoltan wait a moment while he informed the hotel manager, which seemed unusual.

When the manager arrived, he introduced himself and said, "Sir, are you a friend of Monsieur Somkhishvili?"

A perturbed Nasrosoltan responded with a curt "Yes! Why do you inquire?" feeling insulted, wondering what about his appearance this day raised so many questions from the staff.

The hotelier apologized with a somber face. "I am very sorry to inform you that just this morning, we received word that Monsieur Somkhishvili has passed away."

A devastated Nasrosoltan could not believe what he just heard. In a flurried and anxious voice, he stammered, "This can't be! How did this happen?"

The man responded sorrowfully, "It seems that yesterday there was some disturbance outside the Ministry of Commerce, and he was struck by a stray bullet. He was taken to the hospital, but his condition was too grave, and he died in the early morning."

Nasrosoltan was overcome with sadness and looked around in disbelief. Witnessing his terrible distress, the hotelier continued gently, "The police just informed us a few hours ago. I am deeply sorry for your loss. I was just sending a note to inform his business manager of the tragedy."

Nasrosoltan suddenly thought about the family Rustam left behind and asked, "What about his family? They were planning to move to St. Petersburg from Georgia. He was expecting them in the next few weeks!"

The man took in the heartbreaking information and replied, "Hopefully, his manager can get word to them before it is too late."

Nasrosoltan was awestruck. He now realized he had been there at the same moment the shooting took place. He felt terrible that he had gone on to spend the whole afternoon at the museum, while unbeknownst to him, his friend lay dying alone in a hospital bed. How he wished he could have been at his side for those last few moments. He thought how Rustam had so much hope for the future, so many unfinished plans, all silenced in an instant by a bullet not even intended for him.

A thoroughly dejected Nasrosoltan left the hotel, consumed with worry for Rustam's family. He knew the family would not want the funeral in St. Petersburg since Rustam's wish had always been to be buried in Georgian soil.

Dazed and confused, he made his way back home. He spent the next two days entrenched in his apartment in a depressed state, not wanting to see or talk to anyone. He barely left the room, and he kept the shades pulled in total darkness.

The gloom in the air was intolerable. Nasrosoltan kneeled at the foot of his bed and began weeping and murmuring as if communicating with the soul of his dear friend. Within less than twenty-four hours, he had gone from a feeling of confusion to clear-mindedness to now deep sorrow. He spent the rest of his waking hours that evening cursing fate out loud.

On Monday morning, he dragged himself out of bed and made his way to the conservatory. Emerging from his dark apartment and busying himself with his coursework distracted him from his dark thoughts.

***

That afternoon Nasrosoltan once again visited the palace to tutor Irina, but today she noticed he was not the same man she had last seen just a week ago. His eyes carried little of the fire she was accustomed to seeing and instead exhibited a quiet suffering—of what, she did not know the reason. They sat side by side at the piano, and she began to play, but after a few minutes, she noticed his attention was elsewhere, as he was distant and silent.

Curious to know the cause, Irina inquired, "I thought perhaps that you are displeased with my playing, but there is a shade of grief upon your face that points to something other than a few misplayed notes; please tell me, what is troubling you?"

Nasrosoltan turned to her, vulnerable and teary-eyed, telling Irina, "You are quite observant. I apologize if I am not prepared for today's lesson. I did not plan to mention this, and I did not want to disturb you with talk of unpleasant things, but unfortunately, it seems my eyes have betrayed me this day. I am carrying the pain of losing a dear friend so unexpectedly," and he went on to explain the tragic events leading up to Rustam's death. "He was a good man, and I am quite saddened by the calamity that befell him."

Irina, who was overwhelmed at his expression of sorrow and display of love for his friend, suddenly placed her hand upon his in a gesture of comfort and sympathy. Boldly, he grasped her hand and kissed it gently.

This time when they touched, there was no giggling on her part and no pulling away of his hand in fright, just an instant frozen in time. They looked into each other's eyes, sharing this tender moment without a word needing to be exchanged.

That her touch could be so comforting to him at a time when he felt so unguarded was something he had not contemplated. Nasrosoltan never imagined that the loss of his friend could have awakened such feelings within him. A sense of calm engulfed him as he breathed in the scent of lavender on her hand, and he cherished this closeness, as it gave him much-needed solace.

Irina gently pulled her hand away as they both heard footsteps in the distance, worried that someone would witness the display of affection between them. It seemed as if they both wished the lesson would never end, as neither wanted to leave the presence of the other.

Unexpectedly, the grand duke's secretary entered the music room and announced that Grand Duke Alexander wanted to meet with Nasrosoltan. He bid farewell to Irina, whose eyes were glowing with excitement as she leaned in closer to wish him goodbye, already counting the days until next week's lesson. Even though he had left her presence, she was delighted that they were still under the same roof, as Nasrosoltan joined her father in his study.

She rushed up to her room and pulled out her diary in haste to record every emotion she had just experienced. This was the first time she felt so strongly toward a man, and she wanted to safeguard, in her own words, the beauty of each moment of the past hour. She wrote:

> *I am sad to see how Nasrosoltan is tormented by the fate that has befallen his friend. It is surprising that just a while ago, I believed him to be so strict, so indifferent. But now, he shows such tenderness and warmth towards me and has kindled indescribable feelings within me.*

When he took hold of my hand today, I trembled with anticipation, especially when he kissed it—such a gentle kiss. I tried so much not to show my excitement, for I did not want him to think I was alarmed at the gesture. I did not want him to pull away! Sometimes it is unbearably painful to sit close to him and to look into his eyes without being able to express what I can so effortlessly write on these pages. I pray he feels the same way towards me, for I think of him all my waking hours and dream of him while asleep!

Meanwhile, when Nasrosoltan walked into the grand duke's study, he noticed that the grand duke was not in his usual jovial mood and seemed sorrowful. Nasrosoltan was curious to know why but said nothing, waiting for the grand duke to break the silence. After offering Nasrosoltan a brandy, the grand duke, mournful and despondent, told him, "I was disheartened today. I heard terrible news concerning a wealthy industrialist killed a few days ago during a workers' protest. The government officials in charge of the investigation are unsure if it was the Bolsheviks or a lone wolf from the striking metalworkers. Some surmise it was a stray bullet, a case of being in the wrong place at the wrong time, but in any event, the death of this man has saddened me."

Startled to hear of the same event he could not stop thinking about, Nasrosoltan choked up and asked, "Are you referring to Monsieur Rustam Somkhishvili?"

The grand duke replied with surprise, "Yes, that is correct. He was a Georgian, and his company was supplying us with artillery. How do you know of him?"

"He was my dear friend," Nasrosoltan replied as he choked back the tears. "I was there the day it happened. In this whole city, I had no closer friend, but now he is gone."

Then, with his voice cracking, a desolate Nasrosoltan said how much he would miss Rustam and in one fell swoop downed his entire snifter of brandy. The grand duke, wishing to console him, followed suit by raising his glass and saying, "May God rest his soul!"

Grand Duke Alexander witnessed a side of Nasrosoltan that he would not have seen if this tragedy had not happened. He was impressed that the young man had never mentioned his connection with this supremely wealthy businessman. It was a quality the grand duke found refreshing in a city where many considered name-dropping a virtue.

Hearing how Nasrosoltan had just lost his dear friend, in a gesture of kindness, the grand duke offered, "The grand duchess and I would like to invite you to dine with us one evening in the next few weeks when our schedules permit."

Nasrosoltan thanked him for his thoughtfulness and gratefully responded, "Your Highness, it would be an honor and a privilege, and I look forward to the occasion."

The grand duke announced, "Splendid; a formal invitation will be forthcoming."

Having finished their drinks, Nasrosoltan got up and asked the grand duke's permission to leave, as he didn't want to overstay his welcome. Before departing the room, Nasrosoltan added apologetically, "Your Highness, forgive me for showing such emotion today."

With a friendly tone, the grand duke advised him, "Never apologize for shedding tears for a dead friend, for it is not a sign of weakness but a measure of the love and respect you had for another. We lost many good men in the war with the Japanese, and I saw men who shed tears for their compatriots without much grieving and some who suffered without shedding tears. I see the profound sorrow you feel has penetrated deep into your heart. Cherish this and be grateful for the ability to express grief in such a manner. Truly there is no shame in that. But always remember this about death; people only die when you forget them!"

Nasrosoltan, with his hand on his heart, bowed his head in gratitude for the grand duke's heartwarming words. The grand duke, wanting to show respect, especially at such a difficult time for him, got up and said, "Let me walk you out."

They both walked outside the palace entrance and spent another few minutes conversing. Unbeknownst to them both, Irina had found a window within view, stationing herself in position to have one last glance at Nasrosoltan before he left.

That evening he could not sleep once again, but this time, he felt excited, not confused. Nasrosoltan had cursed fate for taking away Rustam in the strangest manner, precisely at a time his friendship was needed the most. But he now realized the irony, that the fate he cursed for putting Rustam in front of a bullet was also the same fate that placed him side by side with Irina at the piano.

To still his mind, he reached for the *Divan of Hafez* and randomly opened a page in the Persian tradition for consultation. To his surprise, he landed on the same sonnet he had read back in Shiraz, at the tomb of Hafez, which at the time had disappointed him. When he reread it now, it seemed the sonneteer's words relayed a completely different message:

> *"Love," I cried, "a little pity*
> *Show to me, a hapless stranger,*
> *Poor and lonely in Love's City."*
> *But she answered:*
> *"Foolish stranger,*
> *Yours the fault, not mine, for losing*
> *Thus, your way; 't is your own choosing*
> *Blame not me, O tiresome stranger."*
> *Once more, O HAFIZ, dawns the morning cup,*
> *Another day in which to seek her face!*
> *Patience! The day will come, in some strange place,*
> *When thy strong hands her veil at last lift up.*

Upon reading this, it was as if a whirlwind of emotion hit him. Had the poet so many years ago foretold how he would feel this night? Might it be that the love Hafez had spoken of was not the pursuit of music but instead the love of a woman?

As if standing before him, he recalled how the mute falgir a summer ago in their Tehran garden pointed to the word *love* on his cloth, adding on a scrap of paper, *You do not believe in fortunes, not even those that poets tell you from the grave!* All in response to Nasrosoltan's mockery of fortune-telling. He reflected upon the arrogance of his ignorance years earlier, passionately believing that love would be the furthest thought from his mind when destiny seemed to be hinting otherwise.

Just as the poet had predicted, Nasrosoltan had been "*a hapless stranger, poor and lonely in Love's City*" back in Shiraz, and he now found himself in "*some strange place.*" He suddenly began to worry about what followed in the same verse, *When thy strong hands her veil at last lift up*, for he did not want any misstep led by such feelings to take him and the princess down a ruinous path.

Pieces of this mysterious puzzle were falling into place right in front of his eyes. Nasrosoltan now accepted that he had powerful feelings for Irina. He also knew that this could put him in a precarious position if he was not careful. But he felt different this time than in Shiraz, where he struggled with his own blindness, leading him to be fearful of loving any woman.

This night, thoughts of Irina did not frighten him. All doubts, despair, and fear had now become insignificant, with Irina on his mind and with her foothold in his heart.

CHAPTER 22

THE INVITATION

A few days later, when Nasrosoltan arrived home from the conservatory, he found a note from Madame Lazar asking him to visit her when he had a chance. He went to her apartment, where she greeted him excitedly. She waved an envelope in her hand and announced that a courier from the palace had delivered a personal correspondence for him.

Upon handing him the envelope, Madame Lazar inquired with curiosity bordering on intrusiveness, "What do you think it could be? I hope it has nothing to do with your tutoring of the princess!" At the mention of Irina's name, Nasrosoltan opened the letter immediately, revealing a formal invitation to dine at the palace.

Madame Lazar was surprised that Nasrosoltan had received an invite to such a formal gathering. Ignoring any notion that she may not have even been invited, she exclaimed, "That is strange. The courier did not deliver an invitation for me; I wonder if he forgot?"

Nasrosoltan felt awkward, knowing how much the Madame desired involvement with the royal family. However, almost immediately after Madame Lazar uttered those words, her eyes met Nasrosoltan's, and it became evident that, unfortunately for her, a shift in position had occurred. He had gained favor while she had not. And for Madame Lazar, there would probably be no invitation.

She became envious, and her feelings were hurt, and she quietly thanked the Lord that Nasrosoltan would be going back to Persia soon. Then, she suddenly blurted out, "You know, Monsieur, I have some good news. I visited the doctor, and his prognosis for a full recovery to my finger was better than expected!"

By offering a veiled threat of her early return, Madame Lazar attempted to shift back the balance by creating uncertainty with Nasrosoltan's position tutoring the princess. Only she knew that there had been no doctor's visit and that her hand was feeling stiffer and actually getting worse.

Nasrosoltan, oblivious to the Madame's games, was happy to hear of her improvement. In an attempt to reassure Madame Lazar, he offered, "It could be that the grand duke has invited me as a gesture of kindness since he learned of my dear friend's tragic death just a few days ago."

Hearing this explanation initially calmed Madame Lazar's anxiety about the missed invitation. But then she turned her agitation to the volatile state of the country. With a heightened nervousness in her voice, she vented, "How can a distinguished man such as Monsieur Somkhishvili be gunned down in the street without reason?"

Madame Lazar started working herself into a frenzy about the political instability and how she did not feel safe anymore. She sarcastically suggested, "Maybe I should emigrate to France, where the people are more civilized."

Nasrosoltan tried to change the subject to keep her increasing uneasiness at bay by asking for assistance on an unrelated matter. Pointing to the bottom of the invitation card, which read, *White Tie, Formal Evening Attire*, he asked, "Madame Lazar, do you think the formal attire I wear when performing auditions at the conservatory is appropriate for such an occasion?"

It seemed his maneuver was successful at changing her train of thought as she refocused and replied definitively, "No, not at all, the outfit you must wear at these functions is quite different.

Really, you must look to acquire the appropriate attire for such an evening, since even the smallest faux pas is readily noticed!"

Luckily for him, his father had finally wired funds to his account for the last few months of his stay, so money was not going to be an issue. At issue, however, was procuring appropriate clothing, which a tailor would need to custom-make.

Madame Lazar added with a dismissive tone, "The invitation for dinner is two weeks from now; there is no way anyone can make it for you in time."

Just as she had pleaded with him months ago to accept the tutoring position, now he begged for her aid. "There must be a way; please, Madame, I need your help. Do you have any idea how I can acquire this formal attire in time?"

Nasrosoltan realized that the more he needed Madame Lazar's help, the more she softened her stance, as she began to see it wasn't Nasrosoltan's fault she had not been invited.

Since the Madame had introduced him to the royal family, she believed the successful outcome of that introduction was in her best interest. So Madame Lazar agreed to do all she could to assist Nasrosoltan in looking his most elegant. But above all, it pleased her that Nasrosoltan felt indebted to her.

She mentioned, "It will be difficult, but I may be able to persuade my late husband's friend, Monsieur Dukemejian, to do it. He is a fellow Armenian and an excellent tailor, well known to St. Petersburg high society. There is a great demand for his exquisite work."

Madame Lazar continued eagerly, "He is a true gentleman. Upon hearing of my husband's death in the war, he was very attentive to me. One truly knows a person's character in such times, for some offer the obligatory condolences, and you never hear from them again. But this kind man was there for me in my darkest moments, sharing my sorrow."

Relieved at her offer to help, Nasrosoltan thanked her profusely and asked, "You say the tailor's name is Dukemejian? That is interesting. In Persian, that means someone who deals with buttons, *dokmechi.*"

Madame Lazar had now fully recovered from her bout of envy and proceeded to impart all she knew about Dukemejian's background. She told Nasrosoltan, "You see, his father was also a well-known tailor who emigrated from the Ottoman Empire, and the talent of this trade has been passed down from the father to his son. It was rumored that his father was so talented that he did not even need to measure, and just by giving a client a quick look-over, he could make him the most fitting attire in a few days."

Madame Lazar sat down and gestured to Nasrosoltan to do the same. "The son, like his father before him, has made quite a name for himself, and because of this, he is a busy person. Even some of the nobility have to wait longer than they would like for their custom-made orders."

Nasrosoltan inquired, "But Madame, if he is so much in demand that even the aristocracy have to wait, why would he do me such a favor?"

Madame Lazar, displaying a confident smile, replied, "Do not worry about that. I will speak to the Monsieur tomorrow, and if he agrees, we will go to his shop together."

Nasrosoltan sensed that Monsieur Dukemejian was not only a friend to her late husband but maybe a more intimate friend to her, seeing the way her eyes lit up when she spoke of the man.

As he got up to leave her apartment, Madame Lazar asked, "Are you by chance familiar with the dining etiquette and seating protocols of the palace?" Nasrosoltan replied that he was not.

She said, "Well then, let us first get your attire in order, and then we will worry about the variety of forks, spoons, knives, plates, and glasses you will find placed in front of you. It can be quite confusing if you have never experienced it. Do not be alarmed; I will teach you!"

Then Madame Lazar, recalling a happier time in her life, added, "When my late husband was alive, we were invited to a few such dinners. I also had to learn all the intricate details, which I will impart to you."

Nasrosoltan thanked her for being so generous. "I had not thought how much I would have to learn in the next couple of weeks, just for one evening dining at the palace."

The next afternoon, Madame Lazar told Nasrosoltan that she had met with Monsieur Dukemejian, and he had graciously agreed to tailor the appropriate clothing in about ten days. She told him, "You should know, this will be no small feat, but it will be in time for your special evening. Monsieur Dukemejian asked that we go to his tailor shop on Nevsky Prospect early tomorrow morning." Nasrosoltan heartily agreed since time was of the essence, and he had nowhere else to turn.

The next morning, they made their way to the tailor shop, with Madame Lazar being exceptionally well-dressed for such a regular visit. This confirmed Nasrosoltan's hunch that there may be more than a flirtatious attraction between them. He wondered whether Madame Lazar wanting to spend more time with Monsieur Dukemejian was the reason she had excused herself from the palace lessons. If this was the case, he was happy for her. Nasrosoltan thought, *Why should she be lonely?* He believed that as a widow, just like anyone else, she also had a right to love and be loved, a topic that was very close to his heart these days.

If tailors were supposed to be secretive about their clientele, Monsieur Dukemejian surely was not. As he took Nasrosoltan's measurements, he shared details about all the famous people whom he prepared attire for. Dresses for high-society ladies, uniforms for decorated military officers, and evening tailcoats and trousers for the well-to-do. It seemed he was trying to impress Madame Lazar with his name-dropping, as his attention was mostly toward her.

Monsieur Dukemejian told Nasrosoltan, "Madame Lazar mentioned that you need the attire in a hurry. You know, if it were not at her behest, I would not have been able to satisfy your request!"

Nasrosoltan thanked the tailor. "Madame Lazar speaks highly of your talent, and I am aware of how much you are in demand, especially with all the important people you just mentioned. I feel honored that you have made a special exception in my case."

Monsieur Dukemejian enjoyed the compliment, and as he continued taking Nasrosoltan's measurements, he replied, "Madame Lazar mentioned you are going to dinner at Grand Duke Alexander Mikhailovich's palace. That is a special honor; they must hold you in high regard. Madame tells me you are doing her a favor by tutoring the princess while she recovers from her injury. That is very noble of you. I am sure you are well aware that Princess Irina is emerging as one of the most eligible women in all of Russia. I know for a fact that she has several impressive suitors who are interested."

He continued, "Why, just the other day, I took Prince Felix Yusupov's measurements. Some say he is amongst her admirers, coming from one of the wealthiest families in Russia. I believe he has the best chance for her hand. I like him very much because while all the royal court exclusively gives their orders to House Brizak, he only wears my custom-made attire and has been a client for many years."

The tailor then added with a proud smile, "Prince Yusupov told me himself that he appreciates my choice of fabric and superior craftsmanship, preferring it to theirs."

Upon hearing this gossip about Prince Yusupov's interest in Irina, Nasrosoltan became disheartened and realized in his naivete that there was formidable competition for Irina's attention. Nasrosoltan questioned if he was living in a deluded bubble orbiting around the princess and ignoring almost everything else. And if so, he worried that he had imagined feelings between him and Irina that did not exist.

If Monsieur Dukemejian had spoken the truth about the prince's attraction to Irina, Nasrosoltan wondered how he could ever compete with a wealthy Russian nobleman of such prominence. Once again, self-doubt and despair engulfed him. He began to think his memory of recent events with Irina may have been nothing but a flight of fancy. He anxiously started to believe that the princess probably did not give him a second thought the minute the lessons ended.

Nasrosoltan questioned whether Irina was simply showing kindness the other day by placing her hand on his, in empathy, when she heard of his friend's death. This made him worry that his boldness in grasping her hand and kissing it in return may have been a colossal error in judgment on his part. He wondered if the reason Irina did not pull her hand away was due to her being caught off guard and not because she was consenting.

As Nasrosoltan was deep in thought about Irina, he totally forgot where he was, and he hunched as if deflated. The tailor then, with a hint of agitation, said, "Please stand straight, Monsieur; I need to measure your chest now!"

In a matter of minutes, a few unsolicited words from this man's lips ruined Nasrosoltan's morning, as he became miserable and was no longer excited by the invitation that had elated him only two days ago.

When the tailor finished his measurements, he told Nasrosoltan he would need to see him twice more to make necessary alterations for the perfect fit, and they scheduled the times and dates.

Upon leaving the shop, Nasrosoltan asked Madame Lazar, "Is what he said about the princess true?"

She replied, "Oh, yes! Her Serene Highness has come of age, and the most eligible bachelors of Russia are pursuing her, as Monsieur Dukemejian mentioned. Nana also told me that many respectable suitors are paying her the most marked attention. She has also revealed to me that Princess Irina is to be introduced to society at a ball in the Salle de la Noblesse later this year."

The hope that Monsieur Dukemejian was just gossiping untruths faded fast with Madame Lazar's confirmation. Although Nasrosoltan should not have been surprised that Irina would be pursued by many regal suitors, he felt the bubble they shared during their weekly lessons had suddenly burst. The tailor's words turned out to be sharper than his needles.

When love rules the mind, the heart only knows what the person wants to believe is real, and Nasrosoltan desperately wanted to trust that Irina had similar feelings toward him. But he now recognized that the odds were stacked against him, as he asked himself: *Why would she ever favor a foreigner of no regal station over a Russian prince?*

How appropriate that Nasrosoltan thought about odds, for it had been the wrong odds at the gaming house that placed him in her presence in the first place. If he had never lost his money that evening, he would have never accepted Madame Lazar's offer to tutor the princess. When the roulette ball avoided his number seven at the wheel, he cursed fate under his breath. Nasrosoltan had come to later realize that by losing there, he was given a chance to possess something far more precious than any winnings he could have imagined that fateful night: the heart of Irina.

However, now it seemed that this fantasy was to be laid to rest. Nasrosoltan once again decided to try to keep thoughts of Irina out of his mind, no matter how difficult a task. The potential obstacles to be surmounted for Irina's affection seemed too tremendous and hung like a heavy veil upon Nasrosoltan's face.

Madame Lazar, who was still unaware of the murmurings of his heart, noticed his silence and suggested that in the evening, if he wished, she could begin his instruction on dining etiquette, to which he graciously agreed.

Nasrosoltan wondered why lately, he seemed to turn from one feeling to another, always uncertain of how he truly felt. One moment he was so strong and self-assured: the next, fragile and full of doubt. Torn between the desire for Irina and stability, it was easy to choose stability when not in her presence. So, he kept himself busy with mundane activities to dull the senses that had awakened within him.

This course of action seemed to slowly work, giving him some relief from his painful week of doubt. However, this lasted only until the next lesson, where once again, his short-lived stability gave way to his desire to be close to the princess. Nasrosoltan began to accept that he could not be indifferent to his feelings, especially sensing that Princess Irina was of the same mindset.

The way she looked at him and smiled rekindled an almost-extinguished hope in his heart, and once again, he began to experience the elusive joy that seemed to be wherever Irina was. She looked even more alluring than he had remembered from just a week ago. Her eyes were the window into her graceful soul, and there was no place Nasrosoltan would rather be than sitting by her side at the piano.

With a serious tone, she turned and addressed Nasrosoltan. "Papa tells me you have been invited to the dinner party we are having next week. He must be very fond of you. I hope you do plan to attend. I would be delighted to see you there, as these affairs can be quite tedious, and your presence would mean much to me."

Then Irina added encouragingly, "I know it is so soon after the passing of your dear friend, and I was worried you may decline, mired in your sorrow. I did say a prayer for your departed friend's soul at church this past Sunday, and I also said a prayer for you, that you gain peace from your suffering."

As she looked at him, her penetrating gaze reached deep into his being, and she effortlessly conveyed thoughts and feelings seemingly above her years.

"How kind of you to think of me and to say a much-needed prayer," Nasrosoltan responded.

Princess Irina replied, "But I am always thinking of you. Lately, I cannot remember a moment that I have not!"

Then she placed her hand on top of his, and he noticed her hand was trembling. He grasped her hand tightly and quietly confessed, "I worried that I was foolish for having the same thoughts about you, but your words just now calmed such fear."

Upon hearing Nasrosoltan declare his feelings for her, Irina lifted her other hand and lovingly caressed his as they stared into each other's eyes. An emboldened Nasrosoltan continued cautiously, revealing what was deep in his heart. "Your touch has instantly washed away any doubt I may have harbored. I have never felt so alive as when I am in your presence!"

Irina said nothing in response but brandished a broad smile, her face blushing with nervous excitement. As usual, when music was not being played for long periods, Nana would make her way to the room to make sure all was right. Luckily, they both heard her footsteps on the wood-paneled floor in the corridor, which they took as their warning.

They immediately extended their distance on the piano bench, and Nasrosoltan began to play the piano to alleviate any of Nana's concerns. This cat-and-mouse play with Nana only deepened the bond between him and Irina. They both laughed as if they were schoolchildren, and the feeling of such awkward moments seemed surprisingly exhilarating.

When Nana reached the music room, she asked if they needed anything so as not to look suspicious. Irina asked for Nana to bring them some tea to buy more private time with Nasrosoltan.

As Nana departed, Irina moved closer to him and once again placed her hand on his, finally uttering what was in her heart. "I have read about feelings such as these in novels, but thought of them as just writers' fancies. I never expected to be so completely consumed with how I feel towards you now." Nasrosoltan took her hand and kissed it gently in gratitude for expressing herself so freely, all the while keeping a fixed gaze into her eyes, stirring her soul.

He then came close to her ear and whispered, "And to an-swer your question, yes, I have already responded to the grand duke's invitation." Nasrosoltan added with a smile, "I look for-ward to spending an evening in your presence, for these lessons just once a week will no longer suffice."

To show her appreciation, Irina did the unexpected and quickly kissed Nasrosoltan's cheek. It seemed fate had deter-mined that his story with the princess would deviate from the sad story of Schubert's unrequited love for the countess, for Irina had now reciprocated his.

Nasrosoltan came to the palace this afternoon devoid of hope because of the tailor's comments, but now he felt on top of the world, brimming with renewed confidence. A confidence that only Irina's love could have provided.

That afternoon, they practiced Schubert's Fantasia for four hands repeatedly, becoming intimately familiar with it. They played the piece with much feeling, completely drawn into it, as the vibrant notes resonated with special meaning for them both.

CHAPTER 23

AN UNEXPECTED GUEST

After a couple of more visits to Monsieur Dukemejian's shop to fit his attire and a few evenings of Madame Lazar's lessons in royal dining etiquette, Nasrosoltan finally felt well-prepared for the palace dinner. He was excited and nervous, wanting to make an excellent impression in this formal setting, but above all, he did not want to commit any social blunder.

He was comforted by Irina's assurance that her mother disliked pomp and ceremony and that she found the glittering Russian court life to be an ordeal. Irina also mentioned that the grand duchess enjoyed intimate gatherings at their home instead, and he reasoned this meant it would be a comparatively quiet dinner without much formality.

As his carriage approached the palace gates, Nasrosoltan noticed a large retinue of bodyguards. This evening, he was not waved through as was customary. Each carriage was stopped, and identification and invitations were thoroughly checked.

Nasrosoltan was surprised to see such security measures in place. He assumed it was careful diligence on the part of the royal family due to the recent disturbances that had killed many, including his friend Rustam. His carriage passed through without incident, and he disembarked and was escorted into the palace, where to his surprise once more, he noticed additional security, including Imperial Guards.

Nasrosoltan was greeted by the grand duke, who welcomed him in and announced, "I am sure you have noticed the high security at the palace. We are honored that His Imperial Majesty, Tsar Nicholas, has decided to join us unexpectedly for dinner. When there is a chance, I would like to introduce you to him."

Nasrosoltan thanked him, and the grand duke continued, "His Majesty is eager for the princess to perform something for him after dinner. I am sure your presence here tonight will add to her confidence. But I must say, it has been your instruction these past few months that has given her a renewed interest in music, and we are thankful that she takes it so seriously now."

After the grand duke moved to the next room, Nasrosoltan was left standing alone, and he became self-conscious and even more nervous. He had never expected the tsar to be there that night, and above all, to be sitting at the same dinner table with him.

It was a small gathering, with only about a dozen other guests in addition to the tsar. Amongst them were two young royal family members to whom he was later introduced. The first was a flamboyant man who Nasrosoltan learned was Felix Yusupov, the prince mentioned by the tailor. The second man was Grand Duke Dmitri Pavlovich, a first cousin to the tsar, tall and well built like most Romanovs. Nasrosoltan already knew that Yusupov had a romantic interest in Irina, but he soon realized that Grand Duke Dmitri was also an admirer.

Since Irina's father had earlier mentioned how Nasrosoltan's presence would make his daughter feel at ease, he wondered whether his invitation was simply to make her more comfortable performing that evening. And, perhaps, not only for the tsar but to Nasrosoltan's chagrin, especially for these potential suitors.

As soon as these disturbing thoughts attempted to derail his confidence, Princess Irina entered the room. She looked around and nodded her head, acknowledging each guest, and then looked in Nasrosoltan's direction and offered him a hurried smile, trying to avoid the attention of others.

Irina looked stunning, outfitted in an alluring evening dress of apricot velvet, and carrying herself with an elegance befitting a princess. Her quick glance toward Nasrosoltan with a reassuring smile confirmed her feelings for him.

At some point before dinner, from the other side of the room, Nasrosoltan's attention became fixated on Prince Yusupov and Grand Duke Dmitri. The two men had cornered Irina near the fireplace as they chatted and laughed together, and by all appearances, it seemed they were having a grand time. He was besieged with envy and extremely displeased to see the way they vied for Irina's attention. But from a distance, it seemed to him that this sheltered and innocent princess was blind to their exuberant efforts, and she was not as savvy at these games of flirtation, in which these two royals were well skilled.

Then the grand duke entered the room and made his way to Nasrosoltan. "Monsieur, let us go, it is time."

Nasrosoltan followed him to the dining room, as did the other guests. To the visible excitement of Irina, the grand duke introduced Nasrosoltan to the tsar. "I would like to present to His Imperial Majesty Monsieur Nasrosoltan Minbashian, who is from the empire of Persia and is a student at the conservatory. His father studied with our dear Nikolai Andreyevich Rimsky-Korsakov. We are grateful that a man from such a noble musical lineage has tutored our dear Irina Alexandrovna these past few months."

The tsar treated him with honor and kindness and mentioned that he was eager to hear his niece perform after dinner.

With a bow to show his respect, Nasrosoltan replied, "I am certain Her Serene Highness will not disappoint His Imperial Majesty. I believe the princess deserves great praise for her talent."

Hearing this, Irina beamed with joy and nervous energy, as she was apprehensive at the thought of performing in front of an audience.

At dinner, Nasrosoltan was seated between Prince Yusupov and Grand Duke Dmitri. The grand duke did not say much, but Prince Yusupov seemed to enjoy talking with Nasrosoltan, who found Prince Yusupov to be charming but also a man of many contradictions. The prince showed much interest in Persia and was curious about life there. He mentioned in passing that even though he had never visited Persia, his residence, the Yusupov Palace, had a bit of Nasrosoltan's homeland in it. "We have a room we call the Persian Room; it is saturated with the aroma of your exotic country and has divans all along the walls draped in colorful Persian fabrics."

Nasrosoltan smiled but said nothing. After a short pause, the prince continued with his small talk, turning his attention to the topic of music. Having heard Princess Irina's father introduce Nasrosoltan to the tsar, Prince Yusupov said, "You know, Monsieur, I am also fond of music. Our family has maintained a private orchestra for many years now. Since I rather enjoy American popular music, I recently suggested they add a saxophone section to the violins and cellos."

Even though Nasrosoltan thought it was a bad idea for the prince to have introduced this newfangled hybrid to his orchestra, he politely responded, "That was a bold move."

The prince smiled, assuming it was a compliment. Attempting to flatter Nasrosoltan, the prince quickly added with a laugh, "Of course, I do not presume to understand music such as one who has studied with the masters at the conservatory!"

In a contest for Irina's affections, Nasrosoltan would surely not worry about going up against the pretentious Prince Yusupov. Nasrosoltan was more threatened by Grand Duke Dmitri, who was quite handsome and less conceited. Dmitri also lived with the imperial family at Alexander Palace in Tsarskoe Selo, and Nasrosoltan had even heard rumors that the grand duke was a favorite of the tsar.

Nasrosoltan's emotions fluctuated during dinner between the now-faint hope that he could attain a permanent place in Irina's heart, and the awareness that he was considered a commoner by the royalty surrounding him. He knew full well that such an affiliation would not be tolerated by them, as he continued the exhausting battle between head and heart while unknowingly being carried forward on a wave of destiny.

As the dinner progressed, the rising political turmoil dominated the discussion. The dinner guests talked about the disturbances of the last few weeks and the many strikes and demonstrations that had become more prevalent. Most of the guests dismissed the real reasons for such widespread discontent, viewing these protests as merely the workers' ungratefulness toward the tsar's recent reforms.

The grand duke addressed the tsar. "Your Imperial Majesty has surely heard the news of the businessman who was tragically killed a few weeks ago, during some agitation at the Ministry of Commerce. He was a dear friend of Monsieur Minbashian and was struck by a stray bullet. Just to think, had he not gone there that day to meet with the minister, he would still be alive today. It amazes me how one can alter his own destiny without knowing it."

Then, turning to Nasrosoltan, the grand duke said, "Monsieur Minbashian, I am sure you must agree."

As if awakened from his thoughts, Nasrosoltan was not prepared for this direct question and initially did not respond. An awkward silence followed, and Nasrosoltan felt he had to say something. In an unexpectedly bold manner, he offered the grand duke an answer that reflected his change of heart with regard to destiny from what he had earlier believed.

"Your Imperial Highness, forgive me, but I do beg to differ, for I feel destiny cannot be altered."

Upon hearing this surprising contradiction to the grand duke's statement, all eyes turned to Nasrosoltan. Suddenly self-conscious and feeling like an outsider, he decided to defend his pronouncement by explaining himself further. "We Persians believe whatever kismet or fate decides, it will achieve, and no man can change that. This was the day my good friend was to die, be it by a bullet or some other means. It was so written long before he was even born."

At hearing Nasrosoltan's reasoning, there were some nods of approval, but then the grand duke replied, "Why do you believe this, Monsieur? I, on the contrary, believe that men, with their own determination and persistence, can change the course of life events. I would be interested to hear a convincing reason as to why you think otherwise?"

Nasrosoltan had not intended to be the focus of attention in this intimidating setting; however, he had no choice but to go on. "Perhaps if the esteemed guests permit, for I do not wish to dominate the conversation, I may be able to better explain why I believe so by sharing an old Persian fable."

The guests seemed to show interest at the suggestion of hearing the tale, so the grand duke encouraged him to continue. "Please do, Monsieur!"

Nasrosoltan proceeded, now addressing the whole table, to tell his story. "One day, as a nobleman walks through a Persian bazaar, he notices in the distance the Archangel of Death coming towards him with a surprised look on his face. The man, realizing the Archangel's intention to take his soul, flees quickly.

"He then immediately seeks an audience with the shah and begs for an appointment to a land far away, so he will not be anywhere near the Archangel. After much insistence on this man's part, the shah finally grants him his wish and appoints him as an envoy to India. It takes the man two months to travel to Delhi. Once there, no longer feeling distressed and believing he is far out of danger's reach, he decides to go for a walk and ends up at the market.

"Surprisingly, again, he comes face-to-face with the Archangel, who was waiting for him, prepared to take his soul and return it to God. The awestruck man says to him, 'How can this be; I thought you were in Persia!'

"The Archangel of Death responds, 'I am also surprised to see you here. When I saw you in Persia at the bazaar a few months ago, I looked at my list, and it said that I was to take your soul a few months later, in a market in India! At that moment, I thought to myself, how could that be possible? For surely you were never going to be able to get so far away in so little time.'"

Nasrosoltan turned to the grand duke. "Therefore, Your Imperial Highness, even though this man tried to change his own destiny, it was kismet that he has a hand in his own unalterable demise."

The dinner guests laughed at his telling of this story, and the tsar, who seemed to be a fatalistic man, said in a light-hearted tone, "I agree, one cannot argue with the will of God. Well said, Monsieur!"

The grand duke turned to the tsar, raised his glass, and declared, "Then we drink a toast to kismet, in thanks that he has blessed Mother Russia with His Imperial Majesty, our revered tsar. May God always protect him and this wonderful country he rules!"

After the toast in his honor, the tsar then got up from his seat, signaling to the guests at the table that dinner had ended. As they all rose, Nasrosoltan went along with the other men behind the tsar to retire to another room for after-dinner digestifs. But no matter how interesting the conversation, Nasrosoltan longed to be elsewhere, in the presence of Irina, who had withdrawn with the ladies to the music room, preparing to perform for the tsar.

After some drinks and conversation, the men joined the ladies in the music room. The tsar seated himself ahead of the others and motioned that those standing out of respect could now have a seat. Nasrosoltan was in the far back, and Irina, who exhibited an air of timidity, sat at the piano alongside the page-turner, ready to perform.

Nasrosoltan could not help but notice how stunning Irina looked, and with all eyes on her, even her demureness was refreshing. He hoped she would flawlessly perform whatever piece she had decided to play.

Before Irina began, she turned to the tsar. "Dear Uncle, I would like to play Schubert's Fantasia. Since it is a piano work written for four hands, will you allow Monsieur Minbashian to accompany me to perform it for you?"

Nasrosoltan was startled since he was not expecting such a request on her part. He hesitated, unsure of what to do. To Irina's delight, all it took was the tsar's approval, who turned around, looking back over his shoulder at Nasrosoltan. The other guests in attendance turned toward him as well, and the tsar smiled, saying, "It seems kismet dictates you also perform this evening, Monsieur," as he motioned Nasrosoltan to come forth.

Then, with all eyes fixed on him and Irina's enticing smile to coax him, Nasrosoltan got up from his seat in the back of the room. He moved slowly and with great focus past the other guests to take his place next to her at the foot of the Tischner.

Once they began to play, it was evident they had practiced often, even though Irina was nervous and played her part a bit hard. Nonetheless, they were able to catch the magical essence of the composition.

As their fingers touched on the keyboard, their anxiety gave way to exhilaration, which was reflected in the beauty of their performance. With every note, their confidence grew, as did the grace and elegance of their playing, to the point that the two were in such unison that they almost forgot where they were, performing for the tsar of Imperial Russia. Instead, they solely cared that they were seated side by side, close together, only aware of each other's movements at the keyboard.

The guests were completely silent. The audience was mesmerized by the music, as they had not expected to experience such an exquisite performance this evening.

Around ten minutes into the piece, as written by the composer, Nasrosoltan completely removed his hands from the keyboard for a brief instant and rejoined Irina on the piano with his right hand only. Then with that one hand, he played several notes in between her two hands, which were still also playing in perfect harmony. This very intimate dance of his hand moving between hers, and the musical ecstasy they were engulfed in, was witnessed not only by the page-turner sitting at their side, but also some in the audience from the right vantage point.

After they finished their performance of the Fantasia, the tsar rose from his seat and began to eagerly applaud his niece's performance, exclaiming, "Brava, brava, my dear Irina Alexandrovna," followed by a long ovation from the guests.

They both got up from the piano and paid the appropriate respects, with a bow on his behalf and a curtsy on hers. Then the grand duke approached Nasrosoltan and shook his hand in appreciation for his inspired work with his daughter.

Irina's remarkable and passionate performance only added to the two suitors' desire for her, and Nasrosoltan even sensed a hint of jealousy directed his way, which ignited his burgeoning confidence.

Confidence is a curious thing, for it sometimes appears out of nowhere and departs the same way. One cannot acquire it with money, though some try, and it cannot be stored for use on a day when it is needed most. Sometimes confidence breeds confidence; as the more one displays it, the more others find it within themselves. However, it is not contagious, for sometimes the more one exudes it, it can have the opposite effect and lessen it in others. Confidence leaves no room for jealousy, for when one feels absolute greatness, there is no need to have hatred toward another. And after such a splendid duet at the piano, Nasrosoltan even felt a bit overconfident. It seemed he had finally broken out of the doubter's castle.

Taking in the moment, Nasrosoltan thought, *Why can't a commoner gain access to a princess's heart? Why can't I be the first to breast the tape in this race?*

Prince Yusupov, who had been watching from afar and listening to them perform with fixed attention, drew closer to them and congratulated Irina on her exemplary performance.

While the princess was speaking to the tsar, Prince Yusupov turned to Nasrosoltan, gently pulling him aside, placing his hand on his shoulder in a friendlier manner than their relationship dictated. As this imposing gesture demanded Nasrosoltan's full attention, Prince Yusupov lingered while Nasrosoltan waited for him to speak.

Looking directly into Nasrosoltan's eyes, the prince said, "It is truly heartening to see our dear Princess Irina Alexandrovna blossoming under your tutelage. That Her Serene Highness has so excelled on this count vouches for the passion your teaching has elicited from her. We in the audience were overwhelmed and aroused by the same feeling of excitement you both exhibited during the magnificent performance."

Then, as if confiding a great secret, the prince moved in closer, with the real intent of encircling and probing for a weakness in Nasrosoltan's defenses.

"Monsieur, please understand that the same passions you have enkindled within her through your lessons may be misconstrued as something more intimate by an innocent and sheltered princess such as she."

He paused briefly to choose his next words carefully. As if he was a cherub with a flaming sword, flashing it back and forth to guard Irina against Nasrosoltan, the prince added this stunning final blow in hopes of turning him away: "In this case, therefore, it may be best for all involved if one does not venture above and beyond the call of duty!"

Nasrosoltan, who just a few moments ago brimmed with confidence, was wholly unprepared for the prince's warning. This tacit threat made Nasrosoltan suddenly feel most vulnerable when he had felt invincible. The tough-hitting words of the prince were like a dagger tearing into the veil of secrecy of his and Irina's relationship, shredding it to pieces. Nasrosoltan wondered whether this threatened prince may expose what others did not yet know about his and Irina's feelings for each other.

Nasrosoltan loathed the way Yusupov had addressed him and wanted nothing more than to offer a strong response. But he knew better, recognizing that he was powerless, and it was neither the time nor the place. Deciding that the best reply was to not show he was flustered, Nasrosoltan brushed off the prince's words as though he did not even hear them.

Trying hard to maintain his composure, Nasrosoltan replied, "I am gratified you enjoyed the performance this evening; it was an honor to make your acquaintance." He then quickly excused himself and left the room.

Prince Yusupov imagined that one blow from his verbal dagger would smite to death Nasrosoltan's ambitions forever. But, unbeknownst to Yusupov, his intention to destroy Nasrosoltan's resolve had launched a mightier weapon, a catapult, breaking down the walls protecting the realm of fantasy Nasrosoltan was living in. The prince's powerful and destructive words did not have the desired effect of making Nasrosoltan fearful so that he would contemplate retreat. Instead, to Nasrosoltan's own amazement, this conversation had the opposite effect, giving him a sense of welcome relief.

For the first time, someone else had discovered what only Nasrosoltan and Irina knew, and he seemed to no longer fear that their secret may be revealed. He decided not to be intimidated any longer by such worries, finding no reason to recoil.

Nasrosoltan recalled Rustam's advice years ago about life and determined to do what his friend had suggested by playing the cards where they might fall. The prince called for Nasrosoltan's surrender, but this, he now swore to himself, he would never do.

Yusupov believed his words had stormed the very fortress Nasrosoltan and Irina had taken shelter in. But by doing so, the prince had instead released this amorous reverie out of their castle in the air, to no longer be trapped there. And now it was unleashed and free to roam the real world.

CHAPTER 24

PEN TO PAPER

This was the most beautiful evening of my life, Irina wrote in her diary. *To sit next to him, in front of all those watching. To play Schubert's Fantasia together, with his hands keeping us steady on the keyboard. Nasrosoltan's presence gives me energy, and I feel alive when I am with him. It seems Papa and Uncle were impressed with him, so I am overjoyed! I just wish he had not departed so soon after our performance.*

When I am with him, I cherish each precious moment. How cruel is Father Time, for he makes hours feel like only seconds when we are together, but a week like many months when I await his arrival. At dinner, in front of all our guests, Nasrosoltan told a funny story about kismet, and with all my heart, I believe in what he said. Can it be that it is this kismet that brought him to me? I am bursting with such excitement that I do not know if I will be able to sleep!

Several weeks earlier, and thousands of miles away in Persia, a father had also put pen to paper. Salar Moazaz had written a letter to his son, which Nasrosoltan just received and eagerly opened to read. Accompanying the letter was a package of pistachio nuts that Nasrosoltan's mother, Khata Khanoom, had sent for him.

His father explained the pistachios were a gift she thought Nasrosoltan would enjoy, considering how he had hurried to procure some before his departure to St. Petersburg. Nasrosoltan welcomed his mother's thoughtfulness, deciding to gift the pistachios to Madame Lazar in thanks for helping him prepare for the palace dinner. His father's letter read:

My dear son, I was surprised not to have heard from you for so long, until last month, when we received your telegram acknowledging the funds I sent you. We eagerly look forward to your return to Persia. The shah has appointed me the Director Madrasaye Muzik— conservatory—at the Dar al-Funun, and I am relying on your assistance. You will be my strong right arm in choosing the appropriate curriculum and training the music teachers and students.

My son, it is also time for you to settle down and start a family. As a composer, I, more than anyone, understand your love of music and the desire to immerse yourself in its study full time. However, at some point, you must think of your duty to the homeland and your family's future. It is worth a great deal to have you back with us at the earliest. Your mother has found you a few suitable choices from good families to meet upon your arrival in the fall. You know how much she prays for you to get married and give her many grandchildren.

You will also be delighted to know that Gholam-Hossein shows excellent musical talent, and we will be sending him to the Geneva Conservatory in Switzerland. It is, therefore, essential that you do not delay your return when you have completed your coursework at the conservatory, for the sake of your family and country.

Even though his father's words were a stark reminder that his time in St. Petersburg was short and that once again, his mother was up to unwanted matchmaking, this did not dampen in any way his excitement for Irina. On the contrary, it made every moment in her presence more precious. With those thoughts, Nasrosoltan began to put pen to paper, not in response to his father's letter, but instead to compose a piano work he wished to dedicate to Irina.

After his and Irina's rewarding duet, notwithstanding Prince Yusupov's warning, Nasrosoltan was jubilant. He wanted to capture these feelings forever with ink and paper as a sculptor would carving a timeless inscription with a chisel on stone. The irony of it eluded him that he was now composing a piece to dedicate to a princess he tutored and loved, just as Schubert had done for a countess—the only difference being that Nasrosoltan's love was requited.

Just a few weeks ago, due to his confused state of mind, he could not compose, feeling the music blocked, not able to write even one line, no matter how hard he tried. But now, the notes poured out of the tip of his pen onto the paper like a waterfall. He was inspired by his love for Irina, and he willed that this work would be a testament to that love.

He soon realized that he had never worked on a composition such as this, so full of emotion, embodying the most profound intensity of expression, and it all came so quickly to him, effortlessly, since it was music that emanated from the depths of his heart and not his head. No professor at the conservatory, not even the greatest, could show him how to compose this way, which only manifested itself through his love for Irina.

Nasrosoltan now fully appreciated the passion with which the great masters used such emotion to compose their timeless creations, transforming their inexhaustible wealth of ideas into sublime works of art.

He spent the next few weeks composing and improving this arrangement. He even mentioned to Irina during one of their lessons that he was writing it, but he added, "When completed, you will get to hear it performed when the moment is right, for I would present you this gift only for a special occasion."

The anticipation was too much for her to bear, and she kept asking Nasrosoltan to perform at least a few notes, just to give her a glimpse into the realm of his creativity, but he would not relent.

To temper her excitement, he said to her, "It is not finished and perfect; how can you ask me to present to you, who are the embodiment of perfection in my eyes, a work that is not yet complete? I plead you remain patient, for with patience, stones are turned into diamonds."

Weeks had passed since the dinner at the palace, performing for the tsar alongside Irina, so Nasrosoltan's presence for weekly lessons drew less attention from Nana and others on the staff. They now considered him not just a tutor but a friend of the family, as they were aware that after some lessons, Nasrosoltan would spend time with the grand duke in his private study, drinking and telling tales. This allowed him and Irina to spend more time alone without the usual curious oversight. These weekly appointments became more of a lovers' rendezvous than piano lessons.

It was during these several weeks that they grew closer through their conversations about all things. When Nana was sent on the usual errand for hot tea from the samovar or some such request, they even found time to get close physically by holding and caressing hands.

On one occasion, as they found themselves alone for an unusual amount of time, the energy in the room was palpable. As the spirit of affection between them grew stronger, they inched closer together on the piano bench. Nasrosoltan could feel the heat of Irina's gaze as she displayed a coquettish smile and moved her head closer to his while they both held tightly to each other's hands. They brazenly felt entitled to this moment, not worried if someone may appear unannounced.

Irina's face beamed with pure joy as Nasrosoltan came close to her and whispered in her ear, "I hope you will forgive me for being so bold, but I would never forgive myself if I were not."

And as their breaths trembled on each other's cheeks, a kiss was set aflame between their two lips. In that one kiss, more was said between them than all the words they had spoken to each other until this point. They lost themselves, surrendering themselves in the silence of the moment.

Nana's footsteps in the distance broke the silence, and as they moved away from each other, Irina hurriedly said, "I wish you would never leave; I love you!" and she handed him a note she had written. He immediately hid it in his vest pocket, out of sight of the approaching Nana.

After the tea was served and Nana retreated from the music room, Nasrosoltan, who was now overcome with emotion, gripped Irina's hand tightly and boldly declared, "My dearest Irina, I also never want to leave your side. I feel agony when separated from you!"

But then, realizing their predicament, he added, "However, as I express my feelings for you, I am also aware that circumstances do not seem to be in our favor. You are a Romanov princess, and I am considered a commoner by your family, no matter how much respect they have shown me."

Having revealed his innermost thoughts, he paused to compose himself and then continued, "My studies at the conservatory will come to an end soon, and I must go back to Persia. My father has been appointed director of the new conservatory, and he needs my assistance. I just received a letter from him urging me not to delay my return. He knows nothing of our feelings for each other, just as your family does not. Never in my life have I been both the most excited and the most unsettled about my future at the same time. I love you and cannot see any future without you, but your position dictates that you be united with someone of a royal background."

Deciding not to share Prince Yusupov's insinuation that their relationship may have already been exposed, Nasrosoltan continued with a warning. "Your family will never allow our love to flourish, and if they even detect a hint of our feelings for one another, I will be banished." He uttered those last words as if the breath left his body.

Irina earnestly replied, "But Papa is very fond of you; if it were not so, he would not have invited you to the dinner where my uncle, the tsar of Russia, was present. I see how he enjoys the time he spends with you after our lessons. Perhaps if you broached the subject with him at the right time, he might be more agreeable than you think. Why would my family wish for anything but my happiness?"

Then, holding back her tears, Princess Irina said, "Why do you even need to return to Persia? Stay here in St. Petersburg with me."

Nasrosoltan, who was caught up in her emotions and unable to reconcile fantasy with reality, replied, "You know it was always my dream to live and compose in this great city. But I now realize I will remain a nobody if I stay here, just a piano tutor to some. Even though I believe I am a worthy composer, there are hundreds of composers in this city who cannot make a living through their work. Back in Persia, I am somebody with a respected family and much honor. We may be asking the impossible; I fear they will never approve of our love. But I also do not know what else to do other than have faith that despite all the obstacles, our love has a future."

Peering into her eyes, Nasrosoltan could see that Irina was distressed. He recognized that his words had the opposite effect of his intention, which was to comfort her. So, in a consoling tone, he offered, "My beloved Irina, do not despair; I will keep an eye out for the right moment and hope the grand duke will be approachable." Though Nasrosoltan had a feeling that this course of action was probably fruitless, he was attempting to protect Irina from further grief.

Since their lesson had ended, Nasrosoltan got up to leave when Grand Duke Alexander's secretary appeared unannounced and informed him that he had been summoned by the grand duke. Nasrosoltan bid a disconcerted Irina farewell until next week. Irina was amazed that her father had called upon Nasrosoltan so soon after discussing the matter. As he was leaving the room, she inquired with a bittersweet smile, "Do you think it is perhaps kismet?"

Nasrosoltan approached the grand duke's study and stopped at the entrance, seeing him reading a newspaper and enjoying a drink, so he waited to be acknowledged. The grand duke raised his head slightly and, with his hand, offered Nasrosoltan a seat. He cordially addressed him, "Thank you for coming. Please pour yourself a brandy."

Nasrosoltan poured the small amount left in the decanter for himself and sat down. The grand duke took a sip of his drink and continued, "I am reading a fascinating article about one of our brave pilots flying a French-made Bleriot XI aircraft to your home city of Tehran. It seems to have surprised the residents there, for they had never seen what they thought was a strange bird flying overhead. Unfortunately, upon landing, the pilot collided with a parked cannon in a field in the city center. Amazingly, Persian technicians were able to repair the plane for him, allowing him to fly back home to Russia."

Nasrosoltan displayed an air of pride hearing about his countrymen's technical ingenuity. The grand duke continued with great emphasis, "You know, it was I who brought the Bleriot to Russia, laying the cornerstone for the first aviation school in our country. I think of these flying machines as instruments of war, to defend the motherland, not as playthings as the minister of war, Soukhomlinoff, mockingly suggests. This flight to your country was a great achievement for our aviators."

The grand duke paused, looking contemplative, then downed the remainder of his brandy in one gulp, adding, "I have strived to make our valiant countrymen prepared for what I fear is to come sooner than anyone expects: a great European war our troops are ill-equipped to fight."

The grand duke continued, slightly slurring his speech, "We do not have the right armaments or enough ammunition, much of it due to the incompetence of this Soukhomlinoff. For the sake of Mother Russia, I hope I am wrong in predicting such a catastrophic event. If this happens, Europe will have committed suicide. You know, my motto has always been 'Russia comes first,' but as I grow older, I realize I only have one life to live, and above all, the protection of my children reigns supreme."

Nasrosoltan realized the grand duke may have had more brandy than usual, as he was divulging intimate feelings about the situation of the country and his family. This day, they were having a more profound conversation than before. He decided it best to just listen and refrain from saying much, as it was apparent the grand duke was looking for a receptive ear.

Grand Duke Alexander then caught Nasrosoltan's attention by confiding, "Your influence on the princess's development has been exemplary, and I wanted to take this moment to thank you for all you have done. As she is my only daughter, her happiness is paramount, and these past few months she has developed a self-assuredness that is evident in her demeanor." He then raised his now empty glass, toasting Nasrosoltan in appreciation.

As the grand duke continued to speak, Nasrosoltan could not believe what he was hearing. Could it be that Irina was right, that kismet was in their favor? Maybe the grand duke was signaling that he was more agreeable than Nasrosoltan had given him credit for. Nasrosoltan's spirit soared like an eagle as he began to believe that maybe there was a chance for their love to flourish.

Irina's father had unexpectedly spoken the words that gave Nasrosoltan a renewed and growing confidence.

The grand duke continued, "The grand duchess and I have noticed how she has blossomed under your tutelage. Thanks to your magnificent performance together that evening, I am happy to say that arrangements are being made for Princess Irina's everlasting happiness."

At first, Nasrosoltan was confused, not knowing where the conversation was leading; however, talk of plans for Irina's happiness intrigued him. But then the grand duke uttered these heart-piercing words: "Prince Felix Yusupov has asked our permission for their engagement. I am sure you are aware I am telling you this in the strictest confidence!"

Even though the grand duke was slightly inebriated, Nasrosoltan had a sense that he would not have divulged such delicate matters to him if he were not leaving for Persia soon. But it did not matter why the grand duke said it, since now privy to this, Nasrosoltan would rather not have heard it. He instantly realized his apparent confidence in imagining he had a chance with Irina had been nothing more than a presumption.

Nasrosoltan felt totally numb and could not hear anything else the grand duke said. Suddenly, as if transported to his childhood, he recalled a poem his father once recited to him by the famous Persian poet Nasser Khosrow.

The poem told the tale of an eagle soaring proudly, high in the sky, admiring the array of his beautiful feathers when a concealed archer launches an arrow that strikes his wing, and he falls from the mist of clouds to the ground. He sees at the end of the arrow one of his own feathers used to make it go straight. The eagle says sorrowfully in Persian, "*Ze ke nalim, ke az mast ke bar mast!*" ("How can I protest, what came from me, returned to me!") And so Nasrosoltan realized that he unintentionally had a hand in his own heart's undoing.

The grand duke's words were the arrow that stopped this soaring eagle's journey mid-flight, tumbling his spirit speedily to the ground. Nasrosoltan could not believe that the same efforts he was recognized for were leading the hand of his true love into the hand of another man.

Dumbfounded and bewildered, he felt like a defeated wrestler without ever setting foot into the wrestling pit. He now fully understood the cruel rules of the game. To enter such a contest, the competitors had to be of the same status as those judging it. Could it be that Irina was right, that it was kismet? However, if so, in this instance, kismet was woefully unkind.

CHAPTER 25

AN AUDIENCE GRANTED

As Nasrosoltan's carriage left the palace, he was in a state of shock and disbelief. Once again, he cursed fate for playing with his emotions—the same fate that created ecstasy and then confusion within him instantly. He wondered why he had not said anything to the grand duke? Why had he silently listened while the words cut through him like a knife, without any proclamation on his part? He regretted his timidity and felt devastated at what seemed to be a *fait accompli* that Irina was to be with another man forever. Having lost track of time, he reached for his pocket watch in his vest but instead found the note Irina had given to him earlier, which he anxiously read.

> *Love is patient, love is kind. It does not envy, it does not boast, it is not proud. It does not dishonor others, it is not self-seeking, it is not easily angered, it keeps no record of wrongs. Love does not delight in evil but rejoices with the truth. It always protects, always trusts, always hopes, always perseveres. Love never fails!*
>
> *This is my favorite verse from Saint Paul in our Bible, and I think it is beautiful and wanted to share it with you, for I rejoice in your love, and I have faith and trust that our love will never fail!*

With the heartbreaking news he had just received from Irina's father, Nasrosoltan felt differently about love. The love that Irina's saint had spoken of was just an illusion, he thought. If he were to write his feelings about love at this moment, there would be no aroma of paradise. Instead, he would say that love is not kind, love delights in hopelessness, love torments, and love deceives. This would be the love he believed every lover, except perhaps a saint, would recognize from having loved.

Nasrosoltan's whole being felt pained, knowing full well there was no remedy: the pain that seems it will never depart the body, which is ever-present and relentless, like a thief, robbing the victim of sleep, appetite, and any joy or purpose. A pain worse than death, for there is a finality in death, a nothingness that is to be expected. But to be kept apart from his love and to know she was to be with another, that was too much to bear.

Nasrosoltan cursed love as the culprit, blaming it for offering him what now seemed unattainable. But what he failed to accept was that love was only an innocent bystander on the path where he had been placed by chance and choice.

With every defeat, there first comes disbelief, then anger, followed by self-pity and finally despair. Until, in the end, one totally succumbs to the grief, or instead, like a phoenix rising from the ashes of pain and suffering, he develops the will to move forward and be reborn with new life and purpose. After several intense evenings of reflection and soul-searching, assisted by bottles of vodka and reading poems of Rumi, Nasrosoltan came upon this verse that deeply touched him and changed his attitude toward love:

> *A damsel said to her lover, "O fond youth,*
> *You have visited many cities in your travels;*
> *Which of those cities seems most delightful to you?"*
> *He made answer, "The city wherein my love dwells,*
> *In whatever nook my queen alights;*

Though it be as the eye of a needle, 'tis a wide plain;
Wherever her beautiful face shines as a moon,
Though it be the bottom of a well, 'tis Paradise.
With thee, my love, hell itself were heaven.
With thee, a prison would be a rose-garden.
With thee, hell would be a mansion of delight,
Without thee lilies and roses would be as flames of fire!"

Rumi's eloquent words were like an ointment rubbed on a blind man's eyes so that he gains sight and can see clearly once again. The poet had reminded Nasrosoltan that he was dwelling in the same city as his love and still had access to her, so he slowly broke from his gloom. Fed up and frustrated, he knew this defeatist attitude was the most unappealing aspect of his character. He decided that hope was not a strategy, but bold action was.

Although Nasrosoltan's hopes had been set aflame with only a few words from the grand duke's lips, he resolved to rise from the ashes of his misery with renewed vigor and a determination to gamble everything for love. He finally understood he had no right to lament his situation if he did not dare fight for Irina. Nasrosoltan had a change of heart regarding love, seeing it as an ally in his quest for the ultimate prize, not an enemy to be despised.

Nasrosoltan gradually felt a resurgence of confidence in who he was. He regained his footing by spending all his free time completing the piano composition for Irina. He poured his soul into this work, and he believed it to be his masterpiece, with the beauty of melody throughout. Nasrosoltan intended to perform this piece at the conservatory's annual public event, which always attracted a broad audience from the public and the St. Petersburg press.

Once again, fate intervened when Director Glazunov called Nasrosoltan into his office, informing him, "Monsieur Minbashian, it is customary for the conservatory to send invitations to the families of Russian students for the public performance.

For foreign students who have no family in Russia, exceptions are made in that the invitation can be sent to another guest if you would like."

Nasrosoltan thought this the perfect opportunity for Irina to hear the work he had dedicated to her, as he had promised for a special occasion.

Nasrosoltan replied, "Thank you, Director Glazunov, for your kindness in thinking of me. I would indeed appreciate it if an invitation could be sent to the family of Grand Duke Alexander Mikhailovich on my behalf."

Upon hearing the royal name, a startled Glazunov inquired, "The Grand Duke Mikhailovich? I am curious to know why, if you do not mind me asking?"

Nasrosoltan responded, "It is my honor to have been the piano tutor to Her Serene Highness Princess Irina Alexandrovna for the last several months, and I have become closely acquainted with the family. Since I am to return to Persia within a fortnight of the performance, I would like to extend this invitation to this esteemed family."

Glazunov was surprised at Nasrosoltan's familiarity with the royal family to the extent that he wished for them to receive an invitation. As Nasrosoltan got up to leave his office, the director reminded him to submit a draft of his musical score for review before the performance.

With such a grueling schedule to prepare for his examination, to unwind, Nasrosoltan spent the little free time he had walking the boulevards of St. Petersburg along the banks of the Neva. He admired the city's beauty, and he knew he would miss it dearly upon his return to an unknown future in Persia. These daily walks became a ritual that cleansed his soul and cleared his mind from the clutter of unwanted thoughts and misplaced doubts.

But now, the one thing that had become quite clear to him was his boundless devotion to Irina. And his feelings for her were no longer accompanied by fear and trepidation of what may or may not happen. Instead, he felt freedom from the shackles that had bound him—bindings that were now cast aside by how he felt toward her and the action he planned to consolidate his position.

On the day of his next lesson with Irina, he arrived at the palace at the appointed time. She eagerly greeted him with a full, beaming smile. "Papa mentioned that we have received an invitation to your performance at the conservatory and has agreed we shall attend. Oh, my dear, I am so delighted and proud; it is sure to be the most wonderful day. I cannot contain my excitement!"

Without taking a breath, Princess Irina continued, "Have you decided on the piece you will be performing for your examination?"

Nasrosoltan took advantage of this opportunity to respond with news she would find pleasing, telling Irina he would perform the work he had created for her. He was aware that at some point during their time together on this day, he would also have to deliver some rather unpleasant news concerning the negotiations with the Yusupov family.

Hearing that Nasrosoltan would be performing the promised dedication to her, Irina spontaneously leapt up with tremendous joy, hugging and kissing him, knowing full well that it was their secret.

Nasrosoltan, uncomfortable that Nana or another staff member may see this display of affection, quickly separated himself from her.

He told Irina, "I have become like Schubert, dedicating a work to the one I love. Just as Schubert, I am also of a different social status than the object of my love. But I declare this love proudly, no matter the consequence!"

With an affectionate smile, Irina replied, "My note the other day expressed my feelings towards you. Did you read it?"

Before Nasrosoltan could reply, Irina excitedly asked him, "So, tell me, where did your conversation with Papa lead to the day he summoned you to his study? Did you mention our feelings for one another?"

Reluctant to break the positive spell, Nasrosoltan had to tell her the truth. "The grand duke imparted some information of a sensitive nature to me that I am not sure you are yet aware of. I cannot help but share it with you, and you must promise to keep this to yourself if it is the first you've heard of it."

Irina was both confused and curious as she asked, "Please tell me, what is it? I promise I will not divulge what you tell me. But please tell me; I am getting worried!"

Nasrosoltan held her hand to comfort her and said, "Prince Felix Yusupov's family is in discussions with your family, asking that you be engaged to him. Once I heard this news, I was flabbergasted and rendered completely speechless."

Nasrosoltan, sensing her uneasiness, continued quickly to try to reassure her. "I felt it would be hopeless at that moment to say anything, and I departed as soon as he gave leave. Later in the carriage ride home, I read your note, which after my initial despair eventually soothed my wounded spirit."

He paused for a moment, as if convincing himself of his next declaration. "I now do believe what your saint proclaims, that love never fails."

With each word Nasrosoltan delivered, Irina's smile slowly transformed into a full pout, eclipsing her momentary joy with an air of gloom, as she was now engulfed in sorrow. Her eyes welled with tears, an outward display of the emotions Nasrosoltan had also felt when he had heard these same words from her father's lips.

It was not surprising Irina did not know of the Yusupov offer, for these matters were kept hidden as much as possible until it was made sure that such a union was to take place. With these arrangements, negotiations between royal families were commonplace, and they would rather not have the news made public until the day of formal acceptance.

Irina was beside herself and began to weep. "No, no, never, I do not wish to spend my life with anyone but you! Please tell me you will tell Papa of our feelings for one another. Please, my dear, promise me!"

Nasrosoltan tried to comfort her by clasping her hands tighter. "Do not let your heart be troubled, my dear, for I have decided not to let my social position deter us from our happiness.

"It may seem the height of arrogance on my part to speak this way, but I deem myself worthy of being with the woman I love, even though she is a princess of the Romanovs. I will not be held back from expressing my feelings to your father. I am determined to seek a private audience with the grand duke after my performance." Then he added with a half smile, "In the meantime, remain collected, and let kismet do the rest."

There was a confidence in the way Nasrosoltan expressed himself that reassured her. He was fearless in the face of insurmountable odds, and this only made him more attractive to her at the moment she felt the most vulnerable. She adored him and was impressed most of all with his willingness to risk everything for her love.

"But what if Papa cannot be convinced?" she questioned. "What will we do then, my love?"

Nasrosoltan replied, "Let us not worry about that at this moment. What is the benefit of worry? As we say in Persian, *Khoda bozorge!*"—God is great!—"We must lean on his grace and the words of your saint who said, 'love is patient.' So we must also be patient and pray for a favorable outcome. We must not do or say anything rash in the meantime if our love is to have a chance."

It seemed Irina had not heard a single word he had spoken when she naively exclaimed, "If Papa is not agreeable, I will run off with you to Persia. I would rather be with the one I love in a foreign land than with one I do not love in my own country! If Papa disagrees, I will talk to the tsar myself because I know he would understand. Even if he forbids it, I will be ready on the eve of your return to Persia to accompany you. You would not leave me behind, would you?"

Nasrosoltan pleaded with her, "My dear, you must control your emotions and contain this talk of eloping!"

Concerned that Irina's emotions could spin the situation out of control, he gently reminded her, "We must not act impulsively, for only one misstep can lead to an unfortunate end to our hope of everlasting love.

"Please, my dear, have faith and allow me to present my case to the grand duke if he grants me a private audience. If anyone hears you speaking this way now, we will never even have that chance."

Irina relented and took comfort in the words he spoke, agreeing to not talk of these things until his hoped-for audience with her father. As Irina leaned in and placed her head on Nasrosoltan's shoulder, she confided, "I have faith in you, and I believe with all my heart that you will find a way to secure our happiness. You have locked me inside your love. I will pray every day from now until then that Papa's heart softens so that he does not resist the words you speak to him."

Irina then smiled as she thought about what she was going to say next, advising Nasrosoltan, "You know, this past Sunday, our priest gave a sermon at church, and he said something unusual. He noted that the same sun that can melt wax can also harden clay.

"So, my love, for our sake, please choose your words carefully when speaking with Papa, for like the sun, the appropriate words can also soften the hardest heart, but misplaced words may unexpectedly harden it further."

Nana's footsteps in the distance alerted them to her imminent presence. They physically separated per their now-perfected routine of acting as if they had been immersed in the music lesson the whole time. Nana, recognizing that this would be Nasrosoltan's final lesson at the palace, had asked the cook to prepare a special Russian teacake for him and Irina to enjoy with their afternoon tea. Today, they did not mind Nana spending a few minutes with them making small talk.

After Nana left them, Nasrosoltan quietly reminded Irina to not mention anything to anyone. Irina agreed by placing her forefinger to her lips as a sign of her vow of silence.

The next day, Nasrosoltan visited Madame Lazar to invite her to his performance, scheduled for the following week. While there, he noticed her injured hand had improved significantly, as she demonstrated to him she could now play the piano once more. Thankfully, it seemed there would be no permanent damage to her hand or her career from the child's bite.

Madame Lazar thanked him. "I have enjoyed your presence here and will remember our many conversations fondly. I am also eager to return to the palace to continue lessons with the princess. Thank you for all you have done, kind Monsieur. I feel enormously proud to have introduced you to the esteemed family of Grand Duke Alexander Mikhailovich."

Nasrosoltan appreciated her words and thanked Madame Lazar for introducing him to the royal family. And in his heart, he silently thanked her for the referral to the woman he now loved.

But Nasrosoltan's deepest gratitude was reserved for his departed friend. If Rustam had not introduced him to the gaming house, Nasrosoltan would have never agreed to tutor in the first place. He found it comical how enraged he was the night he lost his wager while cursing the roulette ball and the unfortunate turn of the wheel. But now, Nasrosoltan saw that turn as a fortunate one.

On the day of his public performance, Nasrosoltan was unusually nervous, eager for the examination to begin. Today, his angst was even more pronounced due to the presence of Irina and her family in the audience. Of the five pianists who were to perform, Nasrosoltan was scheduled last, having to sit through the other recitals before his turn. Nothing can disturb a musician's nerves more than hearing a lack of enthusiasm from the attendees for a performance, which may portend a coldly critical audience.

There was warm applause but no ovation for the first performer, which may have been due to a hint of tiredness, a lack of punch in the artist's playing. But with each successive soloist taking the stage, the crowd began to appreciate the music more deeply, and the responding applause for each performer grew louder and longer.

Finally, it was Nasrosoltan's turn, and he recognized that it had been a blessing rather than a curse to have been last, as now the audience was more expressive and energetic. As he made his way to the piano, Nasrosoltan noticed Irina and the grand duke and duchess in the front row, eagerly awaiting his performance. Of all those waiting to hear him perform, there were only two people he truly wished to impress: his professor, Glazunov, and Irina, for this work was his gift to her, an offering that only she knew of.

As he bowed to the audience, his eyes met Irina's. Nasrosoltan felt a moment of panic that perhaps all could witness his deep connection with her. However, he quickly collected himself and sat down at the piano, and then began to play. Once his fingers touched the keys, he became one with the instrument. Nasrosoltan poured his whole being into his performance, playing the piece with rhythmic energy and dynamic verve. The audience sat in silence, spellbound as the notes touched their willful ears. Princess Irina was thrilled at hearing her gift being unveiled for her one note at a time.

When Nasrosoltan finally finished, he was spent, having mustered all his energy and concentration into playing this piece. At first, he heard no response from the audience. Nasrosoltan suddenly worried that perhaps he had not delivered the impassioned performance he had hoped for. But to his immediate relief, just as he got up to take a bow, he was greeted with more-than-enthusiastic applause and even several shouts of bravo from the crowd. Nasrosoltan was finally able to look toward Irina with a triumphant gaze, and she seemed totally mesmerized by the work he had dedicated and performed for her.

The grand duke and duchess graciously waited for Nasrosoltan to congratulate him. They were speaking with Director Glazunov as he came off the stage and approached them. Nasrosoltan could see on Glazunov's face that he was pleased with the results of the examination. Glazunov shook his hand, saying, "Monsieur Minbashian, you truly emptied your heart into your performance today. As music composition is the hardest and most noble thing a musician can do, surely you must have had a special inspiration for creating this piece. I wish to congratulate you!"

Nasrosoltan had finally achieved what he had wished for when he came to St. Petersburg, but this was not the most important thing for him any longer. He now believed his coming to this enchanted capital city had not been for success in his musical career, but instead for this great journey of love Hafez had foreseen years earlier.

Nasrosoltan quickly approached the grand duke and requested a private audience to discuss a personal matter before returning to Persia. The grand duke readily agreed and said, "I will have my personal secretary contact you in the next few days, once he consults my schedule."

Nasrosoltan thanked him and the grand duchess for coming to his performance. He paid similar respects to Irina, who was still beaming from his secret gift to her. However, Irina seemed even more excited to see Nasrosoltan had secured the audience with her father that she had been praying for.

CHAPTER 26

A CHANGE OF PLAN

Irina spent most of that evening humming the melody of Nasrosoltan's work, trying to recreate it while sitting at her piano. She thought to herself, *Once we can spend more time together, I will surely ask him to teach me how to play it.*

She fantasized about their future together and how Nasrosoltan would do all he could to protect and provide for her. She believed with all her heart that it was God's will, confident that their love story was meant to be.

Irina retired to her room and wrote in her diary, jotting down the nuances of her thoughts of the past few days. She spent the rest of her waking hours that evening praying for a miracle, that Nasrosoltan could convince her father they should be together. During her prayers, she also asked God for strength and faith to do whatever necessary if her father refused.

Early the next day, Nasrosoltan received word via courier that an audience had been scheduled for Wednesday of the following week. This was just a few days before his planned departure to Persia.

Nasrosoltan was eager and excited, albeit nervous. As Irina had reminded him, he practiced delivering, without stutter or stammer, soft words to attain the desired result of unlocking any hardness in the grand duke's heart. Nasrosoltan was a meticulous man and did not want to leave anything to chance. He knew this conversation with the grand duke would be the most crucial discussion of his entire life, not to mention the most difficult.

In his mind's eye, Nasrosoltan visualized sitting with the grand duke in his study, drinking as they had done numerous times. He rehearsed how he would thank Grand Duke Alexander for the courtesy shown to him during his visits to the palace. Nasrosoltan planned that he would gradually direct the discussion toward Irina's progress in playing the piano and how it had been an honor for him to have served their distinguished family in this fashion. Then, if he could garner enough courage to express his true feelings for the princess, Nasrosoltan would do so sincerely and honestly, hoping his words would not fall on deaf ears.

Nasrosoltan knew it would not be an easy task, for Irina's family did not assume him to be a part of her sphere of life. He was not expecting this to be a pleasant conversation but also knew that he would never forgive himself if he did not try to fulfill his impossible dream. He believed a lifetime of unhappiness would be too much to bear, but most of all, he did not want to be a lover solely content with longing.

Meanwhile, Irina had heard that Nasrosoltan was expected at the palace to meet with her father and was ecstatic. With great excitement, she wrote in her diary, *I believe that will be the day all matters will be settled, and my happiness assured!*

As Irina read over what she had written, Nana knocked on her bedroom door, asking permission to enter, so Irina hastily hid her diary behind a pillow. When Nana entered the bedroom, she noticed Irina's unbridled joy and inquired, "My dear Princess Irina Alexandrovna, you seem quite jubilant; share with me the source of your excitement."

Unbeknownst to Irina, Nana had heard the rumor of the recent Yusupov proposal and was hoping to elicit confirmation of the news directly from her. Irina replied, "It is really nothing, dear Nana. I am simply happy today; is it such a surprise to see me in this state?"

Nana replied, "No, my dear Irina Alexandrovna, not at all; it is just that recently you have been within yourself, as if you have much on your mind, but today you seem so free of all concerns. I thought perhaps it is because of—" and then she caught herself mid-sentence, realizing that the princess may not yet know of the negotiations.

Irina, who suddenly worried that her secret was out, demanded, "Because of what?"

Nana became nervous at her own ill-timed comment and responded with added formality, "Nothing, Your Serene Highness, it is not my place to say. Please forgive my insolence; I momentarily forgot myself. I am happy that Her Serene Highness is so joyful without reason. This is a blessed thing!"

Irina started to panic and sensed Nana was trying to cover up something she was not supposed to have mentioned. The princess wondered whether Nana had somehow found out about her plans with Nasrosoltan, and she pressed on, insisting, "Nana, you have to tell me what you were going to say!"

Nana, who was not expecting Irina's overreaction to the words she had just casually spoken, offered the princess profuse apologies for disturbing her peace.

Irina, now sullen, grabbed Nana's arm and, holding back tears, begged her, "Nadezhda Nazarov, please tell me!"

Nana, feeling terrible that she had ruined Irina's mood by unintentionally turning it from joyous celebration to sadness, finally relented. "Dear Princess Irina Alexandrovna, please promise that you will not repeat to the grand duchess what I am about to tell you. If she thinks I have offered information that should have been kept private, no doubt, I will be severely reprimanded!"

After Irina promised her, Nana reluctantly divulged, "I have heard a rumor that Prince Felix Yusupov has asked for the two of you to be engaged. That was why I assumed you were so happy. I thought you had heard the news and were agreeable to the offer with such a noble gentleman."

Irina, suddenly realizing that her secret was still safe, felt relieved and let out a laugh, adding, "Oh, so this was the precious information you were guarding with your life? Do not worry; I will not let Mama know you have revealed this mystery to me. You know I am not a child anymore; I really do not understand why my parents feel the need to keep such things from me. I am old enough now to decide for myself issues that will affect my entire future and happiness!"

Then, as if nothing had happened, Irina regained her joyful demeanor and left her bedroom, telling Nana, "I am going to the music room to play the piano," leaving her perplexed governess to tidy up. Nana was surprised that Princess Irina did not spend even a moment brooding, as she usually would have, upon hearing something that displeased her.

The next afternoon, Nasrosoltan received another note from the palace. The request was to reschedule his private audience to an earlier date, Friday evening, rather than the planned Wednesday afternoon of the following week. The note asked for him to respond with the same courier who delivered the message. It surprised him that the grand duke wanted to see him sooner than initially planned, and in the evening instead of the afternoon. But he surmised the family wanted him to dine with them, which he took as a good omen in anticipation of his conversation with the grand duke. He was delighted to see Irina sooner than he had thought and began to rehearse his address to the grand duke now that time was of the essence.

Nasrosoltan wanted to appear with elegance in attire and poise and to speak from his heart with humility. He diligently read Hafez and Rumi to learn how to talk about love with wit and pleasantry but without blemish. Nasrosoltan desperately needed to convince the unconvinced and persuade the unpersuadable. And to give him strength and confidence, he repeatedly read Irina's handwritten note about love, how love always hopes, always perseveres, and never fails.

On Friday, when Nasrosoltan and Irina's fate was to be decided, he hired an impressive carriage and set off to the palace for the last time. As a parting gift for the grand duke, he brought along a French-language translation of the *Divan of Hafez,* recalling the grand duke's interest in the poems of this famous sonneteer of Shiraz.

As the carriage approached the gates, Nasrosoltan noticed an unusual number of guards, reminding him of the dinner when the tsar was present. It surprised him to see such security measures in place, and he suddenly worried that the grand duke had other guests, which would deprive him of the opportunity to meet in private.

Nasrosoltan was unnerved at the thought that this night may pass with no resolution to his petition. Mired in anxiety, he wondered if he would ever get such a chance again before his return to Persia.

CHAPTER 27

A FORBIDDEN LOVE

"Love is fearless in the midst of the sea of fear"
— Rumi

As Nasrosoltan entered the palace, the butler standing at the front entrance waved to the guards to let him through. Nasrosoltan asked the man if the grand duke was waiting for him in the study.

The butler replied, "No, Monsieur, the family is in the reception room. They have been expecting you."

Nasrosoltan was surprised to hear this and asked, "You mean to say the whole family was awaiting my arrival?"

The butler announced, "Yes, Monsieur, His Imperial Majesty Tsar Nicholas is in attendance!" He then opened the massive doors leading to the room, and Nasrosoltan witnessed a totally unexpected and most terrifying scene, one he was not prepared for.

Irina sat at the foot of the tsar's chair, sobbing uncontrollably, looking disheveled and in a state of utter distress. The grand duke and duchess were seated on each side of the tsar with their steely-eyed gazes fixed on Nasrosoltan. He immediately realized that they had become aware of his relationship with Irina and were outraged at what they knew.

Nasrosoltan saw his whole life flash before his eyes, thinking upon each step of the disastrous net he had entangled himself in, and he feared the punishment that was to come. But mostly, he felt deep suffering, witnessing his love in such a state of disillusion, while he seemed helpless to do anything about it.

Nasrosoltan waited in stunned silence for someone to speak, for somebody to begin the reprimand, as he wondered why Irina had let the secret out. He questioned why she had not heeded his appeal to wait for a chance to discuss the matter face-to-face with the grand duke.

Suddenly, it became clear to him why the date and time of the audience had been rescheduled. This was the last Friday of the month when the tsar regularly visited his sister at their residence for dinner. Whatever message the grand duke and duchess wished to relay to Nasrosoltan and Irina, they wanted it to come from the tsar himself, which alarmed him even more.

The tsar, who was wholly irritated and offended, finally spoke with a disdainful tone. "Monsieur, we are all extremely disappointed that you would take advantage of your position and our welcome into this household to mislead our dear Princess Irina Alexandrovna. You have offered her worthless promises of affection to the point that she has told us she wishes to elope with you to Persia!

"This is utter nonsense, to steal away a princess of the Romanovs without a word to anyone—this is truly preposterous. How dare you, Monsieur? You are lucky you are leaving back to your country in a few days, or else I would have had you banished. The grand duke employed you in a responsible position, and we put our confidence in you to carry out your duties with honor and as a gentleman. However, you have betrayed our trust. This is unacceptable behavior. You should be ashamed of your actions and denounced!"

Nasrosoltan felt humiliated and dishonored at the severe scolding, holding his head down to avert the angry stare of the tsar. He could hear Irina crying in the background, every so often interjecting, "No, no, dear Uncle, please, please, you do not understand, we love each other!"

After the tsar finished speaking, he asked Nasrosoltan angrily, "What do you have to say for yourself, Monsieur?"

Nasrosoltan was caught off guard. He was genuinely terrified in the presence of the irate tsar. But he knew this was not the moment to bow to fear. Whenever he had made a choice out of fear, it had resulted in an unwelcome outcome. He wanted nothing more than to destroy this undesirable emotion that was slowly strangling him. He desired to attain freedom from it now that it had once more reared its ugly head. Nasrosoltan found it hard to breathe, with his heart racing and his palms sweating.

He valiantly tried to present an outward show of boldness, hoping that the elusive confidence he desperately needed would then slowly rise to the surface, allowing him to defend himself. But he was overwhelmed and was not strong enough to fight the fear, so he had no choice but to try to hide it. Though he could not control his feelings, Nasrosoltan hoped against hope that he could at least offer a hint of his fearlessness in the presence of Irina. He knew in his heart, she did not want to see him recoil, but instead, she wanted him to stand up and affirm his feelings for her.

When confronted by the all-powerful tsar, Nasrosoltan wanted with all his being to be courageous. As fear was all that lay between him and his dreams with Irina, he needed to muster enough strength to conquer this insecurity, even if it were only for a few more precious seconds in which he would be allowed to speak. And with that desire came the understanding that courage was not the absence of fear but the overcoming of it.

No longer wanting to be a slave to fear, Nasrosoltan raised his head and gave Irina a confident look to calm her anxiety, then turned to the tsar and proceeded to try to explain himself. But before Nasrosoltan could even say a word, Irina, who had composed herself just enough to speak without sobbing, addressed the tsar while holding his hand tightly. "Dear Uncle, if you love me as you say you do, like one of your own daughters, please allow me to say something!"

Irina's request caught Nasrosoltan by surprise as the tsar, still frowning, unexpectedly nodded his permission for Irina to speak her mind.

Irina thanked him and continued, "You know that I am not a child anymore and that I am of an age that negotiations are already being conducted on my behalf for my betrothal. However, this is all taking place without my prior knowledge or consent. Why is it that I cannot decide for myself issues that will affect the future of my life?

"I love Nasrosoltan with all my heart. He has never given me any worthless promises or false declarations of love. Everything he has said to me is sincere; he is a gentleman. Why should he be ashamed that he has given me much happiness and joy? Is it shameful that he has given me this most precious gift?

"My heart is full of gratitude to him for that. He never once wanted to betray this family's trust by eloping; he even advised me to not speak in this manner. He came here this evening for a private audience with Papa to explain our feelings for one another, like the gentleman he is, not as the coward you make him out to be. Nasrosoltan is not the kind of man to have absconded with me without a word to anyone. It was I who told him I wanted to go to Persia with him if Papa disagreed with his petition. I told him I would rather be with the man I love in a foreign land than with a man I do not love in my own country!"

The tsar listened carefully to Irina's plea. As he was a tenderhearted man, his niece's heartfelt words had some influence on him, lessening the rage he had felt just a few minutes earlier. It may have been that Irina's words reminded him of his own love at a young age to Princess Alix, a liaison that the tsar's parents initially opposed.

Tsar Nicholas's own father, Tsar Alexander III, wanted him to marry another, Princess Helene, to cement Russia's new alliance with France. When Tsar Nicholas finally decided to stand up to his father, he told him, "If I cannot marry Alix, I will never marry at all!" So his father, who became alarmed at the likelihood, eventually agreed to their union.

The tsar knew from personal experience that Irina's words of love held much truth within them. The fundamental difference was that Alix was a princess, while Nasrosoltan was just a commoner. Of even more significance was that the Yusupov family they were negotiating with was the wealthiest in all of Russia.

The tsar turned again to Nasrosoltan. "Monsieur, so what do you have to say for yourself? She is young and does not know better, but you should!"

With the blush of embarrassment heating his face, Nasrosoltan had to once again summon the resolve to turn himself the right way up. He recalled the way Irina eloquently spoke about their feelings for each other just a few moments ago. By unfurling the gracious words from her lips, Irina had defended their love with simplicity and beauty. Words that were intended for her uncle's ears but directly aimed at Nasrosoltan's grateful heart. Irina's spirited confirmation of their love infused power into Nasrosoltan's soul such that he shed his cloak of shame and dishonor for a breastplate of valor and fortitude. Courage emanated from a source deep within him, and with a resolution he had not known a few minutes earlier, Nasrosoltan stood tall as an advocate for himself in front of the emperor of all the Russias.

Cognizant of the truth that to love was no crime, he began to speak in his own defense. "Your Imperial Majesty, Your Imperial Highnesses, I stand before you today respectfully with my sincerest apologies. I have no intention to offend or provoke such outrage with a noble family that has been nothing but kind and most gracious to me.

"As Her Serene Highness Princess Irina Alexandrovna revealed, we never had the intention to elope. I am not a common thief to steal the princess away in the middle of the night."

The grand duchess, who seemed to be the most offended of all the royals, almost did not wait for him to finish his last sentence and interjected mockingly, "Monsieur, please save the theatrics. I can already see this will be a waste of our time!"

Nasrosoltan said nothing, not knowing how to respond to this attack, and awaited a sign from the tsar to see if he could continue.

The tsar waved him on, and Nasrosoltan once again attempted to plead his case. "I came here today of my own volition for the audience that had been granted to me, to speak face to face with the grand duke and discuss these sensitive matters. I was fully aware that it might be a challenging and uneasy conversation. I never had the intent to betray your trust or to disrespect your esteemed family.

"However, knowing that His Imperial Majesty has the power and authority to decide my fate in whatever manner His Majesty chooses, forgive me for having to completely empty my heart before you. I pray this Imperial Family does not condemn me further for doing so. I wish to leave no words unspoken, for I fear the wrath of His Imperial Majesty may never allow me to speak them again. With what I am about to say, I knowingly submit to an inexorable fate to doom me, or God willing, to redeem myself in your good graces!"

The grand duchess exhaled loudly and gestured that she was getting up to leave, proclaiming, "What nonsense!"

Even though Nasrosoltan's expressive words did not seem to impress the royal audience, those words did give him the slightest opportunity to continue when, to the grand duchess's surprise, the tsar threw his hand out toward him and directed, "Proceed!"

The grand duchess sat back down, fuming, hearing her brother's command to Nasrosoltan. He was now fully aware that in what he was going to say, he could not risk trying to chase to the end. He knew his next words would determine the course of his future.

"It pains me deeply to see Her Serene Highness in such despair, for her to be shedding tears in sadness and to be hurting, all because she loves. I never thought I would be the cause of such misery for her, and now instead of bringing her unconditional joy, which is the utmost desire of my heart, I am bringing her unmeasurable sorrow. But why are we to be faulted for expressing this love?"

Suddenly, the grand duke, who until this point had remained silent, interrupted Nasrosoltan and said, "Monsieur, I am shocked. What you are saying sounds absurd for a man of your stature. Why, after all this time, is this the first I hear of this? I feel you have betrayed my trust. Please, for your own sake, reconsider your words!"

Irina turned to the grand duke, and with begging eyes, implored him, "Papa, please, please, I appeal to you, Papa, let him speak!"

The grand duke did not protest further upon hearing Irina's plea, so Nasrosoltan continued addressing them. "Your Majesty, Your Highnesses, neither of us set out to fall in love. Nothing was planned, and we had no scheme.

"For my part, as you know, it was by chance that I accepted the offer to tutor due to Madame Lazar's unfortunate injury. I assure you that for a long while, there was simply a professional relationship between us. But just as life is a gift that determines its own time of when it comes and when it departs, so too is the arrival of love. How can there be blame placed on someone who himself is a bystander while events are taking place around him, once love descends upon him without notice or warning?"

Hearing this, the grand duchess motioned for him to stop speaking and angrily exclaimed, "I cannot believe my ears; do you think, Monsieur, that you will stand there and teach us about love and life? This is ludicrous!"

At this point, the tsar, having also heard enough, put his hand up, signaling Nasrosoltan should stop, and dismissively said, "Monsieur, you both are from different worlds; the union you suggest cannot happen. It is forbidden!"

CHAPTER 28

IF YOU HAVE LITTLE,
GIVE OF YOUR HEART

"The sect of lovers is distinct from all others
Lovers have a religion and a faith of their own"
— Rumi

Once again, Irina began to weep, and with great distress, she appealed to the tsar, "Please, dear Uncle," but then, to add formality as a show of her seriousness, she included his title in her next address to him. Wiping away her tears and with her voice cracking, Irina begged, "I humbly ask that His Majesty grants Nasrosoltan permission to continue!"

Seeing Irina once again falling apart, the tsar reluctantly gestured to Nasrosoltan that he could go on. Nasrosoltan continued, "Your Majesty, this is correct that we have come out of the past, leaving different histories behind. But in the present, perhaps as a result of life's mystery, in our hearts, there is a leaning forward into a future together. This love has blinded me to the princess's station in life and has caused me to neglect my own.

"At first, I fought these feelings with all my power, and I reasoned with myself that it was improper, and therefore tried to suppress such thoughts. I am aware that in the eyes of the royal family, I am just a commoner, and my prospects are modest at best, while Her Serene Highness is a princess of the great Romanovs.

"Here at the palace in St. Petersburg, you view me perhaps as nothing more than the princess's tutor with a conservatory education. However, in my own country, I am well-born and someone with a great future, with a highly respected family—a family that the shahs of Persia themselves have bestowed their grace upon for many years."

Hearing Nasrosoltan going on and on in his long-winded defense, the grand duchess cursed something under her breath. Then, waving her hands, interrupted him and scornfully said, "Well, Monsieur, I think you have shamed yourself enough with your nonsense. We do not trust you, and there is no way back from this impropriety! You are only wasting your breath since none of what you are saying is helping your cause. I grant that you do have a silver tongue, but I am tired of your ramblings!"

Then Xenia turned to her brother and said, "I think we have heard enough; don't you agree, Your Majesty?"

At that moment, Nasrosoltan felt his opportunity for redemption had fallen to the ground. He did not know how to respond, so he stood there in the deafening silence, waiting for someone else to break it.

Suddenly, in defiance of her mother and in defense of Nasrosoltan, Irina intervened. "Mama, please do not do this; please allow him to speak, if you love me!"

The grand duchess retorted, "You know we love you, and that is why we are trying to prevent this disaster of a future you are dreaming for yourself."

And then she continued with a defensive tone while pointing directly at Irina. "Irina Alexandrovna, now that you talk of love, let me tell you, if you genuinely loved me, you wouldn't have betrayed my trust. How could you have kept these matters from me? It is because you are selfish and only care about yourself!"

It was then that Nasrosoltan realized much of the grand duchess's anger was aimed at her daughter for hiding their relationship. Upon hearing her mother's scolding, Irina began to cry, unable to respond to the grand duchess's accusation. Irina was spent, dropping her head into her hands in a gesture of complete surrender.

The tsar did not appreciate his sister taking control of the situation by lashing out at Irina and did not directly respond to Xenia's outburst. Instead, he turned to the grand duke and offered, "Sandro, you are her father. You decide if he is to continue or not."

Hearing the tsar's sudden directive to her father, Irina sensed a hint of hope and addressed the grand duke. "Papa, you and Nasrosoltan had become close while he was tutoring me, so you know his character well. You know he is an honorable man. Why else would you spend so much private time with him, drinking brandy and telling tales?" Irina then implored, "Papa, let him speak!"

As Irina reminded her father of the special relationship he had with Nasrosoltan, the grand duke recalled the last few months where he had developed a genuine fondness for him. In response to his daughter's plea, he gave allowance for Nasrosoltan to continue.

Nasrosoltan, trying hard to control his emotions, added, "I am keenly aware of the customs of nobility and the desire for unions made within their own esteemed circles. It is also such in Persia, where the nobility arranges such betrothals among themselves. However, in many instances, such unions, after much negotiation, arrange all matters except the most supreme, which is the happiness of those involved."

Nasrosoltan then continued with an audacious claim. "I do not mean to intrude, but I believe that holy matrimony is not a game of chance. I understand it is not my place to offer this, but I believe that a house built on the foundation of love is like a house built on a rock, so when the turbulence of life's storms beat on it, it stands firm and does not fall!"

At this point, Grand Duchess Xenia, who had enough of what she felt was Nasrosoltan's impertinence, suddenly rose from her chair. With arms akimbo, she interrupted Nasrosoltan. "That is correct, Monsieur, it is not your place to interfere with our family affairs, and to stand here lecturing His Imperial Majesty in this manner with such insolence! We do not know how subjects address the shah in Persia, but in the presence of the tsar of all the Russias, this is surely not acceptable and is wholly improper! How dare you?"

The grand duchess threw an angry glance toward the guards stationed at the door as if threatening to have Nasrosoltan thrown out by force. She then turned to him and said, "Monsieur, you should leave at once!"

At the shock of hearing her mother heap abuse on Nasrosoltan, Irina, trying to catch a breath through her sobbing, jumped up and shouted, "Mama, please, for the love of God, what are you doing? Do not treat him this way; you are so cruel to him!"

The tsar, who had been listening intently to Nasrosoltan's plea, was vexed at his sister's command that Nasrosoltan take his leave. Apparently, in the heat of the moment, the grand duchess had forgotten that when in the presence of the tsar of Russia, it is only he who decides who stays or goes. The tsar gave the grand duchess a stern sideways look and, not saying a word to confront this disrespect directed at him, motioned with his head for Nasrosoltan to continue. Irina sat back down at the tsar's feet, hoping that Nasrosoltan could transform his circumstance with the next words he delivered.

"Your Imperial Majesty, Your Royal Highnesses, once again, I pray that you forgive these words of mine if they sound impudent, but with this talk of love, I am not building a bridge of dreams and exaggerations. In my heart, I am not living in a fool's paradise. I am not speaking of a love that flames up and then dies out into the darkness of a few embers, but a constant flame. The love that I proclaim for Her Serene Highness is not based on empty promises or meaningless declarations as Your Highnesses believe, but on all that is good and beautiful, compassionate and kind. The love that I offer bears no title or wealth, but what I do offer, and pray to Almighty God falls upon receptive ears, is the most precious gift I possess, my promise of enduring love, for I have little else to give."

The grand duchess, forgetting what she had done just moments ago to anger the tsar, took the reins of the discussion in her hands once again and sarcastically said, "Monsieur, hopefully, you are done!"

But then, before her brother could feel disrespected once more, Grand Duchess Xenia salvaged the situation by turning to him and with respectable formality saying, "Your Majesty, this man should be condemned and never allowed to have any contact with the royal family. He is not to be trusted! What is your judgment, Your Majesty?"

The tsar was about to make his decision when his eye caught Irina looking up beggingly toward him. She took advantage of a moment of quiet and asked the tsar, "Dear Uncle, if you agree with Mama that Nasrosoltan should be condemned, are not even condemned men given a last chance to speak?"

The tsar thought for a second and then said to Nasrosoltan, "Monsieur, let us hear any final appeal now before deciding your fate!"

Before saying anything, Nasrosoltan locked eyes with Irina, giving him the confidence he so desperately needed at this moment. Then with the next few words he uttered, he cast himself about on a sea of chance. "Thank you, Your Majesty. I have spoken all that was in my heart and mind, for love has conquered the very last remnant of any fear I may have harbored. I am not ashamed of my feelings, and I pray, fully aware of the vast space between our two worlds, that these words may find a place within your gracious hearts and gently rest therein.

"I remember how one evening at dinner in this same palace, we spoke of kismet. Just now, His Majesty said he would be deciding my fate. As I believed that night and as I will always believe, kismet has already written what will happen to us. Our love for one another is solely a natural reaction to what blind fate has determined, and we had no choice since we felt hard-pressed to balance the force of such destiny. Therefore, I do now with great humility accept my fate, whatever Your Majesty decides."

As Nasrosoltan emptied his soul with his heartfelt defense of their love, he felt wholly depleted. Irina, spellbound by his plea the whole time he spoke, maintained a fixed gaze upon him.

With a renewed liveliness, Princess Irina turned to the tsar and said, "Please, dearest Uncle, how can you refuse our petition. Do you not want me to be happy?"

Before the tsar could respond, she suddenly blurted out the words the tsar himself had threatened during his own courtship, proclaiming emphatically, "If I cannot be allowed to be with the one I love, I would rather not marry at all!"

Irina's comment startled the tsar. With those words, she inadvertently put the tsar in her shoes, and he began to empathize with her, remembering what he endured from his own family when he first fell in love. This worried him since he did not want Irina's first encounter with love, even a love he disagreed with, to be forever intertwined with pain and sorrow. This was when the tsar would let his cherished niece see his goodness as a loving uncle rather than his greatness as a tsar. Irina would soon witness more of his love than his majesty.

Unexpectedly, with a softer tone, the tsar asked Nasrosoltan, "But then, Monsieur, what was your plan? Assuming the grand duke had acquiesced to your petition, were you going to take our princess from the magnificence of St. Petersburg to your country with no prior planning? That is not how things are done, especially with the nobility of the Romanovs! Does your own family even know of your feelings for our dear Irina Alexandrovna?"

Nasrosoltan, who by now was expecting the worst and had lost all hope of the conversation taking this surprising yet encouraging turn, confessed, "No, Your Majesty, they do not know yet."

The tsar suddenly realized he had been offered a way out of this predicament. One that would not leave Irina devastated but, at the same time, would send this presumptuous tutor on his way.

On the spur of the moment, in an attempt to salvage this uneasy situation, the tsar unexpectedly declared, "Well then, Monsieur, I suggest you go back to Persia as you had planned and discuss the matter with them. If they are agreeable, these matters may perhaps be discussed further. You must understand these things cannot take place on a whim, and much needs to be decided before any more talk of this. That is my final word on this issue!"

The tsar's shocking decision initially left everyone in the room stunned. Irina could not believe what she had just heard from the tsar's own lips, that the miracle she had been praying for had come true. With unbridled excitement, she leapt up from the foot of the tsar's chair and kissed his cheek repeatedly in grateful appreciation. She thanked him over and over for allowing her to be happy, knowing that now, even if her own parents were unconvinced, they would not dare overrule her uncle.

Nasrosoltan, who was absolutely baffled at the tsar's sudden change of heart, bowed low to show his gratitude. "I am forever thankful to His Imperial Majesty. If permission is granted, I shall take leave as soon as possible and act upon His Majesty's advice."

The tsar then dismissed them both. While Nasrosoltan and Irina left the reception room, the grand duke and duchess remained seated and were dumbfounded by what had just transpired. They had expected the tsar to crush this indecency, rather than give it his apparent blessing.

Grand Duchess Xenia, who had continuously scolded Nasrosoltan during his lengthy defense, was extremely disappointed in the tsar's ruling. But instead of confronting her all-powerful brother for his abrupt unilateral decision, Xenia unleashed her frustration on the grand duke, demanding, "Sandro, why did you not say anything? You are her father, for God's sake; don't you care about your only daughter's future?"

Grand Duke Alexander, who was sitting in silence thinking about what had just happened, was pulled out of his thoughts by this unprovoked attack. However, before he could respond to her first question, Grand Duchess Xenia released a sharper arrow. "Why do you think a commoner was emboldened to even think of our Irene in this way?"

The grand duke replied sternly, "Xenia Alexandrovna, what are you talking about?"

The grand duchess angrily responded, "I will tell you why this man felt bold enough to even ask such a thing! It was because you allowed him into our private lives with your invitations for drinking and conversation after Irene's lessons. You have always had a problem with setting appropriate boundaries. And look where we are now!"

The grand duke was shocked at Xenia's anger toward him but most of all at hearing the kernel of truth in what she had said. He felt disrespected by her in front of the tsar and replied to his wife with great seriousness, "Xenia Alexandrovna, His Majesty has already decided their fate. But it was not becoming of you, showing your emotions as you did today!"

Grand Duchess Xenia momentarily caught herself, realizing she may have been too harsh on her husband and therefore did not respond to his comment. Instead, she turned to the tsar and said, "My dear Nicky, I am alarmed. What was the wisdom in your decision? Why afford them this glimmer of hope? I just do not understand."

The tsar tenderly replied, "Xenia Alexandrovna, what would you have done if Father had opposed your marriage to our dear Sandro? Would you have submitted quietly to his wish, or would you have despised him and fought for your heart?

"As you remember, I also had to put my foot down with Father to marry Alix. Irina is young and impressionable; the love she feels for him is pure and innocent. It is prudent that we keep her close to us rather than drive her away with our displeasure for this relationship.

"We are fortunate that the Monsieur is departing for Persia in a few days. Unlike what some say, distance does not make the heart grow fonder. In fact, distance can slowly drain the excitement out of any affection.

"So even though he does seem to be a man with no ill intent towards our Irina Alexandrovna, and their love for one another seems genuine, that love they both so boldly spoke of this evening will not withstand the test of time and distance; two of the fiercest enemies of love.

"Therefore, do not worry, Xenia Alexandrovna, for Irina's fantasies will also fade away with time, and she will soon forget about him when he is gone. In the end, nothing will change. I suggest you continue your negotiations with the Yusupovs!"

CHAPTER 29

THE PANTHEON OF KHOJIVANK

As Nasrosoltan and Irina hurriedly said their farewells outside the reception room, he kissed her hand and urgently told her, "My dear, I thank God that kismet was our friend today. I was truly fearful when I saw you in distress, crying at your uncle's feet. I still cannot believe how events unfolded in our favor. Thank you for the words you spoke in defense of our love. I solemnly vow that you, my lovely princess, are the permanent priority of my life. But my darling, I must ask why you divulged our liaison to your family before I had a chance to speak directly with the grand duke? If you had not said anything, the matter might not have been elevated to involve His Imperial Majesty."

Princess Irina replied, "My dearest, I am also amazed and thrilled that Uncle decided the issue in such a surprising manner. Before you arrived, they made me feel terrible, and I expected a dreadful outcome. I do not want to tempt fate with disturbing thoughts of what might have been, but I only want to cherish this moment and appreciate the beginning of a beautiful future with you. I am so grateful that our love is no longer to be hidden."

Irina then added with a slightly defensive tone, "But it was not me who told my parents, my love. It was Nana who alerted them! She found my diary and read it to Mama. I just found out this afternoon and had no way of getting word to warn you of what they planned. I regret that our secret was revealed in this fashion, but I am not sorry for the consequence, which turned out to be a blessing. As for Nana, I will never forgive her for trying to ruin my life with her betrayal!"

Nasrosoltan tried to console her. "My sweet Irina, don't be too harsh with Nana for what she considered her duty, which is your protection. You should ignore the sin of her deed and forgive her. If Nana had not done what she did, even though I don't condone her having shared your private thoughts, the situation might not have turned out so favorably for us."

Worried that the royals would soon come out of the reception room, and not wishing to be there when they did, Nasrosoltan quickly promised to write Irina every day, and she vowed the same in return. They promised each other they would never forget their love for one another, no matter the circumstance.

Irina kissed him softly on the cheek and bid him a safe journey until they would meet again. She said a traveler's prayer for him as Nasrosoltan departed the palace for what was to be the last time before his return to Persia.

As the carriage carried him back to his apartment, he could not contain his excitement. If not for fear of embarrassment in the company of the carriage driver, he would have certainly let out an exhilarating shout of delight to celebrate his unexpected change of fortune.

What had initially seemed to be the edge of an abyss with no escape had suddenly transformed into a bridge, leading to a future of joy with his lovely Irina. There was nothing to fear any longer, no more doubts, no more secrets, no misery, only happiness—that is all he felt.

Later the next day, as he prepared to leave his apartment to collect his things at the conservatory and bid adieu to his peers and professors, he was surprised at the sound of someone banging at his door. He rushed to open the door and found an irate and anxious Madame Lazar on the other side.

Nasrosoltan invited her in, and without a greeting, the Madame angrily blurted out, "Monsieur, what have you done? Your indiscretion is appalling! Nana informed me of what transpired last evening at the palace, in the presence of the tsar. My reputation has now become tarnished for having introduced you; you have ruined me. I wish I had never referred you to this noble family. I am terribly disappointed in you and in myself!"

Nasrosoltan slowly calmed her down, offered her some tea, and once she regained her composure, he explained to her that perhaps Nana was still not aware of the glorious outcome of the whole saga. That in the end, the tsar had not disapproved, pending his going back to Persia and settling affairs to prepare for Princess Irina to join him there.

Madame Lazar listened with intense curiosity to the details Nasrosoltan shared of this harrowing tale. She could not help but notice his beaming with an aura of elation at recounting the incident and the fortuitous end result. As a savvy lady familiar with the ways of the royal court, Madame Lazar sensed that something did not add up in the story. She wondered whether Nasrosoltan was being sent on a fool's errand. However, if this was the case, she saw no reward in downing his happiness and decided to say nothing further except to offer him congratulations on the news.

Nasrosoltan responded, "How can I ever thank you? If it were not for your introduction, my dear Madame, I would have never been so fortunate. May God bless you!"

The next day, while finalizing his travel arrangements, Nasrosoltan recalled the grand duke's touching words upon hearing of Rustam's death, that people only die when you forget them. With that thought in mind, Nasrosoltan wanted to honor the memory of his dear departed friend. He decided to pass through Tbilisi on his way home to visit Rustam's family and pay respects to him at his gravesite.

When he contacted Rustam's business manager, the man informed Nasrosoltan that Rustam's wife had left Tbilisi and was on an extended stay in Batumi on the Black Sea with her parents. He then gave Nasrosoltan the location of his friend's final resting place, the Khojivank Pantheon of Tbilisi. Khojivank was where many Armenians of great stature, including intellectuals and artists, were buried.

Nasrosoltan spent his last few days in St. Petersburg attending to his affairs, and just before leaving, he asked one last favor of Madame Lazar. Not satisfied with his rushed farewell with Irina, Nasrosoltan requested that the Madame deliver a note to her. He wanted to reassure Irina of his love with words he borrowed from Hafez:

> *Look upon all the gold in the world's mart,*
> *On all the tears the world hath shed in vain;*
> *Shall they not satisfy thy craving heart?*
> *I have enough of loss, enough of gain;*
> *I have my Love, what more can I obtain?*
> *Mine is the joy of her companionship*
> *Whose healing lip is laid upon my lip*
> *This is enough for me!*

On Friday, October 3, 1913, Nasrosoltan climbed aboard a train bound for Persia, an entirely different man than the one who had arrived in St. Petersburg only one year earlier. He now departed with a transformed heart and soul, reveling in all that was delightful. He had a fixed purpose and intended to reach his destination as soon as possible, to prepare for the eventual welcoming of his true love.

As he left this imperial capital city, Nasrosoltan had no idea that barely ten months later, the Great War would erupt and drag Russia into unprecedented destruction and loss of life. Nasrosoltan could not have known that this conflict would affect the futures of many he had become acquainted with during his time in St. Petersburg.

On his journey home, he took a detour to visit the grave of his late friend in Tbilisi. He arrived in the picturesque capital city of Georgia, straddling the banks of the Mtkvari River, a few days later. At the train station, he hired a carriage and proceeded to the pantheon. When he got there, Nasrosoltan was surprised to see the vastness of the cemetery. He later learned that there were over ninety thousand graves in this pantheon, in an area surrounded by a massive boundary wall. This wall also enclosed a beautiful garden and a magnificent church.

Nasrosoltan noticed that most graves had granite and marble sculptures with short, inscribed notes and poems. These engraved words revealed much about the Armenian population of Tbilisi and about their families, their heritage, and different aspects of their social life.

He quickly realized that to find his friend's gravesite, he would need assistance from the keeper of the pantheon. After he spent quite a while searching for him, Nasrosoltan finally located the keeper, who had been busy tending to the expansive grounds, and he introduced himself. In return, the man introduced himself as *bat'ono Grigoryan* (*bat'ono* in the Georgian language being the equivalent of *monsieur*). The keeper was a young and robust man but appeared distracted and aloof.

Nasrosoltan explained, "I have come all the way from St. Petersburg to pay respects to a dear friend, Monsieur Rustam Somkhishvili, who is buried here. Can you kindly direct me to where he rests?"

Nasrosoltan was surprised that just upon hearing Rustam's name, Grigoryan gestured to him to come along, and in a low, gravelly voice and talking dead slow, replied, "Follow me...I know where he lies." Nasrosoltan found it remarkable that the keeper could direct him to his friend's resting place without searching the records.

The keeper escorted Nasrosoltan to Rustam's gravesite. Along the way, upon learning that Nasrosoltan was Persian, the keeper shared the history surrounding this cemetery. He spoke so slowly that it seemed as if it took ages for him to complete each sentence. "As a Persian...you may be interested to know...that the pantheon is built on land given to the Georgians…by one of your kings…Shah Abbas, in 1612." After sharing this historical tidbit, the keeper stopped talking. But because of how Grigoryan lingered over every word he spoke, Nasrosoltan was unsure if it was just a pause or if he had completed his thought.

After a few moments of silence, the man continued where he had left off, once again dragging out each word. "My ancestor was the first keeper…and for generations since then…the eldest son of the Grigoryans…has always held the position. This is something our family…is immensely proud of. People …soon forget the dead…but we take care of them…even when their own families and friends forget them." After another long pause, the keeper continued, "That is why…it is refreshing to see…you have come all this way to pay respects to your friend."

Surveying the multitude of gravestones, Nasrosoltan reflected on the truth that no matter who they were or what they did when alive, they were now all equal. It amazed him that these different lives were now all summed up in the dash etched in stone between their birth and death dates.

Nasrosoltan stopped for a moment, contemplating, but then quickly moved on to where Grigoryan had stopped ahead, waiting for Nasrosoltan to catch up. When he got to the keeper, he noticed a massive marble stone with the inscription, *In memory of our dear husband and cherished father, Rustam Som- khishvili,* but nothing else, except for the number thirty-two chiseled underneath.

A surprised Nasrosoltan turned to the keeper and asked, "Bat'ono Grigoryan, I knew this man! He was much older than thirty-two when he passed, so why did they etch this number on his gravestone?"

Grigoryan became a bit more lively and responded with a laugh, "Oh no, Monsieur…this is not his age. His wife told us…when we inquired…that it had been his wish to have a reminder…on his gravestone."

A puzzled Nasrosoltan questioned the keeper, "A reminder of what?"

Grigoryan grinned. "A reminder of...how many years he had been...happily married to her."

Nasrosoltan laughed and said, "Yes, I can see that is something Monsieur Somkhishvili would have done. Even in death, he makes me laugh when I am supposed to be sorrowful, just as he did in life; God bless his soul!"

The keeper, as if suddenly pierced by sadness, added with a groan, "He was lucky to have had...that many years." After letting out a deep sigh, he continued, "I fear...I will not be...that fortunate."

The keeper's unexpected comment seemed strange to Nasrosoltan, especially from a man younger than he was. Hearing Grigoryan's unsolicited remark, Nasrosoltan sensed he wanted him to ask the reason, and so he inquired, "Bat'ono Grigoryan, why do you say such a thing?"

With waves of swelling grief engulfing him, Grigoryan's face shriveled with anguish as he once again slowly answered, "Because the only woman I ever loved...the woman I knew for many years...and was going to marry...left me for another!"

As tears welled up in the keeper's eyes, he drawled, "We were planning our marriage...when suddenly my father died...and when she learned of our family tradition...that I was to be the next keeper...of the pantheon...she begged me to find other work...since she thought it morbid...that I would be dealing with the dead." He stopped to collect himself before he continued on with his sad tale. "The last time we spoke...was the day... my heart broke forever. She told me... *You stay with the dead; I choose life...I do not want to be known as the wife...of the keeper of coffins.*"

Grigoryan turned away as he strained to compose himself under what seemed to be the weight of the world. Once he felt he could continue speaking without choking up, the keeper turned toward Nasrosoltan and confessed his innermost feelings. "But now…I feel like one of these I have laid down…to sleep in the dust of the earth; the only difference is…that I am dead on the inside…and will forever be."

Nasrosoltan pitied the poor man since it seemed the telling of this tale had left him without soul or strength. He felt incredibly blessed that, unlike the keeper, he was instead enlivened by Irina's love.

Nasrosoltan, aiming to lift Grigoryan's spirit, said to him, "But you are a young man. You have much time left. Do not despair. Surely you will find a new love that will surpass the one who broke you."

The dejected keeper, mired in sorrow, seemed annoyed at this frivolous comment. He dismissed Nasrosoltan's attempt to comfort him and retorted bitterly, "Sir, if you believe that…then I assume…you have never really been in love. How can a love that never went away…ever be replaced?"

Then after another lengthy pause, the keeper made his final pronouncement. "Monsieur…pray that you never have to endure such pain. What I had with her…I have not forgotten…It lives in my spine!"

As the keeper left him to spend a few moments to reflect in solitude at the foot of his friend's grave, Nasrosoltan wondered to himself about the vagaries of life. That, if not for a stray bullet, the number inscribed on Rustam's headstone would have surely been much higher.

Nasrosoltan then posed a question to the heavens: *If I can make the necessary arrangements to prepare for Irina, how many years of living happily in love with her will be engraved on my tombstone upon my passing?*

Chapter 30

The Love Note

Tehran, Persia, 1913

After an uncomfortable journey from Georgia, a travel-weary Nasrosoltan finally arrived at his home in Tehran. He had not telegraphed his arrival date, so his parents and younger brother Gholam-Hossein were surprised and joyous when he showed up.

After only allowing time for some tea, sweets, and small talk, Salar Moazaz, who was eager to assess his son's progress, asked him to sit at the piano and perform something. Nasrosoltan, knowing his father's mindset, was not surprised at the request, and even though he was fatigued, he willingly accepted his father's challenge. After a few moments of warming up, he proceeded to play the work he had dedicated to Irina.

Once he finished playing, Salar Moazaz exclaimed, "Beautiful! Charming! My son, the light of my eyes, I am happy to have you back with us! You performed with such fire and passion that it is delightful to listen to. It was a superbly lyrical piece with great depth. Whose work was this—was it a Russian composer?"

Nasrosoltan smiled and replied, "No, Father, it is my own work; this is what I composed and performed for my examination. It was well received by the audience at the annual public performance. Even Director Glazunov congratulated me personally. Members of the Russian royal family—the grand duke and duchess, sister to His Imperial Majesty, the tsar—were also in attendance."

Salar Moazaz, feeling incredibly proud of his son's accomplishment, was choked with emotion and gratefully acknowledged, "Well, obviously, you must have been inspired to write such a work."

It was a rare moment of praise for his son, as Salar Moazaz brandished a satisfied smile and continued with a confession. "Now that I see your impressive progress, I must admit that I am glad you did return to St. Petersburg, even though it was initially against my will."

Nasrosoltan appreciated his father's compliment and warm reception of his music, which encouraged him to divulge his big news. "Yes, dear Father, I was truly inspired. I could not wait to return home and share with you and dearest Mother my good fortune. My inspiration was the result of falling in love with a woman."

Nasrosoltan paused for a moment to let the news sink in with his now startled parents. They looked at each other with surprise, wondering how to respond to his shocking pronouncement.

Khata Khanoom broke the awkward silence and asked, "Is she Persian?"

Nasrosoltan responded, "No, dear Mother, she is not."

Khata Khanoom was disappointed as she inquired further, "Well, is she at least of our faith?"

Nasrosoltan replied, "No, she is not. She is Princess Irina Alexandrovna, the niece of Tsar Nicholas II of the Romanovs."

The happiness he felt just moments before was wholly shattered when a bewildered Salar Moazaz abruptly demanded, "What are you talking about? This is not the proper way to deliver this news to us, with no warning! What were you doing with this girl and her family? Why did you not write and tell us anything?"

Nasrosoltan's father was now furious and got up and paced angrily around the room. Nasrosoltan had anticipated his parents' surprise, but not his father's anger. He looked to his mother to see if she could say something to somehow soften the blow, but that was to no avail, as she remained silent and deep in thought.

Nasrosoltan continued by offering his heartfelt apologies for keeping them in the dark. "Dear Father, I meant no disrespect, but this was a serious matter that I felt had to be discussed in person. We met and got acquainted when I became her private piano tutor. We fell in love and wish to be married, of course, hopefully, and respectfully with your approval. Events unfolded so suddenly, especially during the last few weeks of my stay in St. Petersburg, that I did not find the opportunity to inform you."

Salar Moazaz stopped pacing for a moment and stared angrily at Nasrosoltan, indicating that he was not convinced. Nasrosoltan quickly added, "I had an audience with her uncle, His Imperial Majesty, and her parents before leaving St. Petersburg. The tsar suggested that I return to ask for your permission before further discussions. Please, my respected father, my kind mother, give your blessings to this intention and to our love for one another. Your permission would be a great gift to me!"

His mother and father were awestruck by their son's request, unsure of how to respond. Nasrosoltan took advantage of their silence, confessing, "I know in your hearts you wish for me to marry a Persian, but I love the princess, and for me, in which country she was born, or to which God she prays makes no difference. All that matters is that she inspires me to do great things, as you have just witnessed with this piece I performed for you.

"She brings out feelings from the depths of my soul that would have remained buried there forever if I had never met her." After Nasrosoltan uttered these words, he looked at his parents to gauge whether to go on. When they said nothing in return, he continued to plead his case.

"I am fully aware that this is not our way and that our traditions dictate that my family find me a suitable Persian wife. Believe me, I would rather be with the woman I love from another country and a different religion than to be with someone I do not love but whom you consider acceptable. I respectfully beg you, do not extinguish the seeds of love that have taken root deep within my heart and have grown to nourish my soul. I implore you to give me your blessing!"

Nasrosoltan was correct that they did not want him to marry a foreigner, even if she was a Russian princess. What he requested was an alien thought to them. Mainly because his mother, with much effort and diplomacy, had already lined up several Persian daughters of well-known and respected families for him to decide upon for a wife. These ladies were just as eager to be the one chosen by this highly eligible bachelor and son of the revered Salar Moazaz.

At a loss for words, his father reasoned to himself that playing for time was the best course of action and declared, "Well then, the tsar is correct in that you cannot begin any sort of discussions about her coming to Persia without proper arrangements."

And then Salar Moazaz added what had been his plan for his son all along. "The first thing you must do is to attain a re-spectable position in your career. Now that you have returned, I can also tell you that I have heard you will be promoted to the rank of *sargord*—major—"in the Cossack Brigade, and that is a good start for the time being. After that, you must find an ap-propriate residence befitting a Russian princess. Once these are accomplished, then we can revisit the issue, considering the way you feel about it. Now go and rest; you must be exhausted after such a long journey. Tomorrow we will discuss a position for you in the conservatory at the Dar al-Funun."

Nasrosoltan was shocked and surprised at Salar Moazaz's change of demeanor when his father suddenly acquiesced to his petition. Now that his father was agreeable, Nasrosoltan bowed down low and kissed Salar Moazaz's hand in appreciation for having consented to his wish. He then asked permission to leave the room to go and rest.

After he left, Nasrosoltan's mother turned to her husband, displaying a palpable uneasiness, and asked, "*Agha*"— sir— "what was the wisdom in such words? Why did you give our son false hope for this relationship when we have already put the wheels in motion with these esteemed families? They will surely take us for fools if, after all this time negotiating with them, we tell them he is to be married to another who was not even in the running!"

Salar Moazaz hesitated for a moment while searching for the right words and then responded to Khata Khanoom by saying something eerily similar to the tsar's thoughts on the future for such love.

"Khanoom, our son is young and impressionable; the love he feels for this woman is pure and innocent. It is prudent that we keep him close to us rather than drive him away with our displeasure for this relationship.

"We are fortunate that he is back in Persia now. You know, my dear lady, unlike what is said, distance does not make the heart grow fonder. In fact, distance can slowly drain the excitement out of any affection. So even though he tells us their love for one another is genuine, that love he so boldly spoke of just now will not withstand the test of time and distance, for these are two of the fiercest enemies of love!

"Therefore, I suggest you continue your negotiations with these families. I believe once he gets acquainted with the one he favors here, all these thoughts of marrying the Russian princess will soon become nothing but a nice memory of his time in St. Petersburg."

Khata Khanoom, relieved that her husband had a plan, responded, "My dear husband, I agree with some of the things you have said."

However, she worried his plan may not go far enough. "I don't believe time and distance are the only enemies of love; the most powerful enemy of love is silence. Distance does not separate lovers; silence does!"

Upon hearing this, Salar Moazaz nodded and called their manservant into the room: "Haji Murad, any letter that Nasrosoltan wants you to put in the post for Russia, and any letter that comes for him from Russia, you will bring to me immediately! You will not mention a word to him, do you understand?" With a bow of his head, Haji Murad acknowledged that he understood.

These two lovers were wholly unaware that in two capital cities, thousands of miles apart, all efforts were being made toward the dissolution of their love. Discounting their love as nothing but a youthful fantasy that would soon be forgotten with the passage of time and the experience of new pursuits. But love is blind to such talk and schemes, and Nasrosoltan was determined to bring anxiety to rest by overcoming any obstacle that would hinder their ultimate reunion.

And so, for the next several months, Nasrosoltan went on about his business and worked tirelessly to secure his position at the conservatory. He also eagerly searched for an appropriate residence to move into with Irina when the time was right. Nasrosoltan spent many evenings writing letters to Irina to remind her of his love, not waiting for a reply before sending another. He relayed his diligent efforts in arranging affairs, preparing for the day they would finally be together again. He wrote, *My dear, it is a wonderful mystery to me that in my heart there was never a time when you were not, since I feel my life began on the day we first met!*

He wrote of many things, like the beautiful places he planned to take her, especially the exotic city of Shiraz to visit Hafez's tomb, to thank the man whose words had given him strength when he most needed it.

Nasrosoltan wrote about his life events, such as his promotion in the Cossack Brigade and the various awards and accolades he had received since his arrival. He noted proudly the gold medal of honor awarded to him by the government for his distinguished service in the music education of conservatory students. He confided that grooming the young generation of musicians in his country was now a source of pride.

Nasrosoltan wrote to her many such affectionate letters, but surprisingly, he received no response from Irina in return. He did not know the reason and began to worry. There was much disruption in mail delivery to Europe due to the severe winter weather they were experiencing, and he hoped that perhaps this was the reason.

Each passing day that brought no news from her added to his distress. But he only needed to take one glance at the keepsake from Irina, the love note she had written to him of her Saint Paul's sayings on love—the reminder that "love is patient and it never fails," that "love always hopes, and it always perseveres"—for him to regain his joyous calm once more.

But reading her note repeatedly delayed his trepidation for only a short while. Finally, in a state of utter desperation, he wondered if he should write to Madame Lazar, the only other person he knew who was in contact with Irina, to inquire about her well-being.

One day soon thereafter, in late January 1914, while at the bazaar, Nasrosoltan noticed a newly arrived shipment of fresh Persian pistachios at one of the storefronts. He recalled how much Madame Lazar enjoyed these delicacies and thought to send her some.

Even though Haji Murad usually did the shopping and shipping of such things, Nasrosoltan purchased the pistachios and shipped them himself from the main post office near the bazaar. He added a short note asking about the princess, informing the Madame that he had not received any of the letters Irina must have written to him.

As the weeks passed, he continued writing to Irina, but his letters started sounding somewhat frenzied. He questioned why he had not heard from her in response to his numerous letters. Nasrosoltan reminded her of the sweet promises they had made to each other, of their vows to love one another no matter the circumstance. He tried to elicit some response from her by quoting

Hafez. Nasrosoltan recalled how she enjoyed his reciting poetry to her every so often, during tender moments together. He wrote: *My dear, this verse so perfectly describes what I am feeling.*

> *The days go by, yet not a word you send;*
> *Of aught befallen you no single word!*
> *Tell the East Wind he is our faithful friend;*
> *Or send a letter by some traveling bird.*
> *Unless you come to meet me, how shall I*
> *The lofty region of your presence scale!*
> *O angel, walk a little down the sky,*
> *And meet me, climbing, lest indeed I fail.*

> *My sweet Irina, out of a sense of hopelessness, I sent a separate note to Madame Lazar inquiring about you, but that correspondence has also remained unanswered. I beg you to do me the kindness of writing at least once to explain what has happened.*
> *Even if you cannot write directly to me, for whatever reason, perhaps you could get word to me through Madame Lazar. I beseech you, tell me, has there been a veil placed upon your feelings for me?*

Nasrosoltan became disheartened and began to wallow in melancholy, preferring solitude to the multitudes. Until one day in late March, a few days after the Persian new year, a letter was brought to him by Haji Murad. It was from St. Petersburg.

Nasrosoltan leapt out of his chair and snatched the letter from Haji Murad's hand, hoping that it was from his beloved Irina. He was about to tear the letter open when he noticed someone had already opened it.

Nasrosoltan asked him, "Who opened this letter?"

Haji Murad responded, "I do not know. Salar Moazaz gave it to me to bring to you."

Nasrosoltan thought nothing of this since it was a known fact that the post office sometimes clumsily opened mail from abroad to inspect letters, without any attempt to conceal their sleuthing. And so, with great eagerness, he read the letter:

St. Petersburg, 28 February 1914
My dear Monsieur Minbashian,

Greetings! It was exceedingly kind of you to send me the pistachios, and I am grateful that you thought of me in this way. I received them only yesterday afternoon and have already enjoyed eating more than I should have. I pray that things are going well for you in Persia, and you are cherishing your family's company.

I have not tutored Her Serene Highness from the time that you departed. I am sure you have not heard this since it happened only a few days ago. On the twenty-second of this month, Princess Irina Alexandrovna married Prince Yusupov in the Anichkov Palace. They have already left for their honeymoon in Egypt and Jerusalem.

I am sorry to be the bearer of such news to you, for I recall your affection for the princess. But such is life, for this is the way with royalty; they prefer to marry within their own circles. In no way is this a reflection upon you.

You are a good and honorable man and a true artist as a composer and pianist. I am sure destiny has other plans for you that, in the end, will lead to your passions and much success. I earnestly hope everything turns out for you as you wish. Do not regret anything, for you have the future!

Sincerely,
Madame Lazar

Nasrosoltan could not believe his eyes. No matter how many times he read the letter over and over again, neither the words nor the devastating message it delivered changed. In complete defeat, he fell back into his chair, in stunned silence for what seemed to be an eternity, with dark clouds of despair hanging over his head.

It is precisely at these moments in life, when one is knocked down so viciously by unforeseen events and unexpected endings, that one must make a choice. To either allow the humiliation and betrayal to crush the spirit or to accept fate and move on. A choice between bitterness or forgiveness.

A resentful Nasrosoltan chose bitterness. He took the keepsake love note from Irina out of his vest pocket, where he kept it close to his heart, and viciously tore it up in sheer disappointment. He threw the pieces into the fireplace to burn until there was no trace of the words of love Irina had so boldly borrowed from her favorite saint to declare her feelings.

Once again, Nasrosoltan recalled that day in St. Petersburg when the grand duke first told him the heartbreaking news of Prince Yusupov's proposal. After reading of Irina's marriage, he felt the same about love as he did at that precarious moment. He again believed that love was not kind, that it delights in hopelessness, and that love deceives.

While wiping the tears from his eyes and with a painful lump in his throat, a tormented Nasrosoltan wondered how Irina could so easily have trampled underfoot the sweet promises of love she had professed. How could she betray him by offering her heart to another with nary a word to him?

If only he could, Nasrosoltan would have stopped at nothing in the search for alchemy to resurrect this love that had suddenly died. As he experienced the gamut of emotion, from rage to dismay, trying to understand the basis of her rejection, he thought, *Who threw you into confusion? Did not what we shared deserve at least a warning of what was to come?*

CHAPTER 31

A CHOICE IS MADE

During the next several months, Nasrosoltan slipped into a dark sadness. He maintained his composure just enough to hide his feelings from his family and friends. He thought of the words the keeper Grigoryan had uttered at Rustam's gravesite, about such love and how it could never be replaced. It was then, humbled to the dust by adversity, that he accepted the truth that nobody understands another's sorrow or another's joy. Just as he had not fathomed the depths of the keeper's misery, believing at the time that his love for Irina was safe.

All his plans of the past months had come crashing down with the news of Irina's marriage. The one thing he did not wish for was to elicit pity from others for Irina's betrayal. So Nasrosoltan acted as if it was his decision to call off the relationship without divulging what had really happened. Nasrosoltan played this role so well that no one suspected anything. And even though Salar Moazaz seemed to have his suspicions, he left the matter alone, elated at the outcome.

As the intensity of what could have been receded, Nasrosoltan felt powerless to resist any longer, and he reached an accommodation with his new situation. He determined not to be a victim of love but instead for love to be a servant of his will.

One Friday afternoon in June, Nasrosoltan asked his mother to find him a suitable Persian woman to marry. His request was music to his mother's ears, and the thought of him settling down and starting a family was her deepest wish. What she did not realize was that this would be a difficult task. Finding what she considered a suitable match had been no problem since she had several young women in the wait.

The complication was Nasrosoltan's persnickety attitude. Every time they visited one of the families, and the prospective daughter showed herself by serving tea, he would find some fault with either the bride-to-be or her parents. Maybe he was comparing them all to Irina, or perhaps his desire to settle down was just a reaction to Irina's rebuff.

But the real reason was that Nasrosoltan felt his trust had been violated by women he loved, first by Madame Shamsi and now Irina. This was the emotional self-defense he used to protect himself from further painful feelings. His inability to trust threatened the potential for him ever having a healthy relationship.

The situation got so unpleasant for his exasperated mother that one day she accused Nasrosoltan of being too picky and exclaimed, "My son, I do not think I can be of service to you any longer in finding a wife. You do not accept any of my choices, but the spurious reasons you offer for dismissing them are ridiculous.

"You say one is too short, the other is too tall, one's hair color is darker than you like, the other's too light. You say one is too shy, while the other is too conceited. In some cases, you do not even like the parents. You will not be marrying the parents, so why is that an issue?

"I think you have been spoiled by the attention a Russian princess gave to you, and now you think too highly of yourself. I feel embarrassed in front of these respectable families. They can easily find many suitable and willing suitors for their daughters. Still, out of respect for your esteemed father's reputation and family name, they have considered their daughters for you. Unless you extinguish the spark of your pride and temper your peculiar taste in what you want in a wife, I will no longer introduce you to anyone's daughter!"

Nasrosoltan tried reasoning with her. "Dearest Mother, if I am to live with someone for the rest of my life, I would rather not be inveigled into an arrangement that I may later regret. I see no fault in wanting someone to be exactly to my liking, instead of realizing years down the road that I have made a mistake that will be hard to recover from."

He added, "If you do not want to help anymore, that is fine with me. If God wishes that I meet a woman pleasing to me to take as my wife, he will place her right in front of my eyes. No need for you to bother yourself any longer with these outdated traditions anyway."

His irritated mother replied, "Well then, God be with you; maybe having lived abroad for so many years in your youth, you feel you are more European than Persian. They do things differently than we do, especially concerning family affairs and traditions!" And then, as she was leaving the room, she delivered her final statement with a sigh of frustration: "*Har che ghesmat bashe!*" ("Whatever fate decides!")

Even though Khata Khanoom had expressed her refusal to assist her son in his quest for a wife, nonetheless, she discreetly kept her eyes and ears open for someone he may find acceptable. She now had a somewhat better idea of Nasrosoltan's likes and dislikes through prior trial and error.

A month later, while visiting the *khazineh,* the public bathhouse, when it was open for women only, she came upon Mrs. Davamolmolk Vaziritabar and her daughter, Hossnieh. Khata Khanoom had not seen the girl since she was but a few years old. She was pleasantly surprised to see that Hossnieh had grown into a beautiful young lady with exquisite features and a sweet disposition. Nasrosoltan's mother asked whether Hossnieh was spoken for. When Mrs. Davamolmolk replied that she was not, Khata Khanoom got more interested in the daughter and proceeded to inquire in greater detail all the facts she wished to later share with her son.

In the relaxed atmosphere of the khazineh, many things were discussed between the two mothers. Besides Hossnieh's appealing features, which Khata Khanoom felt Nasrosoltan would appreciate, she thought her son would also admire that this young prospect studied English and French. But the most intriguing tidbit that Hossnieh's mother had revealed was that she had an ear for music and enjoyed playing the violin.

That evening, Khata Khanoom, already having discussed the matter with her husband, broached the subject with Nasrosoltan, but he quickly dismissed any further talk of it.

Nasrosoltan did not even try to hide his annoyance when he replied, "Dearest Mother, I thought you were done searching for a wife for me. Let us not waste this noble family's time. I do not wish for you to lose face once again. Please do not arrange anything further in this regard!"

His mother replied, "You are correct, my son. I intended to stay out of this affair due to your great expectations and the unique traits you believe the woman of your choice should possess. I am not sure you will ever find any such person—even this girl is probably not going to meet your lofty standards—but since it was by chance that I encountered her at the bathhouse, I thought I should tell you about her.

"She is quite attractive, with many of the features you mentioned you would find agreeable in a wife. She is different than the others I have introduced to you so far. I thought you might like to also know, she speaks English and French and enjoys music, and she even plays the violin."

Her last sentence caught Nasrosoltan's ear. His primary instrument was the piano, but he also taught the violin. Since few Persian women played an instrument, let alone one considered European, Nasrosoltan showed an interest in Hossnieh. To the pleasant surprise of Khata Khanoom, he pondered for a moment and then asked that his mother arrange the traditional introductory tea with the family, to decide for himself.

A few weeks later, Nasrosoltan and his parents were invited to the Davamolmolk estate for tea. After the customary greetings and small talk, Hossnieh entered the room carrying a tray of tea, making an offering to his parents and then her own, as tradition dictated, and then finally to Nasrosoltan himself.

When their eyes first met, Nasrosoltan felt differently about Hossnieh than he had with the other women his mother had introduced. There was something about Hossnieh that he found attractive, with her pale skin and golden-brown hair. And he did notice that she had a certain resemblance to Irina.

He said to her, "Hossnieh Khanoom, I understand you play the violin," and without a hint of any shyness, Hossnieh replied that she did.

Nasrosoltan, not wanting to ask the indelicate, suggested anyway, "If you do not mind, I would very much like to hear you play."

In most cases, at such an early stage of courtship, this could have been considered a strange request. However, Mr. Davamolmolk was an educated and open-minded man and consented that if Hossnieh was comfortable, she should play something. She eagerly agreed and rushed off to fetch her violin.

Hossnieh soon returned and proceeded to play a composition by the Austrian Franz Gruber, a work called "Stille Nacht," or "Silent Night." Nasrosoltan appreciated her talent, but above all, he was curious about the piece she had chosen to perform.

He commended her performance and asked, "How did you come to learn of this song?"

Hossnieh enjoyed his compliment and excitedly replied, "Our Assyrian music teacher at school taught us this piece a few years ago. Ever since then, I have enjoyed practicing and playing it!"

Hossnieh brandished a broad smile and continued without taking a breath, "My instructor would play it for us during Christmas, a day the Assyrians celebrate. I love this holiday with all the joyful singing and music."

Nasrosoltan was impressed by her composure and appreciated how this feisty young woman spoke so freely, unencumbered by the traditional cultural hindrances that seemed to burden other Persian women of her age.

Even though Nasrosoltan's heart was shattered by Irina's betrayal, and he was now only half himself, he recognized the need for a distraction to protect against these recurring feelings of hopelessness. With her sweet spirit, Hossnieh seemed to be the perfect distraction. She was a young and innocent woman who could help him fill the void buried deep within him. Nasrosoltan resolved to outlive the misery and cast aside the endless suffering that bedeviled him. He felt Hossnieh could help him regain the other half of himself he had lost when Irina abruptly left for another.

Soon after their first meeting, Nasrosoltan and Hossnieh were married in Tehran on August 1, 1914. While they celebrated, that same day, Germany declared war on Russia at the onset of World War I.

Nasrosoltan had left a part of his heart in St. Petersburg, and no matter how much he tried to not think of her, Irina's well-being was always on his mind. It was true that he hated what she had done, abandoning their love without notice, but he found it hard to hate her. He worried for her safety, now that the armed conflict her prescient father, the grand duke, had warned of, had finally arrived at their doorstep.

But just as life got in the way of what could have been with Irina, it also had a way of righting itself by offering Nasrosoltan another route for his happiness. Maybe not the same kind of joy, or to the same depths as he had with Irina, but the satisfaction that comes with the ordinary events of living everyday life. Events such as the birth of his first child, a son named Fatollah, in 1915, and his second son, Ezatollah, in 1917. The birth of Ezatollah coincided with an unfortunate arrival far away in Russia, for after the pain and suffering caused by the advent of World War I, a revolution had now been born as a result.

While Nasrosoltan was exuberant with the news of one birth in Persia, the one in Russia caused him much anxiety. He wondered what would happen to the royal family in the chaos the political upheaval would leave in its wake.

In the summer of 1918, when Nasrosoltan heard the Bolsheviks had executed most of the Romanov family, he was devastated. He could not imagine the thought of Irina being killed in such a barbaric way. He grieved for her, and the same raw emotions, the same loss he had experienced upon hearing she had married another, rose to the surface, taking him back to the place he had no desire to revisit. While he had mourned his misfortune when he lost her heart, he came to realize that in the end, she had lost much more: she had lost her future.

Hossnieh, sensing something was amiss, asked Nasrosoltan several times what troubled him. After initially brushing off her queries, one evening, he finally relented and shared with Hossnieh the story of his time with Princess Irina in St. Petersburg.

Nasrosoltan explained that he and the princess had fallen in love and that the royal family found out about their relationship. He recounted how frightened he had been upon the tsar's reprimand and how that fear turned to ecstasy when the tsar seemed to have given his blessing. Nasrosoltan then shared with his wife that for reasons he knew not, Irina had betrayed him for the love of another man. He told Hossnieh, "I tried for so long to fathom the secrets in her head, but I believe her action will remain a mystery to me until the day I die."

He confessed that the reason he was now so dismayed was the news of the murder of the Russian royal family. "I am heartbroken that Irina's final days were so tragic and frightening for her."

Hossnieh listened attentively and tried her best to comfort him, even though it was not a pleasing thought that Nasrosoltan still seemed to love another woman, or at least the memory of one.

After relaying this story to Hossnieh and unburdening himself from the secret he had held all these years, Nasrosoltan unexpectedly felt at peace. It was at this moment that the bitterness he felt toward Irina vanished from his heart. What did remain, however, was the feeling of love he always had for her. Now, for the first time in many years, he no longer felt a victim of a lover's betrayal. He realized that genuine love takes the initiative and forgives with or without apologies for the wrong done to it. It was then that Nasrosoltan finally forgave her, hoping that Irina had not suffered too much in the final moments of her life. Even though she had died, his love for her had not.

In the next few years, Nasrosoltan and Hossnieh had another boy and two girls in rapid succession. The Minbashians were a happy family, with five children, a house full of music, and festive gatherings with friends and relatives. Many evenings, for their own entertainment, Nasrosoltan sat at the piano, and Hossnieh played the violin, as the children joined in by singing along.

Nasrosoltan also had a series of career successes as he moved up in the Cossack Brigade to the rank of colonel. Later by royal decree, he was appointed deputy director of the conservatory under his father's directorship.

One day in 1920, as he read the *Petrogradskie Vedemosti* (*The Petrograd Gazette*) that an acquaintance at the Russian Embassy had given to him, he noticed an article about the fate of the Romanovs (the name of the city had been changed from St. Petersburg to Petrograd in 1914 after the onset of World War I, to avoid sounding too German).

As he read on with interest, hoping to discover any information on what had exactly happened that fateful day in 1918 to the royal family, he was astonished to read surprising news. Irina and her husband, Felix Yusupov, and Grand Duke Dmitri Pavlovich were not executed after all and had survived.

The newspaper article reported that the tsar had exiled them when he found out that Yusupov and Grand Duke Dmitri had a role in the monk Rasputin's assassination. The tsar had not taken kindly to this unauthorized act, asserting that only he had the right to order the death of a citizen of the empire. Ironically, it was this exile that saved Irina's life, as she and her husband were now spending their days at their new home in France. The tsar also spared the life of the less fortunate Grand Duke Dmitri by exiling him to the Persian front as his punishment. Nasrosoltan rejoiced that Irina had survived the revolution and had not been murdered by the Bolsheviks as he initially believed.

Obviously, after being told the story of her husband's love for Irina, Hossnieh was not as excited to hear this latest news. She would have instead preferred that his longing for her remain solely a sweet memory, nothing more. Hossnieh doubted the sincerity of Nasrosoltan's assurance that he no longer had the same feelings for Irina. She sensed that her husband possessed a passion for the Russian princess that had not been tempered by the years.

For his part, now that Irina was alive, Nasrosoltan wished he could see her just once more. Not for the fantasy that anything would come of it, but only to ask her the one question that had plagued him these past few years: *Why had she abandoned him without reason?*

Destiny did not afford Nasrosoltan that opportunity, and so he continued living and loving his life, spending his time teaching and composing music. As much as he tried to create a new masterpiece, he always felt that the piece he wrote for Irina was his best. He yearned for the same degree of inspiration that propelled him to write that work in hopes that he could best it.

Upon Salar Moazaz's retirement in 1931, Nasrosoltan succeeded him as director of the conservatory. A few years later, in 1935, Salar Moazaz died, and Nasrosoltan was appointed inspector general of national military music by Reza Shah, the king of the newly formed Pahlavi dynasty. Nasrosoltan was at the pinnacle of success in his career, having achieved a position of high honor and prestige.

Life had offered much to Nasrosoltan, and like all men, he had his trials and tribulations, but he finally seemed grateful for his many blessings. He began to look forward far into the future, pondering his legacy. Nasrosoltan thought of the many more years he had to live, vowing to leave behind one last work he would be just as proud of as the masterpiece he had written for Irina years ago.

CHAPTER 32

THE ANTHEM

"I did not come here of my own accord, and I can't leave that way.
Whoever brought me here will have to take me home"
— Rumi

The new king, Reza Shah, introduced many reforms during his reign that laid the foundation of the modern state. He now insisted the nation be called Iran, meaning "Land of the Aryans," instead of the historical name of Persia, which dated back thousands of years. He wanted the world to see that Iran was modernizing, and one of the exemplifying features of this development program was the construction of the Trans-Iranian Railway. This railway traversed the entire country from the Caspian Sea, near the Russian border in the north, to the Persian Gulf in the south.

This plan had its critics, who claimed it would have been more economically viable to build an east-west railway line instead of a north-south one. They believed this line only served the purpose of the British, who had a military presence in the south and wished to transport their troops toward the border with Russia in the north if need be.

In any event, the construction of this railway line was a matter of pride for the nation, built solely with Iranian labor and Iranian finance through the taxation of sugar and tea. This impressive achievement required building thousands of bridges and hundreds of bored tunnels along approximately 850 miles of railroad line.

The project was scheduled to be completed by 1939, and in anticipation of this monumental achievement, Reza Shah commissioned Nasrosoltan to compose a special anthem for the inauguration. He also asked Nasrosoltan to conduct the orchestra performing the anthem at the ceremony. The shah wanted the music played while he symbolically secured the last connecting spike between the north and south lines outside the Tehran station.

This was an exceptional honor for Nasrosoltan, especially for such a historic and momentous occasion for his country. He immediately began to work on this piece with great anticipation, hoping it to be the crowning achievement of his musical career. But to his surprise, as hard as he tried, he could not push past the lack of inspiration, as he suffered a creative block with self-doubts haunting him.

At first, Nasrosoltan was not worried, considering he had more than ten months to complete the work. However, as fate would have it, construction of the railway line was not only going to be completed under budget, but it was also going to be finished earlier than scheduled.

Accordingly, the inauguration date was rescheduled to Friday, August 26, 1938, almost six months sooner than initially anticipated. This meant Nasrosoltan did not have the time he expected, and he found it even more challenging to compose under such extreme pressure.

One evening, while entrapped in deep desperation, as time was getting short, he asked himself, *Why not use the melody I created and dedicated to Irina and adopt it as the anthem's foundation? Why should such an incredible piece remain an obscure work that has only been heard once in public at my audition in St. Petersburg?*

As artists often do, Nasrosoltan wanted to share this work with a greater audience for an auspicious occasion as part of his musical legacy. Now that there was a special event in his country's history, he saw this as the perfect opportunity.

Although it was his love for Irina that had ignited the spark of inspiration Nasrosoltan needed at the time to create such a melody, he now felt justified in taking back the gift he had so lovingly offered her.

Nasrosoltan was now composing an anthem, a hymn of praise and loyalty, borrowing from what he had written for Irina. In contrast, she had displayed an absence of such fidelity with her abrupt abandonment of their love.

Cruel fate had determined Nasrosoltan would not perform in celebration of his hoped-for union with Irina, where a princess from the north and a composer from the south were to be joined in matrimony. Instead, as destiny had decreed, his most exceptional work would be performed in honor of a different north-south union.

With his inner critic now silenced and the creative block removed, he worked tirelessly for the remaining days. Several weeks before the inauguration, Nasrosoltan completed his composition, and he titled it "*Sorood Eftetahe Rah-Ahan*" or the "Anthem of the Inauguration of the Railways." He could not wait until this historic day, and instead of fearing its arrival, he now welcomed it with open arms to proudly display his brilliant work.

Inauguration day finally arrived on August 26, a day Nasrosoltan had eagerly anticipated. How he wished his father were still alive and could have witnessed this splendid occasion.

As Nasrosoltan put on his military uniform and medals, he also thought of a way to honor the memory of Salar Moazaz. In remembrance of him, he decided to wear his father's Medal of Honor on his chest alongside his own.

Hossnieh had gone ahead with the children to reserve their place in the stands for the ceremony, and so Nasrosoltan was home with his mother, Khata Khanoom. She was now old and bedridden, being attended to by an aged Haji Murad. To locate his father's medal, he went to his mother's room and asked her where it could be. She directed him to a chest of drawers in Salar Moazaz's private study containing his personal effects, which no one had paid much attention to in the ensuing years after his death.

Nasrosoltan began to acquaint himself with the contents of the three long drawers, which were filled with various items of clothing and other memorabilia. Perusing each article evoked a feeling of nostalgia in Nasrosoltan. After a bit of searching, he found his father's medal that the Qajar Shah had awarded to him when he had been given the title of Salar Moazaz.

Nasrosoltan grabbed it, and after blowing the dust from it, he stared at the medal for a few moments in the palm of his hand. He recalled the greatness of this man who would forever be re-membered as a national hero in Persia, and especially in his family's heart. He then proudly pinned the medal to his chest in fond memory of his father on this historic day.

As he was closing the drawer, he noticed at its edge, almost stuck to the wood, several faded envelopes. There was a corner of one of the letters exposed to reveal most of its return address. As Nasrosoltan moved in for a closer inspection, to his surprise, it was his own handwriting. He pulled the drawer out all the way and snatched the letters, and upon seeing each, he was delivered a shocking jolt. He fell back into a chair and, in utter disbelief and absolute confusion, realized these were letters he had written to Irina that, for some reason, had never been mailed.

Nasrosoltan jumped up from the chair and rushed to the door, frantically calling for Haji Murad. The man hurried into the room, and Nasrosoltan heatedly asked him if he knew any-thing about these undelivered letters since it was he who would usually mail them. A nervous Haji Murad stole a quick glance at the letters Nasrosoltan waved in his hand and hung his head in shame, not saying a word.

Nasrosoltan demanded more forcefully, "Well, speak up. Why were these never sent?"

Holding a downward gaze and in a posture of embarrassment, Haji Murad replied in a barely audible voice, "*Agha farmoodand.*" ("Your father ordered so.")

Nasrosoltan, now bristling with anger, continued questioning, "But why? Do you know why he ordered this?"

Haji Murad, attempting to defend himself, replied, "Forgive me, sir, I do not know why. All I know is that he asked that any letter you wanted me to put in the post for Russia, I should deliver to him, and any letter that came from Russia, I should also bring it to him. I swear to God Almighty, that is all I know, nothing else!"

At that moment, it became crystal clear to Nasrosoltan that his father, to control the situation, had decided to block all communication between him and Irina. He did not know of Khata Khanoom's astute pronouncement to her husband that it was not distance but silence that could destroy a relationship, and Salar Moazaz had acted accordingly.

The only letter his father had let pass through the gates of this nefarious scheme was the one he had opened and read from Madame Lazar, containing the news of Irina's marriage to another. This effort of the father to dissuade his son from continuing his relationship with Irina had worked to perfection. His father's betrayal was a blow that even the strongest of men would find hard to recover from.

As he collapsed into his chair, Nasrosoltan dismissed Haji Murad, not wanting to speak another word for fear of saying something he may later regret. He could not believe the man he had planned to honor today, during the highest point of his own artistic and military career, his own father, had broken his trust in this manner.

And then he felt as if his world was crashing down upon him. Nasrosoltan suddenly realized Irina must have mistakenly believed he had betrayed her since she had never heard from him.

He agonized, thinking that maybe she had written to him but that his father had also intercepted those letters. Considering this, Nasrosoltan quickly sprang out of his chair and clawed through the drawers where he had found his own letters, hoping to find a trace of Irina, but to his dismay, he found none.

He had blamed Irina all these years for his misery, not knowing why she had dismissed the love she so boldly professed for him in front of the emperor. The mystery Nasrosoltan supposed would never be unraveled until the day he died had been unveiled sooner than he thought, and with it came unfathomable pain and regret.

He felt like beating his head against the wall in agony and wailing over what destiny had offered. Nasrosoltan desperately wished he could tell Irina that he had not betrayed her. That he had been faithful to their love and had kept his vows to her until news of her own marriage. He was now hoarding all the guilt as he once again fell back onto the chair.

Nasrosoltan wondered what if just one of his many letters had reached its destination. He felt numb and found it difficult to breathe. How many shocks can a man withstand on the same day, learning that his father had betrayed him, and that Irina had not? Worst of all, she almost certainly thought he had been the unfaithful one.

He tried to get out of his chair but immediately fell to his hands and knees and spent a few moments trying to catch his breath. With his head spinning, Nasrosoltan heard Haji Murad announcing the carriage's arrival to take him to the inauguration ceremony.

Nasrosoltan staggered to his feet, trying to regain his composure. With the little strength he could summon, he angrily tore off his father's medal from his chest and threw it to the ground. He was emotionally bereft.

Nasrosoltan wished the day he had so impatiently waited for had never arrived. Today was no longer a day he wanted to celebrate, especially now that he had torn apart the work he had so lovingly dedicated to Irina, to give birth to the anthem he was expected to conduct in a few short hours.

He prayed to the heavens that he would somehow be saved from performing it, for the melody carried the essence of Irina. Nasrosoltan did not have the emotional fortitude to give of himself when he felt so drained and overcome with grief and despair, confronted with memories of her.

Nasrosoltan slowly carried himself outside to the waiting carriage that his brother-in-law, Allahyar Saleh, had hired to go to the ceremony. As he put his foot on the step to enter the carriage, he heard an unintelligible mumbling in the distance, as if someone was calling out to him. He turned and noticed two men coming toward him. One of them had an awkward smile and flailed his hands wildly, while the other approached Nasrosoltan as if to ask him something. When he looked closer, he suddenly recognized the mumbling man. He was the falgir, the same—but now older—fortune-teller he had met once before at his family's summer home many years ago, the man of the cloth.

All the while, the falgir kept touching his heart, pointing to Nasrosoltan, and then making a sign in the air with his hand, drawing an invisible line from one point to another.

An awestruck Nasrosoltan asked the falgir's companion, "Can you tell me what he is trying to say?"

The man replied, "He asks if you remember that he foretold of a journey you would take, one that involved love? This is the reason he is pointing to his heart!"

The falgir nodded in agreement with what his friend said and then started shaking his head and finger vigorously. It seemed he was trying to say no, but then pointed to himself and nodded his head as if to say yes, which further confused Nasrosoltan.

The falgir's companion then relayed, "He is trying to tell you that you did not believe him then; he wants to know, do you believe him now?"

Nasrosoltan suddenly recalled that day in 1912, several weeks before leaving for St. Petersburg. The fortune-teller had pointed to the word *love* on his cloth, then showed Nasrosoltan what he had written on a scrap of paper: *You do not believe in fortunes, not even those that poets tell you from the grave*, speaking of Hafez and his foresighted sonnet.

The memories this man rekindled delivered another harsh blow to an already crushed Nasrosoltan. He then remembered how the fortune-teller had shown him the word *khanevadeh*, meaning "family," and with his hands had made a tearing gesture, implying a falling apart. At the time, Nasrosoltan, in the height of arrogance, had laughed at what he considered the ridiculousness of this man's prediction.

Nasrosoltan had thought back then, *How can it be that I would ever break with my family?*

And now, years later, as if fate was mocking him, he had received the answer. Just a few minutes earlier this day, he had ripped off his father's medal in reaction to Salar Moazaz's apparent deception.

Nasrosoltan, now pierced with many griefs, was baffled and overwhelmed. He did not know what to think, for he had lost all faith. There was no sign of arrogance in his demeanor any longer, but this was not because he had willed it so; it was a result of the toll the day's events had taken on him.

The heaviness hung in the air, and a dispirited Nasrosoltan took some money from his pocket and gave it to the man who interpreted the fortune-teller's gesticulations. Then, with a wave of his hand, he sent the men on their way and slowly pulled himself into the carriage.

As the carriage moved on, Nasrosoltan looked out the window and saw the falgir, with a fixed stare directed at him. The man still pointed to his heart and then pointed toward Nasrosoltan while shaking his head. By not saying even one word this day, the fortune-teller had spoken volumes.

Allahyar, who witnessed all this in awe, asked Nasrosoltan the meaning of what had just happened. He was curious to know about this strange mumbling man and his connection to him. A drained Nasrosoltan slipped down into his seat, sweating profusely, merely whispering, "My soul melts away with sorrow," followed by a sigh of exhaustion.

From his disposition, as he sat slouching in the carriage, Nasrosoltan signaled that he was spent and in no mood to converse, so the two men shared a silent carriage ride to the inauguration hall.

Upon arrival at their destination, there was great fanfare. Many people had crowded the area to witness this historic event. Military personnel were arrayed in their elegant uniforms, and the orchestra was set, anticipating the arrival of Nasrosoltan. Reza Shah had not yet arrived, but many of the high government officials, including the minister of transportation, were present.

The driver opened the carriage door for the two passengers to disembark, and Nasrosoltan was the first to set foot outside. As he took the last step onto the pavement, he seemed to have tripped, and losing his balance, he stumbled head-first to the ground.

The driver and Allahyar immediately attended to him, hoping that he was not injured, as the curious crowd now noticed what had happened and began surrounding them. As they tried to lift him up, Nasrosoltan grimaced and put a hand on the left side of his chest, indicating he was in excruciating pain. They hurriedly tried to disperse the ever-growing crowd and placed him back in the carriage, rushing him to seek medical help.

Nasrosoltan still had a pulse but was one breath away from eternity as the carriage driver maneuvered the busy streets of downtown Tehran, trying his best to get him to the hospital.

Allahyar kept yelling at the driver to go faster, worried that they were running out of time. The hospital was now within reach, only a few blocks away. As they approached the front entrance to the hospital, Nasrosoltan drew his last breath and let out a final sigh. Allahyar tried desperately to revive him, first lifting his head to see if he was conscious and then frantically shaking Nasrosoltan, searching for any sign of life. Finding none, Allahyar cried out in despair as he sat with Nasrosoltan's lifeless body on his lap.

Nasrosoltan's soul was whisked away by the same Angel of Death he had told the tsar of Russia about at a palace dinner twenty-five years earlier. Nasrosoltan Minbashian died from cardiac arrest, most probably resulting from a broken heart, in the back of a carriage. He did not die, as he hoped, surrounded by his wife and children. Instead, the only family with Nasrosoltan in his final moment was a sole brother-in-law.

That day, the ceremony took place, and the anthem was played in celebration, without Nasrosoltan conducting the band. It may have been that the heavens had mercy on him. Even though Nasrosoltan did not come to his great moment, he was instead granted his final wish. His untimely death spared him from having to hear Irina's melody one last time.

When Nasrosoltan was finally laid to rest, his headstone, unlike Rustam's, carried no etched-on reminder of the number of years of happiness he hoped would be spent with his beloved.

It seems kismet had determined Nasrosoltan was to live a life of restless love. And though Rustam had warned him early on that divine providence was under no obligation to be kind to all, for Nasrosoltan, fate had not been too unkind.

For at least during a few enchanted months in the spring and summer of 1913, Nasrosoltan and a princess had shared a journey of love. A journey of unbridled hope and unfulfilled dreams, accompanied by a hundred sweet promises.

APPENDIX—PHOTOGRAPHS IN CHRONOLOGICAL ORDER

(All photographs are from the Haddad and Minbashian family collections.)

Nasrollah Minbashian (left), standing with clarinet in hand at a café in St. Petersburg with Russian musicians, before his first return to Persia, 1905.

Salar Moazaz (center front row) and the Persian Cossack Brigade military band, Tehran, 1909.

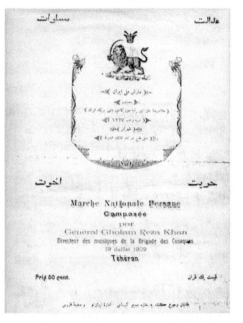

Cover page of the first-ever national anthem of Persia, printed July 19, 1909, composed by Gholam Reza Khan Minbashian "Salar Moazaz," in honor of the liberation of Tehran.

The piano sheet music of the first-ever national anthem of Persia.

Salar Moazaz Minbashian and his youngest son, Gholam-Hossein Minbashian, Tehran, 1911. After Nasrosoltan's untimely death, his younger brother Gholam-Hossein, who had studied music in Geneva and at the conservatory in Berlin, took over as director of the Iranian Conservatory. In 1933, he formed the Tehran Symphony Orchestra, which today still performs works of many of the great classical and Iranian composers.

Nasrollah Khan "Nasrosoltan" Minbashian, St. Petersburg, Russia, 1913, the year he tutored Princess Irina.

Hossnieh Vaziritabar Minbashian "Mami," Tehran, 1919.

Nasrosoltan Minbashian, as an officer in the Cossack Brigade, the second row, left, wearing a white cap, with Russian officials and their families, Tehran, 1923.

Reza Shah Pahlavi (in front) and Nasrosoltan Minbashian to his left (viewer's right), Tehran, 1925. Unbeknownst to them both at the time of this photo, twenty years later, in 1945, Reza Shah's daughter Princess Shams would marry Nasrosoltan's son Ezatollah.

Colonel Nasrosoltan Minbashian, director of the Iranian
Conservatory, Tehran, 1932.

Allahyar Saleh (seated far right), Nasrosoltan's brother-in-law, with Prime Minister Mohammad Mossadegh (far left) on a flight to the United States, 1951. Allahyar, who was the only family member with Nasrosoltan at the time of his death, became a notable personality in his own right. He was a successful politician and was the most trusted advisor of Mossadegh. He was later appointed ambassador of Iran to the United States during the presidency of Harry Truman. After Nasrosoltan's unexpected death, Hossnieh and her youngest daughter, Anvar (the author's mother), moved into the Saleh family home until they could get back on their feet, as they were reeling from the shock of his sudden passing.

Ezatollah (Mehrdad) Minbashian (right), the middle son of Nasrosoltan, who later in 1964 became Iran's first-ever minister of culture and fine arts, did what his father had wished but never got a chance to do—marry a princess. Seen here with his wife, Princess Shams, daughter of Reza Shah, hosting American jazz artist Dizzy Gillespie in Abadan, Iran, 1956.

Fatollah Minbashian (left), eldest son of Nasrosoltan, with Mohammad Reza Shah Pahlavi, son of Reza Shah, during wargames, Shiraz, Iran, 1965. Fatollah was a music composer and an expert at playing the piano and violin. He joined the military like his father and his grandfather, Salar Moazaz. He initially served as commander of the same garrison in Shiraz where Nasrosoltan had served as band conductor sixty years earlier. He eventually rose to the rank of commander of all Iranian Armed Forces as a four-star general.